Til My Casket Drops

Lock Down Publications
Presents
Til My Casket Drops
A Novel by *CA$H*

Lock Down Publications
P.O. Box 1482
Pine Lake, Ga 30072-1482

First Edition April 2014
Printed in the United States of America

Lock Down Publications
Email: **ldp.cash@gmail.com**
Facebook: **Cassius Alexander**
Like our page on Facebook: Lock Down Publications @
www.facebook.com/lockdownpublications.ldp
Follow me on Twitter:
https://twitter.com/cashshtreetlit
Cover design and layout by: **Marion Designs**
Book interior design by: **Shawn Walker**
Edited by: **Shawn Walker**

Dedications

First of all, if you're reading this then it is dedicated to you for supporting me along my literary journey. I thank you sincerely because without you I would be invisible.

Secondly, the book you're about to read is being presented in a friendly battle between a talented and well respected author, Aaron Bebo, and myself. The challenge is the first of its kind in the history of literature. Two authors releasing separate books at the same time with the same title: *Til My Casket Drops.*

We encourage you to read both of our books and leave reviews.

Aaron, you're a class act, bruh. I thank you for riding this journey with me. There were some hurdles along the way, but we leaped right over them and here we are at the finish line. We are both winners because we're doing what we love to do and our readers get a double treat.

Much love, fam.

Special shout outs to my team, too numerous to name but too loyal to forget. I love y'all, *Til My Casket Drops.*

One Love

Chapter 1

Mayhem stood shirtless in the mirror checking out his well-defined body. His pecs bulged and his eight pack was testimony to a religious workout that he had maintained over the past two years while locked up in Fulton County Jail on a murder charge that was recently dropped.

He was tatted up like a mofo, sleeves and all. His body was a canvas that displayed his blood, sweat and tears. Amongst his many tattoos, three bullet wound scars on his stomach was encircled with a tat that defined him and it read: *Get It How You Live.* The red ink looked like blood against his blueberry black skin.

One of the tattoos on his right forearm paid homage to his creed: *90's Baby*. No other generation was like those young boys. They were turnt the fuck up and Mayhem was the worst and best of them, depending on which end of his gun a nigga found himself on.

He turned his head to the side and stared at his mother's name tatted on his neck. Underneath it was *RIP*. Mayhem was only twelve years old when she was beaten to death by her boyfriend but the pain in his heart was eternal, and the memory of that night was seared in his soul. Many believed that it was her murder that had turned him into a stone cold killah.

Tears welled up in his eyes and pain contracted in his heart as he recalled fond memories of her that he held onto with a death grip. A day at Six Flags over Georgia. A ride in a stretch limousine for his tenth birthday. Fresh Jordans and other gear, year round. Anything he wanted, she found a way to give it to him.

"You're my number one man," she had told him every day that he could remember.

"And you'll remain my number one girl," he said, now in a voice strained with years of hurt.

He fingered the platinum name tag with her name engraved on it that hung from a chain around his neck. Damn he missed her. He hated the bitch ass nigga that took her away from him with a passion. She had been a stripper and a prostitute but to him she'd been a Queen. His *All I need,* as youngins referred to their mothers in the 'A'.

"I'll see you soon, Mama," he whispered, biting down on his bottom lip. He grabbed his Glock .40 off of the dresser and tucked it in the waist of his black jeans.

He lived by the gun and expected to die by it too. Any day could be his last, and he was a'ight with that. As long as he went out letting his ratchet spit back he didn't give a fuck.

Mayhem slipped on a black t-shirt then he strapped on an Ultra Lightweight Kelvar bullet proof vest and covered it with a black hoodie. Lastly, he reached in the middle drawer of the dresser and grabbed his black ski mask and a roll of gray duct tape.

His baby mama, Dream, stood in the doorway of the bedroom watching him. "I guess you're going on a lick," she said with disapproval.

Mayhem didn't respond. Things weren't exactly gucci with them. He was only there because it was a place to lay his head and it allowed him to spend some time with his daughter.

There was a time when Dream was his boo, but that time had passed. While he was in county she was out there doing her. She had thought for sure he was going down the road and wouldn't see daylight for a very long time. Dream had let different niggas run up in her and hadn't put a dime on Mayhem's books since the second month after he'd gotten cased up.

Mayhem wasn't the type of nigga to try to regulate his shawdy's pussy from lock down but he had expected her to look out for him after all the shit he'd done for her.

When the murder charge was dropped two weeks ago and he was released, he went to live with Dream but he slept in the spare bedroom and he hadn't fucked her.

"So you're not going to say anything?" She asked, twisting her lips up.

Mayhem turned around slowly and gave her a hard glare. He paid no attention to the short lace teddy that caressed the curves of her luscious body and rested high up on her smooth brown thighs. "What do you want me to say, shawdy? I get it how I live. You know that."

"I know you're going to end up locked up again if you don't find something legit to do." She glared at him with those pretty light brown eyes that hid the disloyalty that resided in her heart.

"Humph," Mayhem chuckled. "What you want me to do, go work at Popeye's or some lame shit like that? I got a daughter to feed in there." He pointed towards the master bedroom where his baby girl, Brandi, was asleep in Dream's bed.

He lowered his arm and looked down from his 6'2" height at Dream who was a foot shorter. "And I didn't hear you complaining when I was hitting licks buying you jewels, designer shit, and that whip that's parked outside," he reminded her.

"Boy, boo," she replied, placing her hands on her hips. "I never asked for none of that shit so don't act like you robbed niggas to take care of me."

"You might not have asked for it but I don't remember you turning it down either," he countered. Keeping his voice low so that he wouldn't awaken his little princess.

"What are you trying to say, Marquis?" She knew that he didn't like to be called by his government name.

Mayhem peeped game. He smiled and moved her to the side as he headed for the door.

"If your ass end up back in jail don't call me because I'm not going to have no holla for you," she hurled.

"I know. That's your get-down. But you had some holla for a whole lot of other niggas that didn't give a fuck about you while I was cased up."

"Fuck you, bitch ass muthafucka!"

Mayhem stopped in his tracks. Steam rose off of his head as he slowly turned around and stepped back towards her with a scowl on his face. "Is that the way you talk to a G?" His tone was as hard as the steel in his waistband, and the vein on the side of his head pulsated like a bolt of electricity had shot through it.

Dream knew that Mayhem wasn't the type of dude to put his hands on a woman so she didn't cower. Instead, she went in harder. "You don't scare me muthafucka!" she spat, shoving him out of her space. "You think I give a fuck about you being a *killah!*" She drew out the last word with special emphasis. "Niggas in the streets might fear you but I don't," added Dream, getting all up in his face.

Mayhem licked his lips and swallowed the anger that bubbled in his chest. Had she been a dude talking reckless like that, he would've sent her ass home to Jesus.

"Lil' mama, when I walk out that door no matter what happens tonight I'm not coming back. You and me are done forever — straight up."

"I don't give a fuck. I hate your ass anyway," she screamed.

"You hate me? Why? Because I won't fuck your ratchet, disloyal ass? You made that bed shawdy now sleep in that bitch."

Dream swung at him but Mayhem easily blocked the blow. He shook his head at her pitifully. "You don't deserve a thorough nigga like me," he said with finality. Then he was out.

"Fuck you! Bitch ass nigga. That's why I fucked your boy, Bebo, while you was locked up."

Mayhem heard that slick shit but he let it bounce off of his back like water off of a duck's ass.

Sliding behind the wheel of his black 2012 Range Rover, he sighed heavily and blocked Dream and her bullshit out of his mind. She was just upset because he refused to dick her down.

Mayhem reached under the seat and pulled out a bottle of Hen Dog that he kept on deck. He popped the top and took a gulp straight to the head. “Ahhhh,” he exclaimed with satisfaction as he felt its heat in his throat.

Pulling off, he turned on some Pac and let that real nigga shit get him in a zone.

Hell, ‘til I reach hell, I ain’t scared.
Mama checking in my bedroom, I ain’t there.
I got a head with no screws in it, what can I do?
One life to live, but I got nothing to lose.

“Hail Mary!” uttered Mayhem.

Starting tonight he was taking no shorts and showing muthafuckas no mercy.

Chapter 2

Bebo was already parked outside of the *IHOP* on Roswell Road in Sandy Springs when Mayhem arrived. Mayhem parked next to Bebo's Lexus IS 250 and got out.

Bebo, a dark-skinned, tall, gangly dude with an egg shaped head, unfolded himself out of his whip and greeted Mayhem with some dap and a chest bump. He smelled like he had just smoked a whole pound of weed.

"What it do, bruh?" he smiled and licked his chapped lips.

Dream's claim rung loud in Mayhem's head. *That's why I fucked your boy, Bebo, while you was locked up.* Even though his love for her was dead, he couldn't help looking at Bebo and wondering if it was true or not. But he tossed it aside and concentrated on the business.

"I'm ready to get these bands. What's up, is it still a go?" He asked, leaning on the hood of Bebo's whip.

"Yea," replied Bebo, lighting up a Newport and taking a pull.

Mayhem's brow furrowed when he noticed a Dread Head in the passenger seat. "Who in the fuck is homeboy?" he asked.

"Oh, that's my nigga, Jabari. He's gonna go up in the house with you."

"What?" Mayhem gritted. "I don't know that mutha-fucka." His mouth was a tight line.

"Bruh, he's official. Trust me," vouched Bebo.

"In God I trust. Everybody else gotta show and prove. Fuck you talking about?" Mayhem spat. "Nigga's always seem official until they get those ghetto bracelets slapped on their wrists, then all the ho come out of 'em."

"I hear you dawg but Jabari ain't that type of nigga. Ain't no ho in his blood. Plus, I need somebody with you when you go up in there because you're stupid with that banger. You can't kill the nigga you're going to jack, he's my wife's twin brother. She would lose her goddamn mind."

"Well, his ass better not buck or he'll lose *his* goddam mind — I'll splatter it up on the ceiling."

Bebo shook his head in exasperation. "See, you're wild as hell. That's why I'm sending Jabari in there with you to keep your young ass calm." He had heard vicious stories of how beastly Mayhem could be. It was rumored that one dude that the youngin had robbed for his chain had ended up in the trunk of his own car with three bullet holes in his head. Body—burned and charred.

Bebo shook his head at the thought of that happening to his wife's twin. He hurriedly waved his boy out of the car and made the introductions.

Mayhem acknowledged Jabari with a slight nod of his head, but he didn't lock fists with him. He didn't know that nigga.

Ten minutes later they were ready to ride out. Bebo looked at Mayhem and held his stare. "Youngin, this is a jack move not a murder. Demetrius is already drunk and y'all gon' have the drop on him so he's not gon' buck. Just get the birds and the money and come on out of there. I'll be parked down the street. Don't kill my brother in-law," he reemphasized.

"You don't have to keep telling me that. I heard you, fam," said Mayhem. He got in his whip and waited for Dread Head to get in.

Bebo put a hand around Jabari's shoulder and whispered, "Don't let that young nigga murk my people. If it come down to it, do what you gotta do."

Jabari nodded his head then walked around to the other side of the truck and slid into the passenger seat.

They drove off with Bebo behind them nervously puffing on his cigarette.

Under the cover of a dark summer sky Mayhem and Jabari moved quietly into Demetrius' backyard. They climbed the four steps that led up to the screened-in back porch and Jabari used a double edged hunting knife to cut a hole in the screen. With a gloved hand he reached in and unlatched the lock on the screen door.

Mayhem walked ahead of him, stepping over a child's bicycle that laid on the floor of the porch. He pressed his ear against the backdoor listening for the sound of movement but all he heard was music. French Montana played in the background.

Nigga, I ain't worried 'bout nothin'
Ridin' 'round with that Nina
Ridin' 'round with that AK, that HK, that SK
That beam on the scope
Window down, blowin' smoke
Niggas frontin' be broke
Try rob me, gon' get smoked
That gun automatic, my car automatic
Ain't worried 'bout nothin'

The irony of the lyrics caused Mayhem to smirk under the black ski mask that covered his face. "Nigga ain't worried 'bout nothin'," he rapped along.

Jabari chuckled.

They slid their bangers out and got ready to do a kick door. Mayhem eyed a spot just under the doorknob. He raised his foot up and smashed the heel of his Timbs at the perfect spot.

The door frame splintered on the first kick and the second one sent the door crashing in. It slammed into the wall with a loud bang. With his Glock held high, ready to spit flames, Mayhem dashed into the den where the music came from. Jabari was right behind him with a pistol grip pump shotgun cocked and locked.

Bebo had said that his brother in-law wouldn't buck the jack but Mayhem was prepared in case he tried. He stepped into the dimly lit den, prepared to hit him in the melon with that heat. Beside him Jabari was locked in too.

They found Demetrius passed out on the couch with his mouth wide open. He was a large, overweight man that snored like a hog. His arms and legs hung off of the plaid couch and his big round stomach rose up and down with every bronchitic breath. Several empty Ciroc bottles and a half-smoked Swisher sat on the glass end table next to a bowl full of loud.

Mayhem stepped as light as a cat burglar. When he was in front of the couch he bent over, stuck his tool in Demetrius' mouth, and slapped him across the face with his free hand. "Wake your fat ass up," he growled.

Demetrius eyes slowly opened and he awakened to a nightmare. When he saw the masked robbers and felt the weight of that banger in his mouth, his eyes popped out of his head.

"How does the steel taste, fat boy?" Mayhem mocked.

Demetrius didn't respond.

"Oh, you hard, huh? You're a G — you ain't giving up shit?" Mayhem said with an overtone of derision.

"You got that right," he mumbled around a mouthful of danger.

Mayhem removed the gun out of his mouth and cracked him across the head with it. "You think this is a game?" he snarled menacingly but Demetrius remained stoic.

With blood running down the side of his face he stared up into the threat of death and mocked it. "Fuck you! You might kill me but y'all ain't leaving here with nothin' but my blood on your clothes. If you was broke when you ran up in this bitch, you'll be broke when you leave out," he spat bravely.

His gangsta caught Mayhem by surprise — Bebo had promised that he would fold meekly — but it didn't deter the young beast from the mission at hand. He had gone up in there to get the nigga's trap and he wasn't leaving out without it. The only question was how much pain and torture Demetrius could endure before he broke.

"You might hold out for a minute but I'ma break your big ass," Mayhem said, leveling the Glock down at him.

The gun clapped twice, echoing off of the walls. Demetrius' winced as hot pain sizzled in both of his shoulders and rendered his arms useless.

"How does that feel?" Mayhem taunted.

"Suck my dick."

"Oh, yea? A'ight, let's see which one of us will suck that muthafucka, you or me." He looked over his shoulder and commanded Jabari. "Duct tape his fat ass. I'ma teach him some respect."

Jabari set the shotgun down and stepped to the business. He slapped a strip of tape over Demetrius' mouth to muffle his cries, then he bounded his hands together behind his back and taped his ankles together.

Excruciating pain surged from Demetrius' wounded shoulders and throughout his entire body as blood soaked his shirt. Sweat beaded up on his forehead and ran down into his eyes.

Mayhem propped him up on the couch. "Suck your dick, huh?" he said again.

Demetrius just stared at him.

Mayhem stared back. *You'll blink before I do*, he said to himself.

He turned to Jabari. "Keep your tool on this nigga, and if he wiggle give him a new hairline," he instructed before leaving the den in search of the bathroom.

He returned a few minutes later with bounce in his step and a bottle of rubbing alcohol in his hand. A large lump formed in Demetrius' throat. He swallowed hard and tried to conjure up the courage to endure the imminent pain that was sure to come.

Mayhem stuck his banger in his waist and unscrewed the top off of the alcohol. Without uttering a word he poured some of the liquid in Demetrius' gunshot wounds.

Demetrius' screamed but it was stifled by the duct tape over his mouth. His large body rocked back and forth as the pain in his shoulders intensified.

"You still hard, my nigga?" asked Mayhem. He poured more alcohol in Demetrius' wounds. Still the only reaction he got out of him were grunts and moans.

"Give me your knife," he said to Jabari. "And turn the music up."

His accomplice complied.

Mayhem put the sharp serrated edge of the blade against Demetrius' face and cut him from the eyebrow to the chin. His jagged skin laid wide open. "Now niggas can call you Scarface."

Blood mixed with sweat and ran down Demetrius's neck. He mumbled something that sounded like a submission.

"He's ready to talk." Jabari quickly cut in. He was relieved because Bebo had explicitly stated that they were not to kill him.

"You ready to tell me where that safe at, Big Boy?" Mayhem asked.

Demetrius nodded *yes*.

Mayhem ripped the tape off of his mouth. "Start talking."

Demetrius knew that his fate was already sealed; he could see that in Mayhem's cold eyes. He didn't fear death, he had resigned himself to that. What scared him was the torture that he was about to suffer. He looked up at Mayhem with contempt and hawked a glob of blood and spit at him.

Had he not been wearing a ski mask it would've struck Mayhem dead in the face. He smiled underneath the mask because he understood what Big Boy was trying to do. He was trying to make Mayhem murk him fast.

"It ain't gon' happen like that, fam. I'ma make you suffer," he taunted.

"Kill me man and get it over with," he pleaded on weak breath.

Jabari was afraid that Mayhem was going to comply. He raised the pump and pointed it at the center of Mayhem's back. *If it comes down to it do what you gotta do.* Bebo's words replayed.

Jabari gently wrapped his finger around the trigger. He didn't owe this lil' jit any loyalty. His allegiance was to Bebo.

"Where is the money and coke?" Mayhem asked Demetrius once more. He was running out of patience and he was about to turn up.

"Suck—my—dick."

Mayhem slapped the lamp off of the end table sending it crashing to the floor. The uneven light casted an eerie silhouette of him on the wall. He picked the knife up off of the table, grabbed Demetrius by the head and sliced off his ear, ignoring the shrill scream that escaped his mouth.

"Muthafucka wasn't listening no way," he spat as he slung the severed ear across the den.

Behind him Jabari was paralyzed by the brutality that he was witnessing. He wanted to blast a hole in Mayhem's back to stop him from murking Bebo's people, but he wanted the money and the drugs more.

He stepped forward and pleaded with Demetrius. "Tell him where the shit at and I promise you after we get it we'll be out. I'll call an ambulance to come and get you and take you to the hospital."

Demetrius was bleeding profusely and death had his name on its tongue. He was weak and fading in and out of consciousness, barely able to respond. But now that he saw his whole life flashing before him, he decided that he wasn't ready to go to that other side. He moved his head up and down indicating that he was ready to cooperate.

Mayhem put his ear close to Demetrius' mouth to hear his faint voice. When he divulged where the stash was at Mayhem caught a bigger rush from snuffing out that nigga's gangsta than he did from the come up he knew he would leave there with.

He sent Jabari to the stash while he remained in the den with Demetrius. After Jabari disappeared out of the door, Mayhem sat the knife on the table and yanked Demetrius's pants down around his ankles.

"I'ma teach you not to tell a G to suck your dick." He picked the knife up off of the table and touched the tip of the sharp blade to Demetrius' chest, drawing a trickle of blood.

Mayhem slowly slid the blade downward leaving a sticky red trail from Demetrius' chest to his navel and he was just getting started.

Chapter 3

Bebo had smoked a whole pack of Newports. He bounced his leg up and down and drummed his fingers on the steering wheel wishing he had another cigarette. Or a blunt! Anything to calm his frazzled nerves.

What the fuck was taking them so long? He wondered as his little beady eyes strained to see up the block.

He rubbed his onion head as every possibility of what could've gone wrong ran through his mind. He let out a sigh and his hands began to shake like a first-time thief.

Fuck these fools at?

Unable to take it any longer, he pulled out his cell phone and called Mayhem's number. When there was no answer he tried Jabari's phone and was relieved when he answered.

"Yo, what's going on in there? What's taking y'all so long? Is everything alright?" The questions came out in rapid fire.

"Bruh, this young boy is cray! He done cut your folks up real bad; slashed his face and sliced his ear off, and that ain't the half," Jabari reported.

"Fuck he do that for?"

'Cause Demetrius wouldn't tell us where the stash was at. I thought you said he wasn't going to resist? It had gotten real ugly up in here."

"Is D dead?"

"Not yet but he's losing blood like a mofo and ya boy Mayhem got that murking look in his eyes." Jabari's harried tone caused Bebo to damn near scream.

"Don't let him do that!" Bebo rested his head on the steering wheel and stifled back tears. That was not how it was supposed to go down. He regretted sending Mayhem's blood thirsty ass on this lick.

"What you want me to do, bruh? I'm in the safe now. You want me to grab the shit and leave Mayhem in this bitch face down?"

“Yea, smash that fuck nigga.”

“A’ight, I’ma blow his whole back out. One.” He disconnected and shoved his phone back down in his pants’ pocket.

“How you plan on doing that?” The voice on the back of his neck was frigid.

Jabari’s head snapped around. Now he too was looking into the eyes of an unmerciful killah.

“What’s—up—fam?” he stuttered.

“I’m not your muthafuckin’ *fam*!” Mayhem shoved his banger in Jabari’s grill. “Bitches get their backs blown out. You calling me a bitch?”

“What you talking about?” He tried to play it off but Mayhem had been standing there listening to his end of the conversation.

“I ain’t talkin’ ‘bout nun,” he chuckled ominously.

Jabari glanced down at his shotgun; he had laid it on the floor to open up the wall safe. “Go for it. Maybe you’re quicker than my trigger finger, we’ll find out,” Mayhem challenged.

Jabari’s hands shot up and Mayhem’s Glock popped off instantly. *Blocka! Blocka!*

Two quick successive shots disintegrated his head, sending brain matter, teeth, blood and flesh spraying everywhere. As his body fell back, Jabari reflexively grabbed ahold of Mayhem’s collar and they crashed to the floor.

Lying on top of Jabari, getting his blood all over his clothes, Mayhem placed the gun point blank on his chest and squeezed the trigger three times. “No new friends,” he spat.

Jabari’s hands fell down to his sides and his bowels released.

Mayhem ignored the stench as he ran Jabari’s pockets and fished out his cell phone. Checking the call log he confirmed what he already suspected.

Soaked in the nigga’s blood, Mayhem stood up and finished emptying the safe. When he had everything inside the duffel bag they had brought along he hurried back into the den.

Demetrius was already dead. Mayhem set the duffel bag down and walked over to the body. He yanked the knife out of dead man's chest and took ahold of his small flaccid penis. Holding it at the base, he severed it away from the scrotum and stuffed it in Demetrius' mouth.

"Suck your own dick, fat ass nigga!" said Mayhem.

Chapter 4

Mayhem bent a few corners, turned off his headlights and parked a block behind where Bebo waited nervously. He eased out of his truck and crept up the street like a night stalker.

Bebo nearly jumped through the roof of his car when he heard a tap on the window. He turned his head to the left and saw a face whose image he would take to hell with him. His eyes bucked and he tried to slither down in the car seat to escape what he had coming to him. But there was nowhere to hide.

Mayhem didn't play no games with that nigga. He fired six shots through the driver's window finding his mark with five of them. Bebo's head and chest exploded in a burst of red, splattering all over the dashboard and the seats. Mayhem snatched the door open and got up close and personal.

He placed the gun in the center of Bebo's heart and sent his ass where all unofficial niggas belonged.

Back in the inner city of Atlanta, Mayhem pulled up at the New American Inn on Cleveland Avenue where he knew the desk clerk that worked night shift. He rented a room and hurried inside to count his loot and wash those niggas' blood off of him.

A half hour later and fresh out of the shower, he sat on the bed in his boxers staring at his come up. He had three birds and seventy bands. He blazed a blunt and reminisced on tonight's kills. Had he left behind any evidence that could tie him to the murder? He asked himself.

A slight stinging sensation on his neck caused him major concern. Jabari had scratched him when he grabbed ahold of him.

Damn, Mayhem fretted.

He got up and examined the mark in the mirror; it was long and pretty deep. They would find his DNA under Jabari's fingernails for sure. "Fuck!"

When he looked closer Mayhem realized that his chain wasn't around his neck. Jabari had snatched it off as they crashed to the floor. The name plate with Mayhem's mother's name on it would seal his conviction.

Now the game plan had changed. Mayhem refused to wait around for those folks to come lock him back up. He had beaten the last murder rap, and he knew there was no way those crackers would let him escape justice a second time.

He grabbed his banger and posed in the mirror, flexing his pecs. With the other hand he touched the tat on his neck. "Mama, I'll make six carry me before I take a chance on twelve judging me," he vowed.

Chapter 5

Mayhem had to move fast and leave Atlanta in his rearview. The only place he could think to go was New Orleans. He had been there a couple of times plotting on a come up with Tank, one of those "Ya Heard Me Boys" that he had met and clicked real tight with in the county jail.

Tank had gotten out and went back to New Orleans but they had remained in touch. Their first plot hadn't panned out but Tank had been trying to get Mayhem to come back. He claimed to have several licks lined up.

Mayhem sat down on the bed and placed a call to Tank to confirm that the offer still stood.

"Yea, bruh. I was just thinking about you 'cause I'm chap, son. A nigga doing bad, ya heard me," Tank clarified.

"A'ight shawdy, I'ma pull up on you when I get there," said Mayhem. He kept the rest of his business off of his tongue. With him, things always remained on a need to know basis.

Tank began telling him about several niggas they could jack. The names meant nothing to Mayhem and he was ready to mash out; sitting in one place was making him jittery.

"I'ma get at you soon, shawdy," Mayhem interrupted. "We'll chop it up when I get there."

"Bet dat."

Mayhem hung up and flicked on the television. He surfed through the local stations and there it was, live on *Channel 2 Action News.* The police had discovered all three bodies but had no suspects as of yet, the news reported.

By the time the forensics' results and the chain pointed them to him, Mayhem planned to be ghost. But he wanted to kiss his daughter goodbye before he got in the wind.

It was almost 3AM when he pulled up in front of Dream's apartment. All of the lights were out inside so he decided to use his door key instead of awakening her. Mayhem entered quietly, locked the door behind him, and turned on the lamp in the living room.

Walking back to the bedroom he bumped into an old ass looking nigga coming out of the bathroom butt naked. Ol' Skool froze in place and threw his hands up in surrender. "Man, she told me she didn't have an old man," he immediately copped deuces.

"She don't," said Mayhem.

"I would've never came over here if I—"

"Relax your ass cheeks, Pops. I told you I'm not her nigga."

Their voices brought Dream out of her bedroom. Her hair was all over her head and the bitch smelled like sex. To make matters worse she was wearing one of Mayhem's t-shirts. He looked at her and wanted to snatch it off of her stank ass, but he kept it playa.

"You're trife, shawdy," he said, shaking his head.

"Fuck you nigga, you can't judge me," she spazzed. "What you doing up in my shit anyway? Give me my door key." She held her hand out.

"I'ma give you your key I just came to get my clothes. Where my baby at?"

"She's in the other room."

"Let me holla at you for a minute," he said, heading in that direction.

Dream turned to Ol' Skool and told him to go back in the bedroom she'd rejoin him in a minute.

She found Mayhem in Brandi's bedroom packing his clothes in the dark. A sliver of light shined in from the hallway illuminating his movements. Dream felt a pang in her heart as she realized that this was truly the end of them.

A tear escaped from the corner of her eye and trickled down her face. She quickly wiped it away before he noticed.

Mayhem sat his bags down on the floor at the foot of the bed and stared at his daughter's sleeping figure. He wondered what would become of her without him in his life. Would

Dream have different niggas running in and out of there like a track meet?

Prolly so.

His chest felt like it was about to cave in. He didn't want to leave his seed but he knew that it would be too dangerous taking her on the run with him.

Mayhem walked to the head of the bed and gently sat down. He pulled his baby into his arms and held her tightly. She instinctively wrapped her little arms around her daddy's neck.

"My princess," he whispered, placing kisses on her soft cheeks. "Daddy loves you so much."

"I wuv you too, Dada," she said in a sleepy voice.

Mayhem closed his eyes and fought to keep the tears from falling. His gangsta was sat on the shelf as he lost the battle to hold in his emotions. When he licked his lips he tasted his own tears in his mouth.

He pressed his face against his princess's and held her securely. After a long moment he laid her back in bed and covered her with the thin blanket. Mayhem leaned over and kissed her one final time.

"Daddy will always love you," he whispered as Brandi drifted back to sleep.

Mayhem took a deep breath then rose up and gathered his bags. He slung a Louie V garment bag over his shoulder and stood looking at his daughter. It was hard leaving her knowing that he would probably never see her again, but he had no choice.

At the door he stopped and stared down at Dream; her face was wet with tears.

"Where are you going?" she sniffled.

"I gotta go away. That's all I can tell you."

Dream looked up at him with apology in her eyes but the words did not come off of her tongue.

Mayhem said, "Shawdy, I don't hold nothin' against you, it is what it is. All I ask of you is not to have different niggas running up in here. You know that shit is mad foul."

Surprisingly, she didn't snap.

"Okay," she muttered.

He flashed her a small smile and wiped away a fresh tear that slid down her face. Things hadn't always been bad between them.

Dream smiled back at him through her watery eyes.

Mayhem went in his pocket and gave her some bands. "Take care of my shorty," he said. "And send that old ass nigga home. You can do better than that."

"I will," she promised.

"A'ight, lil' mama, take care."

As Mayhem drove away from Dream's house that night headed to New Orleans, there was no way he could've predicted everything that was about to pop off.

Chapter 6

By the time Mayhem reached New Orleans it was a little past noon. He had thrown his cell phone away before leaving Georgia just in case po po could track him through the GPS on it.

He pulled up to a pay phone in a gas station on Crowder Boulevard and hit up his nigga.

"Yea, who is this?" answered Tank.

"What it do, shawdy? I'm in your city," said Mayhem.

Tank recognized his voice and immediately got hyped. "Don't fuck wit' me, bruh," he replied excitedly.

"Nigga, I'm not fuckin' with you. Fa real, I'm here. Where you at?"

"At my girl Tweety's house, 'cross the canal."

That was in New Orleans' famous Lower Ninth Ward. Mayhem had been there when he was in New Orleans two months ago so he had no problem finding it.

As he drove through the hoods he saw niggas washing fly whips in their front yards, little kids running up and down the street, and muthafuckas moving like they were up to no good — every day hood shit. Shawdies waved at him from their porches, wanting to fuck his whip. Mayhem honked the horn at them and kept it moving.

When he pulled up in front of Tweety's house Tank was waiting on the porch. Mayhem parked and got out with the duffel bag slung over his shoulder. There was no way he was leaving his loot in the car unattended. *Shid, they don't call this muthafucka Cut Throat City for nothin',* he thought.

He walked up on the porch and greeted Tank with a half hug.

"My nigga!" Tank smiled, reflecting the scorching sun off of his gold grill.

"What's up, Blacker Than Me?" kidded Mayhem; he was jet black himself but Tank was smut.

"Ain't nothin'. Tryna get it how I live but a nigga hurting right now." He patted his empty pockets for emphasis.

"Don't worry, bruh. I got you."

"Whoa nah," he dragged as he happily grinned.

"Yea, nigga I fucks witchu," said Mayhem. He turned around and hit the remote to lock the truck then he followed Tank inside.

"You must've hit a nice lick," guessed Tank as they sat down in the living room.

"You the Feds nigga?" teased Mayhem.

"Picture that." Tank laughed as he reached for a pack of cigarettes on the table. "You want a joe, bruh?" he offered.

"Nah, I don't smoke no more."

"Whaatttt?"

When they were locked up in the county Mayhem had chain smoked to relieve the stress of an upcoming trial that wasn't looking good for him. He had blown a nigga's brains out on MLK and the state had an eye witness to the murder. He had been staring at life in the pen with no parole eligibility for at least thirty years.

The witness was a problem that he had to get rid of or his ass was gonna grow old in prison. Night after night, he and Tank stayed up talking and plotting. Several months passed before Tank finally made bail on charges of aggravated assault. A week later as promised, he made Mayhem's problem disappear.

Mayhem looked around for Tweety. "Where your girl at?" he whispered.

"Winn Dixie, making groceries," said Tank, looking under the couch cushion for his lighter.

Mayhem relaxed; now he could speak freely. He had thanked Tank once before for what he had done, but it needed repeating. "I appreciate what you did for me, that was some real nigga shit," he said.

"Huh, bruh," Tank replied. "I told you that cheese eater would never make it to court to testify against you. I caught that bitch ass nigga coming out of Magic City, followed him home and knocked the gravy out his biscuit. When I hit him with that choppa, son looked like ground beef by the time I eased off of that trigger," he recounted.

Mayhem pictured that shit with a smile on his face. The one thing he despised was a snitch nigga. He had already paid Tank ten stacks for handling that, but the way he saw it Tank had given him back his life so he was forever in his debt.

He reached inside the duffel bag that sat on the floor between his feet and pulled out a brick. Placing it on the table, he said, "That's you, shawdy, and that ain't no flex. That's the Real Deal Holyfield — fish scale, ya heard me." He mimicked the way Tank talked.

Tank looked up at him with a hundred questions in his eyes, but Mayhem put a hand up and stopped him.

"Don't ask, shawdy. 'Cause it don't even matter," he said. He pulled out three bands and dropped the money on top of the kilo.

"You know you don't owe me this, bruh," Tank lightly protested.

"It's all love, family."

"Real shit."

Tank finally found his lighter. He put a flame to his cigarette and pulled smoke into his lungs. Mayhem watched as he blew rings up towards the ceiling.

"Here you go, my nigga," said Tank, sliding a small bowl of loud to him.

Mayhem twisted up a blunt and put some weed smoke in the air as he leaned back on the couch and contemplated his best move. A thorough young nigga named Trouble that he had been in Juvenile with years ago had always preached *Trust No Man*. The heart-wrenching story Trouble told of how his pops, Youngblood, best friend Lonnie's testimony had gotten Youngblood the death penalty reminded Mayhem not to tell Tank why he had left the 'A' so suddenly.

He put the blunt to his lips again and puffed, puffed, passed. "Bruh, I got two more birds and I need you to help me get off of 'em. I also need to get rid of my truck ASAP. Plus, I need a safe place to lay my head while I figure out my next move," he said.

"I got you." Tank leaned back in his chair and pulled hard on the blunt. After a moment of thought he said, "You must've done something real serious up in the 'A'."

"Sum'n like dat."

Tank didn't question him any further and Mayhem didn't volunteer anything. He passed the blunt back to Mayhem and picked up his cigarette out of the ashtray.

"Bruh," he said after some thought, "You can park your truck behind the house if you don't want to ride around in it. And my sideline bitch, Keedy and her girl A'nyah, got a place in the East at Georgetown Apartments on Derbyshire Drive. You can chill there for a minute. Both of them are one hundred."

Mayhem wrinkled his forehead.

"I heard of those apartments before," Mayhem said, searching his memory.

"Yea, Magnolia Shorty got killed over there. But it's cool. And A'nyah is dimed the fuck up. You'll like her."

Mayhem didn't know about that. Pussy wasn't on his mind, and he didn't want to lay his head somewhere that niggas would be running in and out of.

Before he could verbalize his concerns, they heard a car pull up out front. Mayhem was on his feet with his banger in his hand in a split second.

"Damn, bruh, you paranoid as shit. That ain't nobody but Tweety," said Tank, going to the door. He wondered what the fuck Mayhem had done. Whatever it was it had to be serious the way he was acting.

Mayhem slid his tool back on his waist and sat back down.

Tweety came through the door looking ghetto fabulous. She was a thick redbone with an ass that made a muthafucka shake their head in amazement. Her long Brazilian hair weave flowed past her shoulders; her makeup was perfect and her clothes screamed *designer labels*. Her neck sparkled and her wrists and fingers were icy. Mayhem didn't have to guess where much of Tank's money went, Tweety was rocking a nigga's whole hustle.

Shanica, their precious three year old daughter, held on to her hand. Shorty was a little darling. Her cute dimpled self was rocking designer labels already just like her moms. Mayhem thought of Brandi and regret sat on his heart and camped out there.

He spoke to Tweety and the little girl then he and Tank went outside. Tank unloaded the groceries out of the car and carried them inside while Mayhem parked his truck under a carport behind the house.

Fifteen minutes later they headed out in Tank's 2010 Tahoe with Rick Ross' *God Forgives, I Don't* bumping hard.

The first thing Mayhem noticed about the Georgetown apartments was that they weren't hood. The complex looked like condos and certain units had garages. There was nobody hanging out in the parking lot and the lawn was well-kept and free of litter.

"Yea, if shawdy and 'em a'ight, I can rest here," he said.

Tank parked in front of a building where a girl sat outside in a lawn chair. They got out of his whip and walked up the walkway. Mayhem noticed that his nigga had a scowl on his face. As they approached the girl, Tank suddenly stopped.

"What you doing out here with those little ass shorts on?" he asked her. "Fuck is you trying to do, turn a trick?"

"No, baby," she giggled nervously. "I didn't think these were *that* short. You've seen me wear them before."

Mayhem could see fear in her light brown eyes. He lowered his gaze below her waist. The shorts fitted her smooth thighs tightly but he didn't think they were too short at all. *But hey, it ain't my business,* he thought.

Tank thought otherwise, he went from zero to a hundred in the blink of an eye. "Keedy, don't play with me!" He grabbed a handful of her hair and snatched her clean out of the chair, tumbling it over.

"Ahhh," she cried.

"Bring your ass in the house and put some muthafuckin' clothes on," he growled.

Mayhem quickly looked around to see if any neighbors were watching. The last thing he needed was for someone to call the po po's. "Bruh, chill out," he said.

Tank wasn't tryna hear that. He drug Keedy to the door of her apartment and slung her inside like dirty laundry. Mayhem had a flashback of his mother's boyfriend throwing her around the house. He squeezed his eyes tightly to block out the painful memories that still haunted him to this very day.

Tank shut the door behind them and walked over to where Keedy laid crying on the floor. He lifted his foot and kicked her in the side. "Bitch, get your ass up and change out of those ho shorts before I stomp you in your muthafuckin' head," he threatened.

Holding her side and still crying, Keedy struggled to her feet and headed towards the back. Tank turned to Mayhem. "Have a seat, dawg. Bitch gon' make me kill her punk ass, ya heard me."

Mayhem's face was tight. He bit his tongue because he didn't wanna get in that man's business. But straight up, he was not feeling that shit. He respected the next man's get-down but a nigga didn't earn no props with him for beating on a defenseless girl.

"You sure everything is gucci? Shawdy not gon' call those folks is she?" Mayhem asked through gritted teeth.

"Hell no! That bitch know better. I got her ass house trained." Tank's chest was all puffed out.

He sat down on the floral patterned couch and responded to a text that had just came through on his iPhone. Mayhem took a seat across from him in an oversized chair. He looked around the apartment; it was nicely furnished and roomy, and he could smell vanilla incense burning.

When he looked up a bad ass dark skinned shawdy was coming from out of the back. She stood about 5'7" with baby making hips and bow legs. Her 38Ds strained against her wife beater allowing a glimpse of her chocolate nipples. Her dreamy eyes complimented the sensual slope of her mouth and those thin lips of hers looked succulent with that pink lipstick on them. Shawdy rocked her hair in booty braids and her walk could command the attention of a blind man.

Baby girl's leggings hugged her hips like God had put in overtime when creating those curves. She walked over and looked down at Mayhem with a flirtatious smile.

She would've had most niggas stuck right then, but not him. Mayhem had learned through fucking with Dream that what looked good to a nigga wasn't always good *for* a nigga. So immediately he was on guard.

She pried her eyes off of him and turned to Tank. "What's up, cuz?" she referred to him affectionately as she took a seat next to him on the couch, folding her legs up under her.

"Same story different day," he replied nonchalantly

Mayhem tried to ignore that camel toe between her legs that was winking at him.

"Who is this *fione* nigga you got with you?" She asked Tank, cutting her sexy ass eyes at Mayhem and catching him unconsciously staring at the fat kitty.

"That's my *round,* Mayhem; he from the 'A'," Tank replied. "Bruh, this my girl's friend A'nyah." He completed the introductions.

Mayhem acknowledged her with a slight nod of his head and a simple "How you doing, shawdy?"

"I'm okay," she smiled, showing her pretty thirty-twos. "I love the way you say 'shawdy'. Let me hear you say it again."

"Nah, I'm good." *Fuck I look like—a puppet?*

A'nyah stuck a finger in her and mouth and lowered her eyes trying to cast her spell on him. "Oh, you one of those mean ass niggas," she said.

"Nah, I ain't mean, shawdy, I'm just me."

"Oooh, you said it, bay-bae!" Like Keedy her New Orleans' accent was thick. She danced in her seat. "You just said *shawdy.* Aha, I got your mean ass." She cracked up.

Mayhem licked his lips to keep from smiling. A'nyah looked at him with all that sexy and said. "Damn, you gon' be my *trade*, lil' daddy. I'ma have to make you my lil' dip. I hope your baby mamas don't mind."

"Who said I got a baby mama?"

"Oh, nigga you probably got four or five of 'em. Sitting over there with all of that thug passion oozing out of you. I bet you got bitches lined up tryna hit that. Humph?"

"Ain't nobody hittin' *me.* This that real G shit over here, I do the hittin'. And I'm a real selective about who I give the dick to," he put that shit in check.

"I heard that, bay-bae. Humph." She made a little face like she was going to prove him a lie.

"Keedy, come out here and fix me something to eat," Tank yelled as he rolled a blunt.

When Keedy came from the back she had changed into loose fitting sweats and a t-shirt with the words *Tru Ryder Chick* scripted across the front. Mayhem didn't doubt that; shawdy had to ride hard and love even harder to accept being treated so foul. But he couldn't help wondering if she loved herself.

She had re-combed her hair and washed the tears off of her face. He took a good look at her. She had real sad eyes, like it had been a very long time since a smile reached her soul.

Mayhem could definitely relate.

He took in her whole appearance. Keedy wasn't a dime piece but she was far from ugly, too cute to be a nigga's soccer ball. She was light brown and attractive in an understated way. She was slim built with a little bump in the back, and had she made a concerted effort she could've been one sexy ass chick.

Staring at her, Mayhem could tell from her body language that she lacked confidence and self-worth. He shook his head in despair over what had to be wasting away inside of her.

When Tank introduced them, Keedy casted her eyes to the floor. "Hi," she muttered with her head down.

Mayhem didn't know if she was afraid to look at him for fear that Tank would knock her head off or if she was too embarrassed by what he'd just done to her.

"How you doing, Miss Lady?" he asked politely.

"I'm fine." She glanced up at him briefly, looked back down at the floor then she asked Tank what he wanted to eat.

"Hook me and my round up some shrimp po boys," he said.

Mayhem frowned without realizing it. He recalled his mother's nigga handling her the same way. Kicking her ass then making her cook for him and run his bath water just minutes after bouncing her off the goddamn walls.

"Bruh, why don't me and A'nyah just go grab some po boys from a corner store. Your girl don't have to cook," he cut in.

"I'm down, shawdy," said A'nyah playfully.

She assumed that Mayhem was trying to get her alone, but he wasn't doing that for her. He was doing it for Keedy because he hadn't been big enough to do it for his mama.

Chapter 7

Keedy could've hugged Mayhem's neck for rescuing her. She did not feel like cooking shit for Tank's abusive, disrespectful ass. She had the feeling that Mayhem somehow knew that and wanted to spare her the humiliation. That immediately endeared him to her.

She hadn't gotten but a sneak peek at him, but she couldn't even lie to herself—that boy was muthafuckin' mouth-watering. Tank had told her a few things about him so she knew that Mayhem was also street certified. And the look that flashed in his eyes when Tank threatened to stomp her head made her feel that he had a little compassion. There was nothing sexier than a thug with a heart.

Gurl, don't even think about it, she checked herself before Tank read her mind and booted up on a bitch. It didn't take much for him to beat her ass. The wrong word or the wrong tone of voice, the wrong outfit or a casual glance at a nigga that passed by them at the mall—any number of small things could lead to a busted lip or a black eye.

Keedy had worn so many ass whoopings from men, she had lost count. But Tank was the absolute worst in a long line of abusive niggas that she had allowed in her life. He didn't just slap her around, he would fight her like she was a goddamn man. He had spat on her, hit her in the head with a beer bottle and worse. Dealing with him had alienated her from her entire family.

When they first hooked up a few years ago she had poured her heart out to him, telling about all of the abuse that she had endured. He had held her in his arms and promised that he wasn't anything like those bastards that came before him, and he hadn't lied, he was ten times fouler!

The funny thing is that Keedy hadn't even liked Tank at first. In fact, she couldn't stand him. They had grown up together in the Desire projects and were in the same class at Carver Middle before the streets claimed Tank full-time.

Whenever Keedy would pass by Tank and his boys in the projects, he would tease her mercilessly. “You a lil’ skinny, bumpy face, ugly bitch, and yo ass looks like an ironing board,” he would say.

Keedy would stick her middle finger up in the air and pretend to ignore him. But those words used to cut deeply because she already felt very unattractive. Her titties were too small, her nose was too big, and her hair was too short. When she looked in the mirror she used to see a hot ass mess.

Many nights she went to sleep praying that she would wake up beautiful like her girl A’nyah, who all the boys and grown ass men around their way wanted.

A’nyah had always been a pretty girl with a body to die for. Boys would look right past Keedy’s little bitty booty to get at her. That bitch got her pussy popped before she even got her first period.

Nobody was checking for Keedy like that so she didn’t lose her virginity until she was sixteen. And even then she hadn’t lost it to a boy who loved or wanted her. Keedy’s innocence was stolen by an uncle who raped her. More traumatizing than what he did to her was what he said after he had gotten done.

Keedy was balled up on the bed crying. Her stuff hurt so bad it felt like she was split wide open. She could feel something wet running down her thighs. Through tears that stung her eyes like acid she saw him zip himself up. As she laid whimpering and praying that he would leave and not rape her again, he finished fixing his clothes then he walked back over to the bed and scowled down at her.

“Fuck you crying for, musty ass bitch?” he said. “You should be glad somebody wanna fuck your ugly ass!”

He bent over and spat dead in her face. Then, as casually as possible he fired up a cigarette before turning around and walking out of her bedroom.

Keedy never told anyone about what was done to her that night, she just tried to forget that it happened. But she could never forget what he had said. Was she really so ugly that she should be happy to have gotten raped? That's the question that she had been asking herself for the past five years.

Her uncle hadn't just taken her innocence, he had scarred her soul. And every man after him deepened the wound. Even as she blossomed into young womanhood and became cute and sexy, inside she still felt ugly.

Two years ago Tank had taken notice and had begun trying to talk to her. Recalling how cruel he used to treat her, Keedy kept turning him down. She also knew that he had a woman and she was so tired of being a muthafucka's jump off or a sideline bitch. But A'nyah kept prodding her to give Tank a chance plus he was mad persistent. He just wouldn't give up. His determination to get her made Keedy feel truly wanted by a man for the first time in her tortured young life.

Eventually she gave in and fell in love with Tank. In the beginning things were blissful, but as time went on the real him surfaced. He tried to control everything she did and every place she went. Like he thought she was going to turn into a ho the moment she was out of his sight. Keedy regretted telling him what her uncle had done to her because he had only used it against her.

"Ho, you prolly liked it," he'd say when he was in one of his mean moods.

That shit hurt just as bad as when she was being raped. Keedy would lay next to him seething inside, but too afraid to say anything back.

Not long after that the physical abuse started. She kept telling herself that she was going to leave him alone but somehow she never had, and now a bitch was stuck. Keedy figured it was God's way of punishing her for messing with that woman's man. Or maybe she simply did not deserve better. Maybe she was still that musty, ugly bitch that should've felt lucky to have gotten raped.

"What you thinking about, girl?" asked Tank. His voice brought her back to the present.

"Nothing, baby," she said demurely.

"C'mere." He pulled her down on his lap and wrapped his arms around her. "You mad at me?"

"No." She bit down on her bottom lip to hold in the tears.

"You know a nigga love you, yea?" he said, sliding his hands up her shirt and caressing her small breasts.

"Do you?" She asked as a few tears began to fall.

"Hell yea, I love you—you're my bitch. But you gotta stop making me beat on you, ya heard me," he caressed her arm. "Fa real, I don't like doing that shit."

"I'm sorry," she apologized. "I try so hard not to do anything to make you upset."

"It's all good. Give your nigga some of that tongue."

Their lips locked and he played with Keedy's nipples until they hardened. In spite of her anger she felt herself getting wet. She ran her hand down his chest as their tongues explored each other's mouths.

Tank kissed her roughly, making her feel so wanted. Keedy unsnapped his pants and reached inside for proof of his desire. He was rocked up and ready for some of that hot head game of hers.

Keedy stroked him up and down and began sliding off of his lap. "You gotta hurry up, you know they'll be back in a minute," he reminded her.

"Yea."

She went to her knees and fully pulled his dick out. It sprung up and thumped against her chin, causing Keedy to giggle. Tank was impatient as always, he pushed her head down forcing himself inside her mouth and to the back of her throat. She gagged then pulled back a little before licking around the head.

"Put it back in."

Keedy did what he wanted and Tank began fucking her mouth like it was her pussy. She let her spit lubricate him while she relaxed her throat muscles and worked her jaws. Tank closed his eyes and gave in to the feeling. A few minutes later he groaned and nutted in Keedy's mouth.

"Swallow it," he said.

Keedy made it disappear then stuck her tongue out. "All gone, baby."

"That's my bitch," he said.

"Yea, I'm your bitch," she agreed as she got up off of her knees and began sliding her sweats off so that she could straddle him.

Tank's hand shot out, stopping her. "We don't have time for that. Ya dig? My nigga and A'nyah will be back any minute. Go brush your teeth and come back. I gotta talk to you about something."

"Yea," she replied, swallowing her disappointment.

Tank zipped up his pants and fired up a Kool. In that moment he looked just like Keedy's uncle.

Ain't this some shit! She fumed as she leaned over the sink in the bathroom brushing her teeth. Tank had just made her feel like that ugly little bitch again. *Nigga nutted down my throat then dismissed me. Alright!*

He had not fucked her in more than two weeks which caused Keedy's insecurities to soar. She wondered if she no longer pleased him. Or maybe he had found himself another side piece. A bitch much prettier than her.

Keedy rinsed her mouth out and tried not to let it bother her, it wasn't like she would've gotten an orgasm anyway. That was something she hadn't ever had with a man. The only way she could come was with her toy. *I'm going to make a date with it real soon.*

She checked underneath the sink to make sure it was still there but to her dismay it wasn't. "Where did I put it?" she mumbled as she moved things out of the way in search of it.

Am I so fuckin' ugly my dildo has bounced?

Keedy cracked up at the thought of that. Then she remembered that she had put it in the bottom drawer in her bedroom.

She put a hand to her mouth and gave herself the fresh breath test. Yep, her shit was minty fresh. She threw on her game face and went back into the living room to see what Tank wanted to talk to her about.

What have I done now? she worried.

Chapter 8

Riding back from Captain Sal's on Chef Menteur Hwy where they had picked up some sandwiches, Mayhem looked out of the window of A'nyah's Hyundai Sonata as she sang along with Tiara Thomas.

I'll be your bad girl, I'll prove it to you
I can't promise that I'll be good to you
'Cause I have some issues, I won't commit
No, not having it
But at least I can admit that I'll be bad no to you (to you)
Yea, I'll be good in bed but I'll be bad to you
Is it bad that I never made love, no I never did it

"But I sure know how to fuck," A'nyah belted.

Out of the corner of his eye, Mayhem saw her cut her eyes at him but he didn't acknowledge it. She wasn't saying nothin' he hadn't already concluded. But what shawdy didn't know was that he wasn't her average nigga. The power of the pussy had diminished effect on him. The road to the cemetery was lined with easy ass on both sides.

Mayhem continued looking out of the window, deep in thought. What the fuck was he gon' do. Life as he once knew it was over. In just a matter of a few days a nationwide warrant for his arrest on the charges of murder would probably be issued. He thought about calling Dream to see if the police had come there looking for him, but he decided that wouldn't be smart.

A'nyah turned the music down. "Mayhem, are you always so quiet?" she asked. "Or is it that you just don't like me? You can tell me if that's it. I'm a big girl, I can handle it."

"I don't know if I like you or not, shawdy, I just met you. I know you're probably used to niggas drooling all over you but I don't rock like that. With me, you can't just appeal to my eye, you gotta spark an interest in my mind and my soul," he said, continuing to look out of the window at nothin' in particular.

"Damn, bay-bae," she sarcastically chuckled. "I gotta do all that just to hit that?"

Mayhem couldn't help but laugh. At least she was straight-forward about hers.

A'nyah shot him her most hypnotizing smile and sang, "I never made love, no I never did it, but I sure know how to fucccccckkkk."

He looked at her and coolly replied, "You oughta holla at Wale. Maybe he'll let you sing the hook on his next remix."

"You're cray cray," she laughed. "You playing hard lil' daddy, but before it's over you gon' be my lil' dip, yea."

"I hear you, lil' mama, but this dick right here ain't on the table. Your pretty ass can help me get some money though. I know you fuck with some caked up niggas, don't you?" A perfect plan came to mind.

"I'm tryna fuck with *you*," she continued to flirt.

Mayhem saw that dick instead of dollars was on her brain so he aborted the thoughts that flowed through his. While A'nyah sang about how bad she was, he put his nose to the bag and inhaled the aroma of the food they had just bought. Damn, a nigga was hungry as fuck.

The food hit the spot for everyone. Tank smashed his then reached over and grabbed half of Keedy's without asking.

"You want another cold drink, Mayhem?" asked A'nyah on her way into the kitchen from the dining area where they were seated.

"Nah, I'm good. Thanks," he declined.

"What about you?" she asked Tank, giving him the side eye.

"Keedy gon' get it for me," he said and like presto shawdy was on her feet.

Mayhem and Tank walked out on the back balcony and put some loud in the air. Looking out over an expanse of trees,

Tank told him that he had talked to Keedy about letting him chill there for a minute and it was all good with her.

"Shawdy seems like good people," Mayhem said.

"Yea, she one hundred. And A'nyah ain't gonna have a problem with it, she all on ya dick anyway. But don't sleep on her, lil' mama play niggas like dominoes, ya heard me."

Mayhem wasn't worried about that. His only concern was whether or not she would have different niggas running in and out. If so, he wouldn't feel comfortable resting his head there longer than a day or two.

"A'nyah don't get down like that," Tank assured him.

A'nyah was down with the move. She agreed to let Mayhem have the third bedroom for as long as he needed it, and she confirmed that she did not entertain company there. He gave her and Keedy both three hundred and went outside to get his things out of Tank's truck. The shower and the bed was beckoning a nigga. When he finally laid his head on the pillow he was out like a light.

Mayhem was resting peacefully until a recurring dream invaded his sleep. His mama was trying to gulp air into her lungs and pry that nigga's hands from around her throat.

"Please, Carlton! I can't breathe!" she coughed.

"I don't give a fuck, bitch," he growled. Then he punched her in the face.

Little Mayhem saw her fall in slow motion, and her head hit the floor with a sickening thump. Her boyfriend looked down at her with no mercy and kicked her in the head, again and again.

Mayhem ran up behind him and jumped on his back, but he was a little, skinny nigga so the man easily slung him off of him and continued to stomp her head with the heel of his construction boot.

"A dead bitch is better than a hard-headed one," he spat as blood poured down her face.

Mayhem pounced to his feet crying. "Leave my mama alone!"

He quickly looked around the room for something to hit the nigga with. Finding one of his aluminum baseball bats in the corner, he grabbed it and flew at him screaming, "I'ma kill you, muthafucka!"

The huge man spun around and snatched a gun off of his waist but Mayhem didn't stop. He drew the bat back and swung with all his might.

Boom! The gunshot echoed like a cannon in the cramped apartment.

Mayhem's small body flew backwards and he crashed to the floor on his back. A ball of fire coursed through his stomach like a rolling inferno.

"Nooooooo! Not my baby," she cried out as she desperately tried to pull herself up on her feet.

Carlton turned and scowled. "You should've taught his little ass to stay out of grown folks business!" He raised the gun over his head and brought it down with force, cracking her skull wide open.

"Muthafuckin' hard-headed bitch. Didn't I tell you I was gon' kill your ass the next time you disobeyed me!" he spat.

Whack! Whack! Whack! Whack! He slammed the butt of the gun across her head over and over again until, ignoring the blood that spurted up in his face. He was in a rage and the cocaine that he had snorted seemed to enhance his fury.

"Die bitch!"

"Leave her alone, muthafucka," groaned Mayhem. His small hands tried to stop the blood from gushing out of the big hole in his stomach.

Carlton was headed over to where Mayhem lay to finish him off when loud banging on the door brought him out of his murderous frenzy.

"Jacole is everything alright in there? It sounded like I heard a gunshot." It was the voice of Miss Priscilla, their upstairs neighbor.

Carlton snapped out of the trance and looked down at the destruction that he had caused. Sweat ran down his face and his hands began to tremble as the weight of his actions stared him hard in the face. In a panic he snatched his car keys off of the mantel and dashed out of the back door leaving it as wide open as he had left his girlfriend's head.

A gust of wind blew into the house, moving the curtains and whisking across Mayhem's brow. He ignored the hot, intense pain that blazed in his stomach and the blood that gushed out as he willed himself to crawl over to where his mama laid.

So much blood covered her head and face, Mayhem couldn't even see her eyes. "Mama," he cried out as he tried to lift her head.

It was as limp as a Raggedy Ann doll and her mouth was slack. "Please don't die, Mama," Mayhem cried.

He laid his head on her chest like he often did as an infant, listening for that precious beat of her loving heart. A sound that was no more.

"Jacole! Jacole! What's going on in there?" Miss Priscilla yelled through the front door.

But Jacole couldn't answer her, she had gone to the other side.

Mayhem bolted up out of his sleep, knocking the lamp off of the nightstand. He swung his legs over the edge of the bed and sat there with his head down in his hands. The wetness on his face was nothing compared to the ache in his heart.

"Mama, I wish I would've been big enough to help you," he mumbled over and over again.

Chapter 9

Tank had gone home to Tweety and A'nyah was off somewhere digging her hands down in some trick nigga's pocket. Keedy was lying across her bed reading *The Pussy Trap* by Nene Capri on her Kindle. The main character Kayson had her clit in a fit with "The Enforcer".

Lawdieee, what I wouldn't do to be that bitch Koko right about now. "Whew!" She fanned herself at the thought of all that good dick attached to a true Boss.

As quickly as the image passed through her mind, her insecurities kicked in. Who was she kidding, if Kayson came alive off of those pages he probably would've took one look at her and jumped his ass right back into the fictional world.

Keedy was so fucked up she couldn't even enjoy a fantasy without ruining it with self-doubt.

As she continued to read she unconsciously slid her hand inside her sweats and touched her sensitive pearl. She moaned when Kayson strapped Koko in that "electric chair" and turned her ass out. *For some of that he could execute my ass for real—for real, and a bitch would die with a smile on her face.*

Keedy squeezed her thighs together and pretended that she was Kayson's rider chick, Koko. Not only was she getting all of that good dick, she was a Boss in her own right. Kayson had taught her well, and she didn't play no games with a nigga. There was no way Tank would beat a bitch like KoKo's ass and dog her out; he would get his whole muthafuckin' wig pushed the fuck back.

If only I had KoKo's courage, Keedy chided herself.

A loud bang came from the guest bedroom, snapping her out of her little fantasy. She sat the Kindle down and went to investigate.

"Are you okay in there?" she asked as she tapped lightly on the door of the guest bedroom.

A few seconds later the door opened and Mayhem stood there bare-chested and rocking basketball shorts. He was all hard body and tats. His dark chocolate looked like a Hershey's bar. A wisp of hair ran from his navel and disappeared into the waist of his shorts. Keedy's imagination followed it.

She had to put her hands against the door frame to keep from fainting. She shook her head trying to regain full consciousness.

"Are you okay?" they asked each other at the same time.

She giggled like a little school girl. Mayhem smiled but when she looked up and into his eyes they were red.

Nah, can't be, she discounted her first thought. It had to be from the weed.

"Are you okay, Mayhem? I thought I heard a loud bang?" she asked again on a shaky voice.

"Yea, I'm good but your lamp ain't. I knocked it over and I think it's broke." His eyes turned apologetic. "Hold on, let me give you the money to buy another one."

"Huh?" Damn, she had slipped back into a fantasy.

"I think I broke your lamp. But I'll replace it. My bad," he repeated. His voice was hoarse from sleep, making him sound like Jeezy.

Keedy's knees felt weak.

"It's okay, you don't have to do that," she somehow managed to say.

Mayhem shook off her response and went over and grabbed his pants off the back of the chair by the bed. He returned with some money in his hand but Keedy refused to accept it.

"You don't owe me anything for that cheap little lamp," she insisted.

"Take the money, shawdy, it's all good," he softly pleaded.

She shook her from side to side like an insolent four year old, but her response came out sugary sweet. "I just wanted to make sure you were okay in here," she explained.

Out of habit he licked his lips.

"Thanks for checking on me. And thanks again for letting me rest here. I really appreciate it."

Keedy's breath got caught in her chest. "You're wel—come," she stumbled over two itty bitty words. And even after she got them out she had to pry her eyes off of that man, he had her hypnotized without even trying to do so.

Later that night she went in her bottom drawer and pulled out her trusty dildo with the thick vibrating head. Feeling hotter than a furnace down there, she dove under the covers and hurriedly slid her panties off. She spread her legs wide and turned on her toy. She became more excited as it started buzzing. Closing her eyes, she traced her puffy lower lips with the tip and her juices began to flow.

"Ummm," she moaned as she inserted a few thick inches inside her buttery cup.

Her hand moved up and down, and her walls accommodated the toy's width. Keedy opened her legs more and arched her pelvis off of the bed.

"Yes," she moaned. It felt so good as the width filled her and the length touched her bottom. She moved it in and out and rotated her hips to match the rhythm of her hand. "Oh, god," she moaned as her hand began to move faster and faster.

Keedy squeezed her eyes tighter and allowed her imagination to run free. She envisioned him on top of her pounding away. "Fuck me. Make me come," she cried.

Her pussy was on fire and sopping wet. She could hear it gushing and she felt an orgasm coming on fast. With her other hand she grabbed a pillow and covered her head just before she screamed out in ecstasy.

"Oh, my god! Oh, my god! Sweet muthafuckin' Jesus!" It felt like the top of her head had blown off.

Take me Lord I'm ready to go.

She was limp as a wet noodle. Keedy didn't have the strength or desire to move and her pussy was still jumping. It felt so good she fell asleep with the dildo inside of her. Wishing it was Mayhem.

Chapter 10

Keedy awoke to the mouthwatering smell of bacon frying in the kitchen. Her stomach growled as she threw the covers off of her, swung her feet over the side of the bed, and rubbed sleep out of her eyes. She stifled a yarn and looked under the tangled sheets for her toy. Locating it, she held it against her chest. "You did that shit last night, yea." She uttered fondly.

For a minute she thought about pleasuring herself again but her stomach overruled her coochie. She didn't know what had gotten into A'nyah, it had to be snowing in hell for her to be up cooking breakfast. Then Keedy recalled that Mayhem was there. That was the reason A'nyah was up early and in the kitchen.

Bitch, you know you do the most.

Keedy giggled as she headed to the bathroom, took a quick shower, and handled her other morning ablutions. She threw on an oversized t-shirt and a pair of leggings, and bounced into the kitchen ready to crash A'nyah and Mayhem's little romantic breakfast. She wasn't trying to block, all she wanted to do was get her a plate and retreat to her comfy bedroom.

As she followed the scrumptious aroma, it dawned on her that today was Thursday not Saturday. A'nyah must've called off of work, she figured. If she was doing it like that, the bitch must've came home late last night and jumped Mayhem's bones. And he had to have put something brand new on that ass for her to call in sick because A'nyah was serious about her money.

"Alright, girl," Keedy mumbled as she went to investigate the smells.

When she reached the kitchen she was thoroughly surprised to see Mayhem standing over the stove. "Good morning," he said.

"Good morning," she returned. "Where is A'nyah?" She looked around for her girl.

"She said she had to go to work."

"Okayyyy. Hmmm. What's for breakfast?" She walked up, got on her tippy toes and peeked over his broad shoulders.

"Let me see," replied Mayhem stunting a lil' bit because he was wicked in the kitchen. He had two pans going at once and he was working them effortlessly. "Uh, I got some bacon, of course. Egg omelets with cheddar and chives, and a sprinkle of bell pepper and diced onions. Then I'ma have you some hash browns fried, smothered and covered. Buttered biscuits with some muthafuckin' grape jelly—and," he drug the last word out. "A big ass pitcher of Minute Maid orange juice. Now what you know 'bout that?"

Keedy covered her smile with her hand but a little giggle escaped from behind it. "You're a mess," she said with a wisp of breath on his neck. "Who taught you how to throw down?"

He half turned towards her. "I'm self-taught, shawdy," he lightly boasted.

Keedy put a hand on her hip and looked at him suspiciously. "Am I going to have to call 9-1-1 after I eat your cooking, Mayhem?" she half teased.

"Nah, I'm that nigga. After this you'll be tryna get me to hook you up every morning. Fa real shawdy, I'm a beast in the kitchen."

"Humph. We'll see."

"Never doubt a man of my many talents." He flashed her a confident smile. "Just hold up a minute, I'm about to make you eat your words."

"Yea? They'll probably taste better than what you're cooking," she teased.

Mayhem licked his lips and Keedy's pussy almost pulsated out of her leggings and landed at his feet. She had to take a step back or her ass would've been singing, *Please Excuse my Hands.*

Mayhem turned the fire down low and escorted her into the dining area. He pulled a chair out for her at the table and waited for her to be seated. Keedy was cracking up because he was being all theatrical about it.

"I'll be right back, shawdy," he said after scooting her chair closer to the table.

When he walked off Keedy fanned herself and mumbled, "Lawdieee."

"Mayhem, that was delicious. I'm too full," Keedy complimented as she washed down the last of her fluffy omelet with a swig of orange juice. "Boy, you missed your calling," she said sincerely. "The food was scrumptious."

"Thanks. I told you I'm 'bout that life," he replied as he pushed away from the table, stood up and began gathering up their plates.

"Oh, no you're not! You might as well sit down, I'm not having it," she protested.

"I got this, lil' mama. If a nigga can't clean up behind himself he needs to stay out of the kitchen."

"No, Mayhem."

He gave her a look that underlined his response. "Chill, shawdy, I got this. Take it as my way of thanking you for letting me rest here." He knew that not many girls would've went for that even if the nigga was their man's friend. "Plus I gotta make up for breaking your lamp last night."

"Will you stop it?" said Keedy.

She watched Mayhem clear the dishes off of the table and carry them into the kitchen. A few seconds later she heard the dishwasher and water running in the sink. All she could do was shake her head in amazement. *If only Tank did things like this*.

"Thank you again for the wonderful breakfast," she said awhile later as they sat in the living room discussing Mayhem's plans for the day.

"You're welcome." He twisted up a blunt and brought it to his nose, inhaling the scent. "So, you sure you don't mind being my chauffeur for the day?"

"Not at all," she said truthfully.

Tank had called to say that he was spending the day with Tweety and wouldn't be able to come through until tomorrow. Keedy was used to being the side chick so that didn't bother her. Hell, she hadn't ever had her own man, all to herself anyway.

Mayhem thought about her driving him around and wanted to make sure Tank was good with it, he wasn't trying to disrespect his man, he told her.

Knowing that Tweety was probably around him, Keedy decided to text Tank instead of calling. Less than a minute later her phone rang with Tank's ringtone. "Hey, baby," she affectionately answered.

"Fuck you want, bitch? Didn't I just tell you I'm chilling with wifey today? Damn!" he snapped.

Keedy's feelings were hurt but as usual she held in what she wanted to say. "Ya boy wanted to talk to you." Her voice cracked and she passed the phone.

Mayhem noted the instant change in her expression. He winked an eye at her like *don't let it get you down* and placed the phone to his ear. "What's cracking?"

Tank's tone instantly improved. "What's up, round?" he said.

"Nothin', bruh. I just wanna make sure you don't have a problem with shawdy driving me around. I need to grab a cell phone, a small safe and some other shit."

"That ain't no problem. Tell her I said it's all good."

"Fa' sho." Mayhem got ready to give Keedy the phone back.

"Aye, what happened with you and A'nyah last night, did you hit that?" Tank asked.

Mayhem chuckled. "Nah, I went to sleep and lil' mama went out."

"Bruh, you need to get at A'nyah. I heard that bitch is the truth. They say a nigga ain't never had his dick sucked like lil' mama do that shit. Fa real, one of my mans told me that ho is a brain surgeon *and* she got that wet. A half'a band will get your dick sucked, yo booty hole licked, the whole nine, ya heard me."

Mayhem laughed. "I'm good, fam," he said, shaking his head.

They chopped it up a little while longer then Mayhem said, "A'ight fool, here's your girl." He extended the phone out to Keedy.

"He don't want to talk to me. I'm just his bitch," she said in a hushed tone. She was right. When she placed the phone to her ear Tank had already hung up.

She blinked back the tears that tried to well up in her eyes while chiding herself. *Don't get all sensitive now, bitch. You knew what it was when you started dealing with him. Just be happy that you have a man, even if he isn't really yours. Your ugly ass don't deserve that.*

Mayhem noticed the sadness that came over her face. She saw him studying her so she forced the corners of her mouth up and bounced to her feet feigning happiness that didn't reach her eyes.

"Looks like I'm at your service today," she said. "I don't have anything else to do until much later when I go over to my girl, Lenika's house, to do her hair but all she wants is a Chinese bun with some bangs. That's nothing."

Mayhem smiled.

Keedy covered her mouth. "Oops, sorry. I was rambling on and on, and you probably don't have the faintest idea what I'm talking about, huh?"

"Yea, I do. A Chinese bun is a honey bun with nuts, fried rice and dead cats on it."

Keedy burst out laughing and this time her smile reached her eyes. She playfully punched him on the shoulder. "You know what—your ass is *re re*."

"That makes two of us but you're a lot prettier than me," he said.

The minute the compliment left his mouth Mayhem regretted uttering it. Keedy felt a flutter in her heart. Tank had never told her that she was pretty. She lowered her eyes and stood there stuck.

Mayhem stood up and put a friendly hand on her arm. "My bad, shawdy, that was out of bounds. But you're still throwed off," he kidded.

Keedy looked up at him without lifting her head and playfully punched him again. She flashed a shy little smile, and then excused herself to go get dressed.

As she walked away Mayhem found himself staring at the sway of her hips. She stopped and looked over her shoulder and their eyes met, communicating something that neither one of them wanted to think about.

Chapter 11

Late the next evening Tank called to tell Mayhem that he was on his way to scoop him up; he had found someone that wanted to buy both birds that Mayhem had. As he waited for Tank to arrive, Mayhem went to the closet and retrieved the kilos from inside of the small safe that he had purchased yesterday. He placed the birds in a black backpack and re-locked the safe.

As he stepped out of the closet, he looked up and saw Keedy staring at him through a crack in the door. As soon as their eyes met she turned and went into the living room.

Mayhem got up and went out there to see what was up. He found her in the living room sitting in a chair with her Tablet on her lap. "Did you want something?" he asked, standing in front of her with the bag in his hand.

"No, Mayhem." She looked up. "Just be careful tonight, okay?"

"A'ight, shawdy. I appreciate your concern and I'll watch my back," he promised.

"Please do," she muttered and gave him a reluctant smile.

Mayhem smiled back at her as he took a seat on the couch and waited for Tank to arrive. They heard keys in the door a short while later and Tank came in with another dude behind him.

Mayhem rose up from the sofa and gave Tank a gangsta hug. "What it do, shawdy?" he asked.

"'Bout to help you get off of those birds for $22,000 apiece, ya heard me."

"That's what's up."

"I told you I got you, my nigga," said Tank, checking his wrist for the time.

Out of the corner of his eye he noticed Keedy sitting there quietly. He looked down at her and Keedy stood up and went to the back, leaving the men to discuss their business in private.

"You got that bitch well trained," remarked Peanut, he and Tank laughed.

"My dude," said Tank, talking to Mayhem, "this my round, Peanut, who I told you about. He's official."

Mayhem hit him with a head nod.

"What's up, May-hem?" said Peanut, pronouncing his name as if it was two separate words.

They locked fists and bumped chests then Mayhem stepped back and assessed him. He was a lil' scrawny, red, freckled-faced nigga with brown dreads that came down to his shoulders. He was rocking a Pelicans jersey, fresh jeans, and throwback Adidas shell toes. His wrist was icy and the platinum chain around his neck held a diamond encrusted medallion shaped like the state. "The Boot" was written across it in blue diamonds and red rubies.

"So are these *your* people we're going to see?" Mayhem asked him.

"Yea, but Tank know 'em too. Like he said, they one hunnid. I put my life on that."

"You most certainly do," Mayhem quipped, but he was very serious. If anything went wrong he was blaming Peanut.

"Bruh, you don't have to threaten me. I don't play those kinda games. This nigga, Julius, we 'bout to go see—me, him and Tank go back like a bad hairline. He's an older cat that's been in the game a long time and he well respected. Ya feel me?"

Tank nodded in agreement and Mayhem relaxed. "Let's get to it then," said Mayhem, grabbing the backpack and heading out of the door behind Tank and Peanut.

When they reached their destination they parked and went to the door of a house in the Seventh Ward on Annette Street. The yard was dark and the street was quiet except for the sound of a dog barking somewhere up the block.

Tank and Peanut got out of the front and Mayhem slid out of the backseat. His eyes scanned the block for any danger that lurked but he saw nothing. Paranoid by trade, Mayhem said to Tank, "Let me get a tool before we go up in here. If something pops off I wanna be able to pull out more than my dick."

Tank took a Nine off of his waist and passed it to Mayhem. "Here you go, dawg. Cock and lock that bitch."

Peanut frowned. "Bruh, that ain't the move. You're gettin' booted up for nothin'. Julius don't play no games. Trust me."

"I hear you but you ain't saying shit," Mayhem checked him. "I trust in God. Every other muthafucka is suspect. Straight up." He took a pair of dark Ray Bans out of the backpack and slid them on his face.

Peanut walked up the driveway without responding. Mayhem turned to Tank. "Nigga on his period, ain't he?"

"Don't trip. Let's just get this money and be out, ya heard me."

They caught up with Peanut at the side door where his coded knock was answered after a few minutes of waiting. "Who is it?" asked a deep voice from the other side of the door.

"It's Nut."

A light came on illuminating the area. They heard bolts being unlatched and the door swung half open. A dark-skinned, dude named Larron stood in the doorway with a ratchet down at his side. His arms and shoulders bulged with thick muscles. "What's up, my nigga?" he greeted Peanut with a fist bump then stepped aside to let them in.

"I'm gucci," Peanut replied. "Where Julius?"

"He in the den waiting on you." Larron tucked his banger then secured the double locks on the door and turned to Tank. "What's good, son? How's Tweety and that little girl of yours?"

"They good. You know I'ma always make sure they straight even if I gotta starve myself to do it." He and Larron gangsta hugged.

"I hear that shit," acknowledged Larron. He looked over Tank's shoulder at Mayhem. "This your round?" he said.

"Yea," replied Tank.

Larron looked Mayhem up and down trying to get a read on him. But he was hard to get a handle on because Larron couldn't see his eyes and that *act up* shit oozed from his pores. "Bruh," Larron said, "I don't know you so I'ma have to pat you down. No disrespect."

"Nigga, you not patting shit over here," spat Mayhem, instantly establishing that he was not with the fuckery. "Fuck you mean you don't know me? I don't know you either." He stood with his feet apart and his hand close to his waist, trained to go.

Larron's brows furrowed. He looked at Peanut and Tank. "What's up with y'all boy? He must not know who the fuck I am." He deepened his voice but Mayhem just grinned at his attempt to intimidate.

"Why you talking to another man about me? I'm right here. Ask me if I *give* a fuck who you are. All niggas bleed," Mayhem scowled as he moved his hand closer to his heat.

Larron did the same.

Tank threw an arm around Larron's shoulder and chuckled. "Be easy, killah. My man is good peoples, he's just a little paranoid, ya heard me."

"More than a little," Peanut snorted. Already he didn't like Mayhem.

"A'ight. But somebody better teach him some respect," said Larron, looking back at Mayhem with a hard mean mug.

Mayhem didn't reply. He was done talking. The next words out of his mouth were gonna be followed by the clap of his tool. He and Larron held each other's stare; two killahs ready to go at it to the death.

Larron was the first to look away. "Let's go handle this business so y'all can be out before I catch a body tonight," he remarked to Peanut.

As he turned to lead them to the den, Tank fell back with Mayhem. He pushed his palm towards the floor and whispered, "Turn your gangsta down some, these niggas are my A1's from day 1."

Mayhem wasn't studying his ass either. He was gonna stay *turnt up* until the deal was completed and they were out of there.

As they proceeded through the living room, down a short hallway that led to the den, Mayhem remained on alert. His eyes rotated from side to side and his hand was wrapped firmly around the handle of his heater.

The room they entered was brightly lit but clouded with weed smoke. Mayhem fanned the air and pressed his back to the nearest wall while Peanut and Tank dapped Julius who was sitting in a leather recliner smoking real good. His eyes were red and they sat close together inside a head that looked like a black lemon.

"Have a seat," Julius offered as he pulled hard on the blunt.

Tank grabbed a chair and straddled it backwards. Peanut sat on the sofa and Larron remained standing, still mean mugging Mayhem. Julius looked back and forth between the two hard faces and lifted an eyebrow. "What's your round's name?" he asked Tank, passing him the blunt.

"Mayhem." Tank accepted the loud and put it to his lips.

"Mayhem," Julius repeated his name in a friendly tone, "when I invite you into my home we're family. I can respect your caution but you can relax. Have a seat and smoke one with us."

"I don't mix business with pleasure. That's like two dicks and no chick," spat Mayhem. "It always leads to a lot of shit."

Julius chuckled. "I like that."

"Let him stand there then," Peanut said in a whisper.

Mayhem overheard that slick shit and tucked it for later. His expression remained stone as he watched Julius get up, walk over to a bar in the corner, and return with a bottle of Henny and three glasses.

Mayhem and Larron remained posted up as Julius, Tank and Peanut shared drinks and blazed several blunts while talking back and forth. Finally, Julius cracked his knuckles and announced that he was ready to handle business.

Mayhem flexed his fingers as Larron moved to the closet and opened the door. He relaxed when the muscled goon brought out a Nike shoe bag and walked it over to Julius.

Julius dumped the contents out on the wicker and glass table in front of him and a few stacks of money fell over onto the floor. Larron picked them up and dropped them down on the pile, and then reposted by the door.

"Y'all wanna count it?" Julius asked.

"Nah, I wouldn't insult you like that," Peanut volunteered.

"I was really talking to Mayhem," Julius clarified.

Mayhem acknowledged the respect with a nod. Then he said, "Tank, handle that for me."

One by one, Tank flipped through the bands of Franklins and Grants, just doing a quick guesstimate. "Everything looks official, bruh," he declared as he stood up and walked over to Mayhem.

Mayhem handed him the backpack and Tank returned to his seat. He took the two kilos out and sat them on the table before Julius. "Here you go. That's one hundred percent fish scale, the same as the brick I sold you yesterday."

Julius pulled out a small pocket knife and cut a picture window in the wrappers of both kilos. He peeled back the V-shaped flap and dug a small sample out of each brick and held it up to the light. The coke glistened like crushed glass. When he tasted the product it froze his whole mouth and the potency surged straight to his head. "That's that fi', ya heard me." Julius smiled. He was going to flip that work in no time at all.

He stood up, walked over to Mayhem and shook his hand. "Nice doing business with you, whoadie," he said in his throwback lingo.

"You too," replied Mayhem as he watched Tank put the stacks in the duffel bag. His eyes and nerves remained on alert until he had that dough in his hand and they were out of the door.

"You know you gotta break Peanut off for setting up the deal," said Tank as the three of them headed to his car.

"I'ma fuck wit' him," Mayhem agreed even though he didn't like the lil' bitch ass nigga.

As they reached the front of the house three masked gunmen stepped out of the darkness. "Reach for the mutha-fuckin' sky!" One of gunmen barked as his pistol grip pump shotgun moved from chest to chest ready to put anyone one of them on their ass.

Beside him, one of his partners held a choppa and the other one brandished a Desert Eagle. All three seemed anxious to wet a nigga's chest if they so much as breathed too hard.

"Ain't this a bitch?" Mayhem spat under his breath. It was the ultimate disrespect—a jack-boy getting jacked. *Fuck that, these niggas gon' have to leave here with a body.* He was ready to test fate, but before he could make a move a fourth robber stepped up behind him and put that chrome to his dome.

"Not tonight, nigga. I'll spray your muthafuckin' brains out so I can see what's on your mind before you pull *that* bitch out."

Mayhem froze and gritted his teeth as he felt the dude reach around him and take his banger off of his waist. "Let me get this too," he taunted as he grabbed the money bag.

Mayhem held on to it a second too long and the boy cracked him over the head with that steel. Mayhem's shades flew off and landed at his feet. The robber yanked the bag from his grip and raised the gun to his head. "Say one word and I'll make it your last," he threatened.

"Fuck is y'all doing?" Tank snarled.

Ol' boy with the pump shoved it in his face. "Shut the fuck up before I blast your punk ass. Matter-of-fact, all y'all niggas kiss the muthafuckin' dirt."

Tank and Peanut dropped to the ground on command. Seething, Mayhem followed suit but before his chest touched the pavement he took in whatever features he could of the crew. The nigga with the pump was tall and thin and the other two that he could see were average height but one of them had a pot belly.

"Check their waists for guns and run their pockets and if one of 'em flinch, bust his muthafuckin' head, son," commanded the one with the pump.

Mayhem watched as they took Tank's gun off of his waist and the money out of his pocket. Peanut wasn't strapped but he got jacked for his dough and his jewels. Mayhem just laid still, bristling inside as hands ran through his pockets relieving him of a stack but leaving a few loose bills.

"Thanks for the donation," said the dude that had put the gun to the back of his head. *Whop!* He kicked Mayhem in the face. Then he and his friends moved quickly to a black van that was parked two houses down.

Mayhem had noticed that the fourth nigga had an unusually large head. He stored all that in his memory and promised himself that he would find each and every one of those bitch muthafuckas.

They should've never left me alive!

As the van drove off with its tires squealing, Mayhem climbed to his feet. His chest heaved up and down, and his nostrils flared in and out as he retrieved his Ray Bans off of the ground.

Tank and Peanut had stood to their feet too. "This is some muthafuckin' bullshit," Tank scoffed as he dusted himself off.

"Somebody gotta answer for this! I'ma kill me a bitch muthafucka and I mean that shit." He paced back and forth in a ten foot square.

Humph—that ain't the half! Mayhem put his hand to the side of his head and it came back sticky with his warm blood. Anger coursed through his body hot and thick. Mayhem didn't utter a word, he just clenched his jaw and went to the car and climbed in the back seat.

A few seconds later Tank leaned in the window. "Bruh, me and Peanut 'bout to go back and holla at Julius. This fuck shit happened right here in his muthafuckin' front yard and he's gonna have to straighten this shit out, ya heard me."

"Whatever, shawdy." Mayhem stared straight ahead.

Tank could feel the intense heat coming off of Mayhem's bloody brow. He knew that if his round had a banger right now he would light the street up like the Fourth of July. "I'ma try to get this nigga to give me the bricks back 'cause somebody had to have talked and it damn sho' wasn't me," Tank said earnestly as his nostrils flared in and out.

Mayhem remained silent, looking straight ahead as the vein in his neck pulsed with blood as hot as lava.

Tank slammed his hand on the roof of the car and spat, "Niggas must think this shit is sweet! I'm finna act the fuck up." Then hurried back over to where Peanut waited and together they went to confront Julius.

Twenty minutes later they returned with no answers, dope or money. Julius and Larron had sworn that they hadn't had anything to do with them getting jacked and they had no idea who the robbers could've been.

Mayhem chuckled. The next time they saw him he was gonna get some answers in blood.

As they drove off Tank and Peanut argued heatedly. Peanut would not believe that Julius had pulled a greasy move like that. Tank's opinion had quickly shifted; his finger was now firmly pointed at that nigga, Julius.

Mayhem still hadn't uttered a single word. When they bent a corner and he spotted a Walgreens he asked Tank to stop so that he could get some Peroxide and bandages for his head.

As soon as Tank pulled into the lot and parked Mayhem was out of the car. He went inside the store and made his purchases with the twelve dollars that the robbers hadn't taken.

"Fuck you looking at?" Mayhem growled in response to the cashier's questioning stare.

"Nothing," she replied meekly and handed him his change.

Mayhem pocketed the coins, snatched up his bag and bounced out of the door.

As they drove to Keedy's, Mayhem rattled around in the bag while Tank bent corners and continued to debate with Peanut. When they pulled up in front of Keedy's apartments the lot was quiet and there was no one loitering about. Tank and Peanut had stopped arguing but they were still in disagreement.

From the front passenger seat Peanut looked over his shoulder into the backseat and apologized to Mayhem. He promised to get some answers. "Somebody set that shit up," he said bitterly. "I don't believe in no goddamn coincidence."

"Yea," Tank agreed. He half turned in his seat and looked at Mayhem with apologetic eyes. "Round, you alright? he asked.

Mayhem finally spoke. "Fuck no, I'm not a'ight. Niggas took my shit like I'm a ho." He was breathing fire.

"Don't worry, dawg. We gon' make those niggas feel it," vowed Tank.

"I hear that shit but somebody gon' feel me right muthafuckin' now." Mayhem wrapped his arm around Peanut's neck. His other hand came out of the bag tightly gripping the handle of the cheap butcher knife that he had bought from the store.

“Hold up!” Peanut gagged.

“Pussy ass muthafucka, I’m not the one to test.” Mayhem breathed on the back of his neck as he applied pressure to his windpipe.

“Bruh, what the hell you doing?” screamed Tank.

“Fuck you mean? This nigga put his life on it, now I’m about to collect in blood.” Mayhem forcefully plunged the knife into the side of Peanut’s neck.

Blood skeeted in his face and all over the headrest. The taste of that crimson red liquid and the loss of his money quickly unleashed the beast in Mayhem. “You wanna test my muthafuckin’ get-down?” he growled as he stabbed Peanut repeatedly in the base of his skull.

Peanut tried to squirm a loose but Mayhem had that death lock on him. He drew back and drove the knife in the back of Peanut’s neck so viciously that the knife broke off at the tip.

Peanut opened his mouth to scream but it quickly filled with blood, and when he tried to move his arms and legs wouldn’t work. “Fuck ass nigga!” Mayhem gritted as he continued to stab him over and over again.

Tank reached up to try to stop Mayhem from bodying his man but Mayhem’s fury was on one thousand. The further Peanut’s body slid down in the seat, the further Mayhem leaned over it to drive the blade in and out of him.

“What the fuck you do that fo’?” Tank cried as Peanut slumped lifelessly down to the floorboard. “Nigga you trippin’!”

Mayhem hopped out of the back and snatched the passenger door open. Blood dripped off of the knife and onto his shoe but he was beyond giving a fuck. He leaned in the car and rushed the knife so deep into Peanut’s heart that only the handle was visible.

Mayhem looked up at Tank. “You should’ve warned ya man I ain’t the one to fuck with.” He pulled the bloody knife out of Peanut’s chest and wiped it on the nigga’s shirt.

Tank looked down at the corpse of a friend that he had ate noodles off the same fork with. "Nawl, man. Nawwwll," he moaned in disbelief.

Peanut stared up at him through eyes that saw nothing.

"Fuck! Fuck! Fuck!" Tank banged his fist on the steering wheel.

Mayhem felt no remorse. "You better get that bitch ass nigga outta my face before I murk his ass all over again."

He rose up and slipped on his shades and headed up to the apartment without glancing back. He didn't give a fuck what Tank did with his boy's body.

Y'all muthafuckas gon' learn today!

Chapter 12

Keedy was up late finishing up a weave cap that she was sewing for a client whose hair she was doing tomorrow. She looked at the clock on her nightstand and saw that it was almost midnight. She needed to take her ass to sleep because her first appointment was at 7:30AM. That was a long trek across the river on the Westbank in the city of Westwego.

She had tried to lay down and close her eyes about an hour ago but sleep had been as elusive as happiness. For some reason that she couldn't explain she was worried about Mayhem. The trepidation rose up high in her chest but she forced it back down. Tank wouldn't let anything happen to him and she had never known Peanut to be on the bullshit.

She was worrying for no reason, Keedy concluded.

After finishing the cap she put the materials away and went to use the bathroom. As she stood washing her hands in the sink, Keedy thought that she heard a rap on the door. She turned the faucet off and listened closer. Someone was definitely knocking.

Keedy squirted a dab of skin moisturizer in her hand and rubbed it in as she went to answer the door. On the way she grabbed her robe off of the bed and slipped her arms into it.

The hallway and living room was dark. A'nyah had turned off the lights before going to bed, but the light shining in from the kitchen allowed Keedy to see her way. She stopped and flicked on a lamp then proceeded to the door. "Who is it?" she asked, looking through the peep hole.

"Mayhem," he said, hiding the knife under his shirt.

Keedy turned off the alarm and opened the door with a relieved smile on her face. But it quickly melted and her mouth fell wide open when he stepped inside and she saw that his clothes were saturated in blood. Her eyes moved up to his face; splatters of blood was all over it and she could see that he had suffered some type of injury to the side of his head.

Keedy gasped and covered her mouth with her hand. "Oh, my god, Mayhem, what happened?"

"Nothin'," he replied. "I'm a'ight."

"Where is Tank?" Her face was etched with worry.

"He's good, shawdy." Mayhem stepped around her and headed back to his room.

Keedy looked out of the door and saw Tank's tail lights fading away. She closed and locked the door, turned the alarm back on, and went to investigate.

Mayhem's door was closed but she could hear him in there moving around. She didn't want to pry but she was really concerned. She raised her knuckles and started to knock but thought better of it. Mayhem didn't seem like he was in the mood to be fucked with. And who was she to get all in that man's business anyway? She chastised herself.

Back in her bedroom Keedy searched under her covers until she found her cell then she quickly called Tank but the phone just rung until she was sent to voicemail. Frustrated and filled with deep worriment she redialed his number and tried to will him to answer, but once again all she got was Tank's recorded greeting.

Keedy hung up and sent him an urgent text. *Babe plz call me I'm worried!*

As she sat on the bed staring at her phone praying that Tank would return her call, Keedy heard Mayhem's door open. She leaned forward and peeked through the crack in her door. Mayhem had stripped down to a pair of basketball shorts and he was headed to the bathroom.

Minutes later, Keedy heard the shower running and she came up with the perfect opportunity to check on Mayhem's condition. She had done laundry earlier but hadn't set any clean towels out.

When Mayhem peeked his head out of the bathroom door, Keedy was already standing there with a fresh towel in hand. "Thanks," he said.

"No problem."

Their eyes held each other for a moment. Keedy noticed that blood was still trickling from his brow. Pointing, she said, "Mayhem, you're bleeding. When you come out of the shower I'm going to put a bandage on it for you. Okay?"

"That's what's up." His voice was hard but she knew that it wasn't intentional. Obviously, he was still heated over whatever had happened.

Keedy returned to her bedroom and checked her phone for a response from Tank. Still nothing. She shook her head in despair, his shit was really starting to get old. She sat the phone down on the nightstand and stood there staring at it with her arms folded across her chest. If Tank didn't want to be bothered at least he could call and let her know that his black ass was alright. *Damn, am I really that insignificant to him?* she scoffed. Didn't he know that once she saw his friend covered in blood she would worry about *his* safety?

That muthafucka don't care. I'm just convenient pussy and the bitch that he knows he can count on when his sugar turns to shit.

Fuck it, he would call if he needed her. That's how it always went; he stayed having time for this, that, and the third bitch. But as soon as that ass got locked up or when he hit a streak of bad luck and his pockets were leaking, her number was the first one he dialed. But let her call him and it took a hope and a prayer for him to answer.

Keedy told herself that she was tired of being muthafuckin' tired. She turned on her heels and went into her bathroom to search the medicine cabinet for her First Aid kit. At least Mayhem would appreciate her assistance.

She was dying to know what had happened. She had overheard him talking on the phone to Tank earlier and had pieced together that they were going to serve somebody some weight. Mayhem had left with a bag in hand and returned with nothing but blood all over him; that added up to trouble. And the look in Mayhem's eyes told her that he hadn't bitched up in the face of it.

Keedy liked that gangsta shit in a nigga but it also troubled her. If somebody had crossed Mayhem, that was probably their blood on his clothes. And Tank was probably drenched in it too, she resolved.

Keedy didn't know what to think about Peanut, he was a good dude but she had never known him to bust his gun. In her wildest imagination she would've never guessed that it was that bitch nigga's blood all over Mayhem.

As she waited for Mayhem to come out of the shower she went into the kitchen to get a bottle of water. Her throat felt dry and her nerves were frazzled. She uncapped the bottle and took a few swigs then screwed the cap back on tightly and placed the bottle back in the refrigerator.

She encountered Mayhem in the hallway as she returned to her bedroom. The towel was draped over his shoulder exposing the beads of water that coated his well-toned chest. The wound over his left eye was still bleeding. Talking in a whisper so that she wouldn't awaken A'nyah, Keedy told him that he might need to go to the ER and have it stitched up.

"Nah, shawdy I'm not going to no hospital," he rejected.

Keedy didn't argue with him. She could see that he meant that shit. Besides, the last thing he probably needed right now was a confrontation. "Okay, I'll hook it up for you. Let me go get my kit," she said.

As she moved past him in the tight space her breasts rubbed up against his arm. Mayhem didn't seem to notice it but Keedy damn sure did. A tingle coursed from her nipples straight to her clit. She admonished herself for the thought that followed the sensation. She was supposed to be concerned about his injury not getting wet between the thighs.

On weakened legs she continued into her bedroom to retrieve the First Aid supplies. As she gathered them up her kitty squished with her juices. Keedy stood straight up, took a couple of deep breaths and counted to ten.

When she felt composed enough to move she went across the hall to play nurse. Hopefully she could bandage Mayhem up without allowing her hands to wander.

Keedy sat down on Mayhem's bed and spread a towel over her lap. "Come on. Let me bandage you up so we can both go to bed and get some sleep."

Mayhem walked over to the door and opened it wider, for Keedy's sake. If A'nyah woke up to go to the bathroom he didn't want her to get the wrong idea and run back to Tank with no fuck shit. The light was on in the bedroom and there was nothing to hide. He stretched across the bed and laid his head on Keedy's lap.

"Close your eyes so this Peroxide doesn't run down into them," Keedy said softly as she put on a pair of rubber gloves.

Mayhem closed his eyes and breathed slowly out of his nose as he conjured up a hideous death for Julius and Larron. There was no way he would ever believe that they hadn't set up the robbery. The night's chain of events replayed in his head with cinematic recall. He still couldn't believe that those bitch ass niggas had brought the weakest shit to the strongest enemy they'll ever face. He was going to show them how an ATL souljah rocked. And by the time he rolled up out of New Orleans he planned to leave behind a trail of destruction with his name tatted all over it.

Keedy could feel the tension in his shoulders pressed against her leg. She tried to think of some wise, comforting words to calm the beast that seemed to be threatening to leap out and engulf everything in its path. "Mayhem," she began as she washed the gash with Peroxide. "I don't know what happened tonight and you don't have to tell me. But you have to be careful because these niggas are grimy as hell."

"I hear you, lil' mama," he replied.

Keedy hushed. Mayhem was a street nigga and probably already knew that most people weren't hitting on shit. After cleaning the gash thoroughly, she dried it with some gauze and used some Steri-Strips to close the wound. Lastly, she applied some anti-biotic cream explaining that had she applied it first the strips wouldn't have stuck.

"There," she said, "that will prevent infection."

"Thanks. Is my shit swollen?"

"Yea," she replied, looking down at him with compassion in her eyes.

A voice came from the doorway causing Keedy's head to shoot up. Mayhem lifted his head off of her lap then he sat up.

"Keedy, c'mere," said Tank. He stood with his hands against both sides of the door frame.

Keedy popped up like a Jack in-the-box. Her heart pounded with fear and even though she hadn't been doing anything foul it felt like she had been caught creeping. She nervously collected her First Aid kit and hurried to the door.

Tank took up the whole doorway. Keedy stopped in front of him and looked up into his eyes. What she saw told her that he was going to kick her ass.

"I-I-I was just putting a bandage on his head, baby," she explained nervously.

"Go in the bedroom. I'll be in there in a minute," he said nonchalant-like. Which meant he was going to really fuck her up. Keedy swallowed her spit and looked at him pleadingly.

"Get your ass in the room, bitch," he mouthed.

Oh, my god, he's going to kill me. Keedy's eyes teared up and she wanted to blink them and disappear off of the face of the earth. Her legs moved on their own accord and she heard him close Mayhem's door behind her.

She stood there in her pajama shorts trying to decide what to do. Should she wait around for a beating or get ghost? If she ran, she would have to keep running forever. Because if she ever returned the punishment would be harsher. If she stayed, judging from the look that she had seen in Tank's eyes, he was capable of killing her ass tonight.

Tears slid down her face as she walked into her bedroom, sat down on the bed and waited to get beaten half to death.

Chapter 13

Keedy sat with her arms wrapped around her shoulders, rocking back and forth, praying that Tank's temper would cool down before he came into the bedroom. If history was a true indicator of what was about to happen, she might as well lay down on the floor right now and close both of her eyes because that was how he would leave her, knocked out with both eyes swollen shut.

She felt like a defendant who had been falsely convicted without ever being allowed to testify on her own behalf. And since Tank was the judge and juror there was no way to appeal his verdict. Now the only thing being decided was how cruel her punishment would be. The best she could hope for was that her life would be spared.

Fear rushed up on her chest and caused her shortness of breath when she saw the doorknob rotate to the left. A second later Tank entered wearing a blank expression on his face.

Keedy had to think quick. She stood up and rushed up to him, wrapping her arms around his waist, "Baby, I was worried about you." She looked him up and down. There was splotches of blood on his clothes but she didn't see any wounds. "Are you okay, baby?" she asked in the most affectionate tone she could effect. Tank grunted but she didn't give up. "Come on, let me get you out of these clothes. You have blood all over you," she said.

"I'm about to have some more on me in a minute and it's gonna be yours." He moved her aside, closed and locked the door.

Trembling uncontrollably she asked, "Why? What did I do?"

"Bitch, get naked then bring me 'The Belt'."

Keedy knew exactly what he meant. Tank had braided three thick leather belts together and he used them to whip her like a slave.

"No, Tank. Please," she begged. She rather he beat her with his fist than whoop her with the belt. Not only did that shit hurt like hell, it was so humiliating.

"Save that shit. I'm about to teach you about letting another nigga lay his head on your lap." Tank walked over to the iPod and turned some music on to drown out the cries that she would soon make.

Keedy was paralyzed with fear. She thought about bolting for the door but he would strangle her if she wasn't successful.

Just when she was about to make a break for it Tank came back over to where she stood. He grabbed her by the face and gritted. "Get. The. Belt. Bitch." He roughly shoved her towards the closet where he kept it.

Keedy tripped over her own feet and landed on the floor on her hands and knees. Instantly she felt the carpet burn against her skin. Tears poured from her eyes and snot ran out of her nose as she looked up at Tank silently begging for mercy.

The hard thump of Mystikal played in the background as Tank hovered over her like the black hand of death. "Ho get up!" he spat.

"Please, baby," she cried. "I didn't do anything. You know you're the only one I want."

Her pleading seemed to infuriate Tank even more. He reached down and snatched her up by the collar and drug her over to the closet. Slinging her inside, he barked, "Get the belt or I'ma beat your punk ass to death."

Keedy searched the closet high and low but couldn't find it. "It's not in here," she said, turning to him with a petrified look plastered across her face.

"What do you mean it's not in there? Fuck did you do with it?"

"Nothing. I swear."

Tank didn't want to hear that. He stepped in the closet and searched it himself but he couldn't find it either. Now he was bubbling with anger. "Sit your ass in here while I look for it, and if you move I'ma snap your muthafuckin' neck," he threatened.

Before leaving out of the closet he made her sit on the floor. He stepped out, closed the door then pulled a chair over to the closet and propped it under the doorknob so that she couldn't escape.

This bitch bet' not have thrown that shit away with her slick ass.

Tank stormed over to the dresser, snatched the drawers open, and began slinging Keedy's panties and bras over his shoulder as he searched for the braided belt. When he got to the bottom drawer he came across an object that sent his fury soaring out of the top of his head.

Gripping it tightly he stalked back over to the closet, kicked the chair out from under the doorknob and snatched the door open.

Keedy was shivering with fear. She knew that he couldn't have found the belt because her girl, Kim LeBlanc, had thrown it away the last time she was over there. *"Gurl, I'm not letting you keep nothing for that nigga to beat you with,"* Kim said, shaking her head at her pitifully.

Keedy had told her that Tank would murder her if he looked for it and couldn't find it, and now her fear was about to come to past.

"Bring your ass here," Tank gritted.

As she climbed to her feet and stepped out of the closet, Keedy put her arms up to her face expecting a sudden punch to come flying at her head.

Tank snatched her by the arm, pulled her over to the bed, and threw her down on her back.

Straddling her, he held up the dildo that he had found in her drawer. "Fuck is this?"

Keedy breathed a sigh of relief. "Baby, that's nothing. It's just my toy. I use it when you're too busy to come through."

Whack! Tank punched her dead in the mouth.

"Ahh!" she cried out as she tasted the blood from her busted lip.

"What? You a ho now?" The scowl of Tank's appearance defied logic.

"No, baby, it's just a toy." Confusion resonated across her face as she tried to defend her position.

"So you been fuckin' yourself? Ain't that a bitch? Your ass that muthafuckin' hot, huh?"

"No." Keedy shook her head from side to side.

"Yes it is! That's why you were in there tryna fuck my nigga."

"No, I wasn't. That man don't want me."

Whack! "Who the fuck you raising your voice at ho?"

"Nobody." She sniffled as the room started spinning.

Tank sat the dildo down and ripped her night shirt off. "Get naked!" His eyes were crazy with jealousy. She had never seen him so angry.

Tank got up off of her and allowed her to take off her clothes. Keedy didn't know what he was going to do but she knew that it would be something foul. The last time he had punished her this way he had abused her anally. It had hurt her to go to the bathroom for a full week, and just thinking about it now sent a sharp pain shooting through her rectum.

"Lay down and spread your legs," Tank commanded.

Keedy didn't ever consider disobeying him. She put her head on the pillow and opened her legs. Tank stuck a finger in her pussy then held his finger to his nose and sniffed it. She obviously passed his sick smell test so he came at her with some other dumb shit.

"Your shit feels loose. Who you been fuckin', huh?"

Keedy narrowed her eyes at him. *This fool is losing it.*

"Spread your legs wider," he ordered.

"Tank, what are you about to do?"

Whop! He punched her in the eye. "Shut the fuck up, bitch, and do what I say."

When she began to scream, Tank wrapped both hands around her throat and cut off her breathing. “Be quiet,” he whispered tersely.

Keedy fought to free herself but the more she squirmed, the more pressure he applied. She gagged and coughed as her lungs screamed for oxygen.

Fuck it, Keedy said to herself. She was just going to lay still and let him end her retched life. What did she have to live for anyway?

When she stopped moving Tank slowly released the pressure and removed his hands from around her throat. He climbed on top of her and used his knees to force her legs wider apart. “You gotta have something in your big ass pussy 24/7, huh?” he asked derisively.

Keedy just laid there crying.

“I’ma put something inside you,” he said ominously. Then he wrapped his finger around the dildo and shoved it violently up inside of her.

Keedy cries boomed over the music but Tank quickly grabbed a pillow and covered her head with it to muffle her screams. “Shut the fuck up, ho,” he gritted as he rammed the dildo in and out of her with force, ripping her vaginal lining. “This what you wanted, ain’t it?”

Keedy whimpered as she felt blood running down her thighs.

Tank removed the device from inside of her and took the pillow from over her head. Holding the bloody plastic penis in front of her mouth he ordered her to lick it clean.

Bile rose up in her throat at the thought of putting that in her mouth. “No, Tank,” she refused. “You’re just going to have to kill me.”

“You think I won’t,” he said right before his fist slammed into her already battered face.

Keedy’s head crashed against the headboard and the room began to spin again but Tank was just getting started. By the time he finished beating her she was curled up on the floor in a fetal position, bleeding severely from up top and down low too.

In a final, painful insult Tank viciously rammed the dildo up her ass.

Chapter 14

Mayhem was awakened out of his sleep at the crack of dawn by A'nyah's piercing scream. Rolling out of bed, he grabbed the knife off of the nightstand and ran towards the frantic sound.

He found A'nyah standing over Keedy who was still sprawled out on the floor of her bedroom in the condition that Tank had left her in hours ago. Mayhem moved A'nyah aside and went down to his knees, placing his face close to Keedy's mouth. He could feel her breath on his cheek so he knew that she wasn't dead.

When he looked down in her face it was hideously swollen and bruised. Mayhem felt the same lump in his chest that he had felt when he was younger and his mother's boyfriend had left her battered and unconscious. He bit down on his knuckles to stifle the emotions that threatened to come out the wrong way.

As he lowered his eyes he noticed the object sticking out of her backside. When he realized what it was, he almost wanted to go kill Tank. He had heard them in there fighting last night but he had never expected to find Keedy in this condition.

Mayhem cradled Keedy's head in his arms and looked up at A'nyah. "Take that out of her," he uttered through clenched teeth.

He respectfully turned his head as A'nyah removed the lodged dildo out of Keedy's behind.

"That dirty muthafucka," she spat.

Mayhem reached up and pulled the comforter off of the bed and covered Keedy's nakedness. "We have to put some clothes on her and get her to a hospital."

"Okay." A'nyah moved quickly to the closet to grab something to slip on her girl.

Mayhem looked down at Keedy and teared up. Both of her eyes were swollen shut and her head was almost twice its normal size. A moan escaped her blood-crusted lips.

"Shh. Don't try to talk," he said.

"Am I going to die?" she asked barely above a whisper.

Mayhem's heart contracted against his chest. "No, shawdy, you're not gonna die. I got you." His voice cracked with sentiment.

Mayhem had killed men in gruesome ways but this sight gripped his heart and squeezed it so tightly that his chest felt close to caving in. He had only known Keedy a few days but he knew that she didn't deserve this—no woman did. He held her firmly in his arms and a tear escaped from the corner of his eye, cascaded down his face, and dripped onto her forehead.

He let out a long sigh as painful memories forced themselves to the front of his mind. In the next second he was rocking her in his arms like he had rocked his mother, promising her that he would not allow her to share that same fate. He looked up when he felt A'nyah's hand on his shoulder.

"Let's hurry," she said.

Mayhem lifted Keedy up like she was a newborn baby and gingerly laid her on the bed. While A'nyah dressed her, he went to throw something on himself.

Five minutes later they were speeding to University's ER in A'nyah's car. Mayhem rode in the backseat with Keedy's head on his lap. He held her hand and promised her that everything would be okay.

A'nyah was cussing as she bent corners. "I hate Tank's bitch ass. He's always jumping on my girl for no reason, but he treats that trick bitch he has at home like she's a fuckin' queen. I swear somebody needs to blow his muthafuckin' head off."

Mayhem didn't comment. Tank was his mans and he had done him a real solid to help him beat that murder rap. But this shit was real foul and there was no way to defend him on this.

"When we get to the hospital I'm going to tell them who did this to her so they can lock his punk ass up," A'nyah fumed.

"No, shawdy you can't do that."

"Why not?" she challenged hotly. "His bitch ass needs to be in jail for this shit right here." A'nyah wiped at the tears that streamed down her face.

"No," Mayhem reinforced. As much as he despised what Tank had done he could not condone snitching. "Just tell them you don't know what happened. You came home and found her like this. I'll deal with Tank."

"What do you mean you'll deal with him? Are you going to beat him close to death and shove something up his ass like he did her? Because if you're not, I'm having his dirty ass locked up." The heat coming off of her words was smoldering.

"Just let me handle it, a'ight," Mayhem barked. He didn't know what he was going to do but he wasn't letting her put those people on Tank.

They shouted back and forth before the strength of Mayhem's manliness overruled A'nyah's emotions and she reluctantly agreed to let him deal with Tank.

When they turned onto Perdido St. where the hospital was located, it suddenly occurred to Mayhem that the nurses might look at him suspiciously as if he was responsible for Keedy's condition. He could not chance an encounter with po po. He leaned forward in the seat and said, "A'nyah, pull over and let me out. I can't go to the hospital with y'all. I have some warrants and a nigga can't take no chances."

A'nyah was still upset that he had forbade her to drop a dime on Tank's grimy ass. But she didn't question him. She slowed down and let him out.

Mayhem looked down at Keedy and shook his head. Baby girl was fucked up. He sent a quick prayer up to heaven where he believed his mother sat with other angels, and then he placed a soft kiss on her forehead. “Be strong, shawdy,” he said on strained breath.

As Mayhem climbed out of the car and closed the door, he kept his eyes locked on Keedy until A’nyah sped off. Unconsciously, he reached up and dried his eyes with his hand and shook his head in disgust at what his boy had done to that helpless girl.

Keedy was the furthest thing from Tank’s mind; he didn’t give a fuck what state her health was in. Next time he was gonna shove a knife up her hot ass.

His sole thoughts were on Peanut. He had been forced to discard his nigga’s body on the side of the road like trash. *Damn, Nut. I’m sorry, dawg. It was not supposed to have popped off like that.*

That nigga, Mayhem, had snapped and now Tank was left to face the repercussions. Lying in bed with his arms around Tweety and her ass up against him, Tank closed his eyes and tried come up with his best move. Peanut had family that was sure to come knocking on his door as soon as his body was found and those niggas weren’t bitch made. *Fuck it. I’m not no ho, either.*

Tank resigned himself to an eventual interrogation by Peanut’s people. He sighed heavily and pulled Tweety closer. A quick nut might relieve some of the stress that he was feeling.

He reached around and rubbed Tweety’s nipples and pressed something rock hard up against her ass. “Umm,” Tweety moaned and wiggled her but against him as his hands traveled down her body.

When he tried to rub her pussy Tweety said, “We can’t. It’s that time of the month.”

Tank drew his hand back and his dick instantly began to deflate. Damn, he couldn’t catch a muthafuckin’ break. He closed his eyes and wished for sleep that came slowly.

Just when he began to drift off, his phone began lighting up with back to back calls. "Who the fuck is this?" he grunted. It seemed like he had just closed his eyes thirty seconds ago.

Tank reached over his girl and answered the persistent call. "Yea." His tone reflected his irritation. Until he heard Mayhem's voice on the other end of the line then he reduced his bass. "What's up, round?" he asked.

Mayhem immediately started going in on him. "Hold up, bruh," said Tank. He slid out of bed and walked into the bathroom.

Tweety woke up and was right on his heels. "Who the fuck is that?" she asked accusatorily as he held the phone in one hand and his dick in the other.

After relieving himself he answered, "This my nigga, Mayhem."

She eyed him with distrust and remained rooted in her spot. She had caught his ass doing way too much in the past not to monitor his calls.

Tank shook his head at her suspicious ass. "Fa real, Tweet, it's too damn early in the morning for this."

"Whateva." She held her hand out, palm up.

Tank handed her the phone because he knew that if he didn't Tweety would pack her shit and bounce. "I told you it's my round. You're on some new shit," he said.

Tweety put the phone to her ear. "Hello." She already had her fist balled up. If a bitch responded she was going to pop him dead in his mouth.

"Yea, what's up," replied Mayhem.

Tweety twisted her lips up and gave Tank his phone back. "That don't prove shit, nigga, he could be calling for one of your little sideline hos. Let me find out," she threatened.

"You ain't gon' find out nothin' like that because I'm not doing nothin'." He slapped her on the ass as she left out of the bathroom and went to climb back in bed.

Tank waited until Tweety was under the covers then he whispered into the phone. "I'm back, bruh. Where you at?"

Mayhem didn't know where the fuck he was at so he had to put Tank on hold and ask a lady who had just walked up to the bus stop where he waited.

"Thanks," he said, flashing her an appreciative smile.

"You're welcome," she smiled back while glancing down at her watch.

Mayhem stepped off and relayed his location to Tank in a clipped tone.

Tank heard the anger in his voice but he didn't give a damn how he felt. Shit, he was hot too. "We'll talk when I get there, ya heard me," Tank said.

"Yea."

Tank drove Tweety's whip to pick up Mayhem; he had left his own at a detail shop around the corner from his house to have the upholstery replaced. There had been too much blood on the front seat for it to be cleaned.

Mayhem recognized Tweety's car as soon as Tank pulled up. He slid into the front passenger seat and shut the door. Tank fired up a joe, turned the music up, and pulled off. Neither of them spoke for about five minutes.

Finally, Mayhem turned the music down. "Shawdy, why did you do that girl like that?" he asked.

"What?" replied Tank. "Nigga, I know you're not tryna check me about how I handle *my* bitch. Fuck kinda shit you on?" He looked over at Mayhem with a lowered brow.

Mayhem sent the same heat right back at him. "You know how I feel about that fuck shit. I told you what I saw a coward ass nigga do to my mother."

"Keedy ain't your mother though. And I know you're not calling me a coward because I'll do the same thing to a nigga," Tank spat.

"What you saying, shawdy?" asked Mayhem. "'Cause you can pull this muthafucka over and we can get to it."

"Bruh, this ain't what you want, ya heard me."

"I see your mouth moving but you ain't pulled this bitch over yet," challenged Mayhem as he sized up Tank's jaw.

Tank blew smoke out the side of his mouth then thumped his cigarette out of the window. He looked over at Mayhem and abruptly jerked the wheel to the right, bringing the whip to a stop. He threw the gear in park and hopped out. "Let's get to it," he spat.

Mayhem was already out of the car too. He snatched his shirt over his head and tossed it on the seat. As they met at the front of the car ready to throw blows a police cruiser approached.

Thinking quickly, Tank walked back to the driver's door and leaned in and popped the hood. Mayhem lifted the hood and pretended to be checking the engine.

The police car slowed down as it passed by and the officers glanced at them with suspicious eyes but pushed on without stopping. "Bruh, let's get the fuck out of here," said Tank.

Mayhem didn't object, he took it as a sign to let that shit go. The moment had passed and the anger in both of them had dissipated with it. When they got back in the car and drove off Tank passed Mayhem a blunt and they blew some smoke in the air and calmed the fuck down.

"Whatever happens we can't turn against each other," said Tank, staring straight ahead as he drove. "Me and Keedy gon' be a'ight so don't even stress over that, ya heard me."

"I hear you but shawdy is good people. I don't see why you treat her like that."

"Nigga, you need a cape or something?" Tank chuckled. "Money over bitches. Believe it or not she likes me to beat on her. It makes her know that I love her."

Mayhem couldn't even wrap his mind around that. He pulled hard on the blunt then passed it back. "All I ask is that you don't do that shit in my presence, shawdy," he said.

Tank reached in the compartment between the seats and handed him tissues. "Blow your nose when you finish crying," he joked as he stopped at a traffic light.

Mayhem balled the tissue up and slung it out of the window. Tank was laughing but he was dead ass serious. The next time he was going to show him how it feels to be defenseless.

Tank saw the expression on his mans' face. He didn't want to beef with him; shit was already about to get serious and they didn't need to be at each other's throats.

The light turned green and with it he pulled off and changed subjects. "Bruh, you reacted too quick last night. I don't believe Peanut had nothin' to do with that setup."

"Fuck that nigga, he's dead," Mayhem spat out of the window onto the ground as if the mention of Peanut's name tasted like shit in his mouth. "If I could I would slump him again. A man is responsible for the actions of whoever he vouches for."

Tank knew that Mayhem was spitting real talk but he still felt a pang in his heart for Peanut's demise.

"And I'ma get those other niggas too," added Mayhem, wringing his hands in murderous anticipation.

"I'm down," said Tank, co-signing Julius' fate. "We gotta get some ratchets."

Mayhem nodded his head in agreeance, he felt butt naked without a banger on his waist. They went back to the apartment for Mayhem to get some money. Then they hit the streets to come up with guns to replace the ones that they had lost last night.

Throughout the rest of the day as they went about purchasing guns, not once did Keedy cross Tank's mind. But she remained in the forefront of Mayhem's.

Chapter 15

Keedy used the control on the side of the bed to incline it so that she was sitting up as if in a chair. Her whole body ached and both of her eyes were still swollen shut. Her head felt like it was the size of a pumpkin and she could still feel a sharp pain in her rectum. But none of those aches and pains were as intense as the pain in her heart.

Two days had passed since she had been admitted but the memory of what Tank had done to her was still fresh in her mind. He had beaten her many times before but this was the worst. Before she had always blamed herself for upsetting him or for not playing her position like a real bitch should. But now she had to face the truth, that cold-hearted muthafucka didn't give a fuck about her.

Tears slid down her bruised face as reality struck hard. The social worker that had visited yesterday had spoken some real shit. "When love leaves you laid up in the hospital it's time to let go."

Keedy didn't know if she was strong enough to do that but the fact that she was thinking about doing so was a lot more than she had done in the past. Her sore ribs hurt every time she took a breath and served as a reminder of how sadistically Tank had assaulted her. *How can he claim to love me and beat me like I'm less than a dog?*

She didn't even want to recall what he had done to her with the dildo, but the pain back there wouldn't let her block it out. Fresh tears spilled down her face and tasted salty in her mouth.

When Keedy began to sob her head pounded like somebody was beating Congo drums inside of her cranium. She uttered a silent prayer for God to take away the pain and give her the strength to leave Tank alone. It would take divine intervention, she was sure of that because she was a weak woman.

"You okay, hun?" The kind voice of the elderly day shift nurse interrupted her self-pity.

"Yes ma'am," she lied.

The truth was she was all fucked up. Not just physically but her mind was in conflict with her heart and her spirit was crushed. But if there was one thing Keedy was good at, it was putting on pretenses.

"Good," the nurse replied. I brought your lunch." She adjusted the tray holder over Keedy's bed and sat the food on it.

Keedy couldn't see out of her swollen eyes so the nurse placed the fork in her hand and guided it to the tray. "Okay, let's use the clock method. Your chicken is at twelve o'clock, your potatoes are at three, and your peas are at six o'clock. If—" She stopped abruptly when a visitor entered the room.

He walked over to the bed and smiled at the nurse. "I'll feed her," he said, gently taking the fork out of Keedy's hand.

For a fraction of a second the nurse wondered if he was the one that had beaten Keedy but the compassion in his eyes conveyed that he was not that type of man.

"It's okay. I'm a friend," said Mayhem.

The nurse put her hand on Keedy's arm. "Baby?"

Keedy nodded her consent and the nurse left them alone.

Mayhem looked down at Keedy and felt an ache in his chest that threatened to cut off his breath. He wanted to wrap his arms around her and promise to protect her. Instead he held the vase of roses that he had brought her up to her nose.

Keedy inhaled their fragrance and teared up. She turned her head away feeling ugly and pitiful. Mayhem reached out and stroked her hair.

"It's okay," he whispered consolingly.

The tears flowed nonstop and Keedy covered her face with both hands. "I don't want you to see me like this," she muttered.

"I don't. I see you the way that I know you are—a beautiful person."

His words brought more tears from her eyes. Mayhem sat the vase down on the table by the bed and grabbed some Kleenex out of a box nearby. He reached down and dabbed at her tears tenderly. "Don't cry, shawdy. Everything will be a'ight. C'mon, try to eat something for me. Okay?"

"Okay," she sniffled.

"Hold up." Mayhem set the fork down and went to wash his hands.

Keedy heard the water running and was touched by how considerate he was. When she heard him returning from the bathroom she lowered her head.

Mayhem pulled up a chair and picked the fork up and removed the lid off of the tray. "This looks good." He speared a chicken strip and held it up to Keedy's mouth.

She bit off a piece and chewed slowly. It hurt to swallow but she endured the discomfort because suddenly she was hungry. Next Mayhem fed her a fork full of mashed potatoes. When a bit dribbled out the side of her mouth he wiped it away with a cloth napkin.

Keedy smiled.

Mayhem was patient with her and took his time, always allowing her time to chew her food completely, swallowing it before offering her more. In between bites of chicken and forks of potatoes and peas, he held a glass of water up to her mouth as she sucked through a straw.

When Keedy had enough she waved off the last of the chicken fingers. "You want dessert?" he politely asked.

"What is it?"

"Jello with fruit."

"No, thank you."

"Good. I'm about to fuck this up," he said, eliciting a little smile from her.

A second later she asked playfully, "Why are you smacking like that?"

Mayhem chuckled. "'Cause this shit is fi', shawdy."

Keedy shook her head in amusement.

"Here." He held a spoon of Jello up to her lips. "Taste it."

"No, Mayhem, I don't—"

Before she could complete the sentence she tasted the sugary treat on her tongue and just like Mayhem said, it was good. "Umm." She licked her lips.

Mayhem smiled. "Now look who's smacking," he kidded.

"Shut up. Why you do me dat?" Keedy moved in slow motion and play-punched him on the shoulder.

Mayhem loved the way she talked, her New Orleans accent was sexy as hell. They shared the Jello until it was all gone then he placed the tray out of the way.

"Thank you, Mayhem," she said with sincerity. She didn't know what she had done to earn his kindness but she truly appreciated it.

He asked about her bills since she was in no condition to do hair anytime soon. Keedy told him that her bills wasn't a problem but he could hear the uncertainty in her tone.

"Why you gotta wrestle with me, shawdy? he asked. "Just let me do what I do."

"No, Mayhem, you've done enough." She choked up.

Mayhem took her hands in his and spoke softly. "Keedy, I haven't done anything but showed my concern for a girl who welcomed me into her home without even knowing me. That may seem small to you but it meant everything to me. We've only known each other for a few days but I can tell that you're platinum. So let me look out for you, a'ight?"

"But—"

Mayhem put a finger to her lips, hushing her. "Shh. No *buts,*" he said with a tenderness that liquefied her heart.

"Okay, she relented. But can I ask you a question?"

"Yes, you can."

"Why do you care what happens to me?"

Mayhem closed his eyes and squeezed her hands tightly within his as he bared his soul.

When he finished telling her the story about his mother's death and the guilt he carried with him over not being able to save her, Keedy's face was wet with tears.

"I'm not going to let that happen to you," he promised.

Chapter 16

Mayhem leaned against the door frame of the bathroom watching A'nyah wrap her hair up and prepare for bed. She had just come home an hour ago and they were discussing his visit with Keedy.

"Bay-bae," A'nyah said, "you can't rescue a bitch that don't want to be saved. Tank has kicked Keedy's dumb ass more times than I can count on my fingers and toes, and every time she goes running right back to him. I'm so over it."

Mayhem lifted an eyebrow. "If that's how you feel why were you so bugged out when you found her the other morning?"

"Oh, that's my girl so I would never watch her lay on a floor and die without trying to help her but I'm not wasting my breath on her and Tank because she's not going to leave him alone." She rinsed the cream off of her face and patted her skin dry with a towel.

"So what you just give up on her? And when he ends up killing her you'll be the first one standing over her casket crying," he predicted.

"Humph," remarked A'nyah. She hung the towel on the rack and turned toward him. "Why are you so worried about Keedy anyway? Don't you see all of this woman standing right here?" She was wearing a t-shirt that stopped mid-thigh with no panties underneath it. She ran her hands over her hips and traced her lips with her tongue erotically.

"Yea, I see," Mayhem replied nonchalantly. His disinterest in her was torturing which made A'nyah want him all that much more.

She stepped toward him and pressed her body against his. "I don't want to talk about Keedy," she said, lowering her voice seductively. "I want you to take me in the room and make me scream your name."

Mayhem looked down at her. The swell of her breasts and the softness of her body was tempting. He hadn't tapped any pussy in a minute. But easy chicks were a complete turn off so it was nothing for him to resist her. "Why are you so hot in the ass?" he asked, ignoring the heat coming off of her body.

"Because you make me hot. I can just think about you and my pussy will start dripping. Wanna see?" She took his hand and guided it between her legs.

A'nyah hadn't lied, her shit was sopping wet and it was fat to death. "Do you see what you do to a bitch?"

Mayhem pulled his hand back but A'nyah was determined to get that dick. She reached down and grabbed a handful of what he was packing. "Dayum, lil' daddy, you can fill a bitch all the way up with this," she remarked.

A'nyah stroked him through his pants and slowly went to her knees. Looking up at him with lust filled eyes, she rasped, "Let me suck this big dick."

"Shawdy, don't even play ya'self," he said, removing her hands off of his wood and pulling her up to her feet.

"Are you serious?" She folded her arms across her chest and frowned at him.

"Dead ass," replied Mayhem.

A'nyah threw her hands on her hips and twisted her face up. "Why you handling me like I'm a duck? Let me find out you scared of pussy."

"Scared?" Mayhem shook his head. "Nah, shawdy, I keep telling you I'm not your average nigga."

"Ain't nobody said all of that," she sulked, poking her lip out. Mayhem fixed his mouth to say something but A'nyah cut him off. "Ugh! Can we fuck now and talk later?" She stomped her feet like a cute little brat.

"Goodnight, shawdy," he said, dismissing her.

A'nyah rolled her eyes and brushed past him on her way out of the bathroom. Mayhem watched her t-shirt rise up high on her ass as she walked down the hall.

Feeling his eyes on her ass, A'nyah stopped outside of her bedroom door and turned around. "That dick felt good in my hand. I can't wait to feel it inside this wet pussy," she said with a naughty smile on her face.

When her bedroom door closed Mayhem went to his room and laid across the bed and fired up a blunt. The weed got him high and made him feel depressed at the same time. What the fuck am I doing? he asked himself.

His life had no direction; no meaning or purpose other than day to day survival. And he missed Brandi and Dream like crazy. Yea, *Dream* too. In spite of everything she had done, she had still carried his seed in her belly for nine long months and had endured the pain of pushing his baby out. For that reason alone he would always carry love for her.

When the reverie became too strong to resist Mayhem sat up on the edge of the bed and grabbed his cell off of the nightstand. He stared at the phone with the realization that he would be taking a huge chance by calling home. But it didn't matter, he just needed to hear their voices.

Mayhem punched in Dream's number and after several rings he heard her familiar voice. "Hello," she answered, sounding groggy.

"Hey."

"Who is this?" Dream asked as she rubbed sleep from her eyes.

"Your baby daddy."

"Oh, my god! Mayhem are you ok? I've been so worried about you and Brandi has been crying for you every day."

Mayhem felt a sharp pain shoot through his heart. "I'm good. What about y'all?" he asked.

"We're okay."

"I miss y'all, shawdy," he admitted and waited for her to say the same back to him.

When Dream didn't respond it hurt him a little, but he brushed it off and asked, "Did any heat come your way?"

"A little at first but I told them I didn't know where you were. They haven't been back since but niggas in the streets are talking."

"Fuck them."

"Exactly," she chimed.

Damn, her voice sounded good. Mayhem thought about swallowing his pride and going back to get his family. If he was living on borrowed time he might as well spend it with them.

He checked the clock on his phone and saw that it was after midnight but he had to hear his baby girl's voice. After that, he would talk to Dream about coming back for them.

"Is Brandi asleep?" he asked.

"Yea, but I'll wake her up. Hold on."

"A'ight."

As he waited for his daughter to come on the line, Mayhem could hear Dream getting up out of the bed. Then he heard a nigga's voice in the background. Dream and the dude started hollering at each other and all of a sudden the phone call ended. When Mayhem tried to call back he kept getting sent straight to voicemail.

As much as he tried not to give a fuck it still hurt him. *The bitch just ain't no good.*

Mayhem sent her a text.

Just let me talk to my daughter.

A minute later a reply came back.

Nigga don't call or text her phone no more.

Mayhem became heated. He redialed Dream's number hoping that cell phone gangsta that she had over there would answer. But again and again he was sent to voicemail.

The fact that Dream would allow some bitch made nigga to regulate him talking to his seed had Mayhem's head pounding. If he would've had a whip, he would've drove back to Atlanta and murked her and that lame nigga and took his daughter.

Wrinkles lined Mayhem's forehead as he let the phone slip from his hand and fall to the floor. Sighing heavily he got up and went to the kitchen to get a bottle of Jack to wash away the rage that had risen up in his chest.

Back in his room as the loud clouded up the room and the liquor heightened his anger, Mayhem smoked and drank himself into a murderous rage. But with no one around to unleash that beast on, all he could do was keep turning up the bottle of Jack until he was passed out across the bed.

As sleep drifted down upon him visions of Dream's dirty ass and A'nyah's insistent seductiveness formed an unwanted visual collage behind his eyelids.

In the middle of the night Mayhem heard soft whispers in his ear and felt his dick rise. Either Dream or A'nyah stroked him and no matter how hard he tried to resist he couldn't move his hands or open his eyes.

He felt her warm mouth encircle the head then her tongue traced it slowly. When she took him deeper into her mouth then all the way back to her throat, slurping and gagging, Mayhem couldn't help but grab her head and hold it in place. His harder than steel dick was coated with her spit.

"Fuckkkk," he moaned as she gently rubbed his balls while messaging his wood with her throat. It felt so good Mayhem didn't ever want to awake from the dream.

"You like the way I suck your dick, Daddy?" she garbled.

Mayhem moaned incoherently.

She bobbed her head up and down, took the whole thing out of her mouth, spat on it, and then licked it clean.

Mayhem's toes curled. He felt her spit the dick out and slap it up against her face. Then she put it back in her mouth and made him moan like a little bitch.

She ran her tongue down the underside of his length then across his nut sacs, and before he realized what her intentions were she was licking his ass.

That shit felt weird and good at the same time but even in his dream Mayhem was too G'd up too lay there and let Dream/A'nyah eat him out like he was a bitch. He reached down and pulled her up.

"You don't like that, baby?" she coed.

"Hmmm," he grunted.

"Okay," she whispered in his ear. I'm about to give you some of this fat pussy. You'll love that."

He felt her straddle him and place the head of his dick right on her soft slippery lips. He arched his hips up hurrying the insertion. His girth caused her to moan out in pleasured pain as she paused to allow her body to slowly accommodate his size.

"Oooh, you feel so damn good," she cried.

Mayhem grabbed her hips and pulled her all the way down until he was touching bottom. "Yesssss," she panted as they began to grind in harmony. "Get this pussy."

"I'ma get it," he said in a hoarse tone, speeding up his pace.

"Yes, hit this shit, Mayhem. Fuck me like you own me. Make me do whatever you say, nigga."

She threw her head back and bounced up and down on his pole like a gymnast. Her gushy wet sheath felt so hot and tight, Mayhem could hardly hold back from busting all up inside of her.

She felt him swelling up inside of her walls and his desire increased hers. She leaned forward, placing her palms down on the bed, and gyrating her hips in a hard circular motion to get every inch of that hardness inside of her.

Her nipples grazed back and forth across his chest as her pussy gripped that dick and made it hit every one of her spots. "Ooh, yes muthafucka, now you're fucking this pussy like it's yours. Make me come on this big, black dick. Oh, yes, here it come. Come with me! Nut in this pussy, nigga. Nut in this shit," she cried out as an orgasm the size of Mount Rushmore came down on her. "Awwww, sheeiiitttttt."

Mayhem couldn't hold back any longer, he let out an animalistic growl as his nut exploded and he sprayed his seeds deep inside of her pussy.

The power of his eruption brought him fully awake. He could feel wetness all over himself. *Damn that shit felt real as fuck!* Mayhem blinked open his eyes and reached for the

Jack but his movement was thwarted by the weight of A'nyah's sweat drenched body on top of his. When he realized what the fuck had happened his brows knitted together and he pushed her off of him.

A'nyah sat up and smiled at him. "I told you I was going to make you my lil' dip." She laughed triumphantly.

Chapter 17

Mayhem stood under the shower feeling like he had been raped. He shook his head and laughed at the thought of that. He promised himself that he would never fuck with Jack Daniel's again, that's for sure.

Lathering his body with soap and rinsing A'nyah's lascivious scent off of him, he faintly recalled what had happened. He couldn't lie to himself, shawdy had that heat but it absolutely wouldn't happen again. Like he had told her, that shit didn't count no way because he hadn't given her the dick voluntarily.

"Boy, please," she had laughed. "You know your ass wasn't that drunk. You was throwing that dick back on your own free will."

Mayhem still disputed that but what was already done couldn't be erased and he still wasn't gon' be her lil' dip, her trade or none of those tags she put on her conquests. He was a muthafuckin' boss and now he was determined to reinforce that in her mind.

When he had showered and dressed he followed his nose into the kitchen. A'nyah was standing over the stove in boy shorts and a wife beater, singing. "Is it bad that I never made love, no I never did it—but I sure know how to fuck."

She looked up to see Mayhem standing there rubbing his chin and watching her. "You think you did something, don't you?" he asked.

"I did—I got some of that dick and it was the bomb dot com." She giggled.

Mayhem lowered his brow and tightened his mouth but said nothing.

"Ahh, lil' daddy, don't worry I'm not gon' tell nobody. It will be our own little secret," she continued teasing.

Mayhem was looking at her like he was contemplating taking a warrant out on her ass for sexual assault.

A'nyah cracked up. She lowered the fire, sat the spatula down, and walked up to him and wrapped her arms around his waist. "Bae, why you gotta look so damn mean? You did that shit last night. You see a bitch is in here making you breakfast."

"Nah, I'm not eating your cooking," he joked as he disengaged himself from her embrace. "Y'all do that voodoo shit down her. Fuck around and have me checking for you fa real."

"Okayyy," she sang as she did a little dipsy-do back over to the stove.

The breakfast turned out good. A'nyah had made blueberry pancakes, scrambled eggs with cheese, and lots of bacon. Afterwards Mayhem helped her wash the dishes and put them away.

A'nyah was acting like they were now a couple but Mayhem maintained that what had happened last night wouldn't happen again.

"We'll see, boo," she said confidently as she went to get dressed for work.

As soon as she was gone Mayhem went into the kitchen and poured out the last bottle of Jack that he had in the cabinet. *Never again,* he reiterated.

Back in his room he sparked a blunt and called the hospital to check on Keedy. For some reason it felt like he had just cheated on her.

After three rings a nurse answered and asked him to hold on.

Keedy came on the line sounding much better than yesterday. "Hello," she said.

"Good morning, shawdy. How you feeling?" he asked.

"Good morning. I'm better," she replied. The sound of his voice washed away the aches that she had been feeling before his call.

Mayhem asked if she had been given her pain medicine.

"Yea," she replied.

"They better take good care of you or I'ma come there and turn up," he said, causing her to giggle.

"You so crazy," she said.

Yea, about you, Mayhem thought but didn't say. He felt a strong connection to her but he knew that he had to respect her relationship with Tank even though he treated her so foul.

"Why are you just holding the phone?" Keedy asked.

"I don't know," he admitted. "I didn't want anything. I just wanted to call and tell you good morning."

"Thank you. That's so sweet of you."

"It's nothin', shawdy."

"Yes it is. It means a lot. Thanks again for checking on me."

Keedy's response went unanswered as they both grew quiet. Mayhem sat the blunt down in the ashtray and watched it burn while trying to think of something to say to keep her on the phone.

Keedy's heart was beating fast; that's what his voice did to her. She knew what she wanted to say to him but she wouldn't dare put herself out there like that. He would think she was crazy. All he had done was show concern for her.

Say it girl, urged her inner voice.

Keedy closed her eyes and took a deep breath. *Okay, you can do this,* she told herself.

Another deep breath and she was ready. She opened her mouth to utter three little words but nothing came out but a squeak.

"You okay?" asked Mayhem.

Keedy nodded her head up and down as if he could see her.

"Shawdy?" he called.

"Mayhem, I have to hang up now," she said.

"A'ight. I'ma try to come and see you later."

"Okay," she replied and quickly ended the call before he realized that she was crying and asked why.

Keedy knew the answer to that but she didn't want him to know. She held the phone to her chest as if it was his head lying there. It had been so long since anyone cared about her.

She allowed herself to dream about being Mayhem's woman even though she knew that it would never happen. And if it did, once he found out about her past he would kick her dumb, ugly ass to the curb. No real nigga wanted a bitch that so many others had been with.

Nope, she was not wifey material. Tank was right, she would never be more than a nigga's jump off.

As the tears began to flow harder, Keedy wished that Tank had killed her. Then she wouldn't have had to deal with the agony anymore.

Chapter 18

Tank had something to deal with too. He was about to attend what is called a second line and he knew that he would encounter Peanut's people there. A few of them would probably give him the side eye and it was possible that the tools might have to come out.

Tank wasn't sweating it because his round was with him to watch his back. His only concern was keeping Mayhem from bustin' his gun unnecessarily.

"Bruh, I'm here to pay my respects and you're here in case Peanut's people try to bring the drama. But they don't know shit so let's just play it cool," Tank cautioned as they climbed out of his whip and joined the crowd.

Mayhem agreed to tone down his gangsta but that quickly changed as soon as they spotted Julius and Larron a short ways up the block.

Both men were part of the crowd that was congregated outside of the church on Washington Avenue as Treme Brass Band began playing the blues version of Al Green's, *For the Good Times*.

Like many of Peanut's homeboys they wore t-shirts with his face emblazoned on them. Even Tank wore a shirt decorated with happier times of the life Peanut lived as they proceeded the mahogany coffin he was put to rest in.

Initially, they stepped slowly toward the horse and carriage that was to lead the second line funeral. Once the song came to an end, brief silence befell the multitude and then the music erupted in a more festive tune.

Mayhem and Tank walked side by side, in step, with about a dozen funeral goers between them, Julius and Larron. "I'ma do those bitch ass niggas right here," Mayhem whispered as he reached for the new fo-fifth that was tucked under his shirt. He figured that after he hit those niggas in the head he would be able to escape in the mass pandemonium that would follow.

Tank quickly grabbed his wrist preventing him from whipping out. "Bruh, you must be crazy," he gritted. "Don't you see them people right there?" He nodded towards several uniformed cops that were congregated not far away.

Mayhem let his hand fall to his side but his eyes bore into Julius and his boy's backs. The minute he got a chance he was gonna pump something hot in their spines.

For the time being he bridled his anger as they got swept up in the crowd that marched and danced down several blocks. They traveled the circumference of Peanut's hood, from Robinson St. down to LaSalle Avenue ending up at Shakespeare Park where the hearse awaited to take the coffin. From there the celebration of Peanut's life continued. The deejay made it feel as if it was a block party instead of the mourning of a loved one.

Amidst the dancing Mayhem lost track of Julius and Larron but he knew where they rested their heads so they were just living on borrowed time.

An hour or so later as the celebration came to a close, Mayhem and Tank were headed back to Tank's whip when two of Peanut's cousins stepped in their paths.

"Tank, what's up?" asked Kendrick, the taller of the two. His tone and the scowl on his face immediately put Mayhem on alert.

Mayhem watched both boys' hands closely. If either one of them flinched it was gonna get mad ugly in a hurry.

"I'm fucked up, son. I still can't believe my lil' nigga gone," said Tank, wearing a poker face.

Doobie, a short dark-skinned youngin' with a mouthful of gold teeth and a Glock .40 on his waist that he was known to let pop off, stepped up in Tank's grill. "I'm hearing that my big cuz was with you earlier that night before he got killed," he stated almost confrontationally.

Tank looked down at the half-pint gangsta and met his glare with a harder one. "Nigga, you accusing me of some fuckery?" he spat.

"However you wanna put it," Doobie stuck his chest out. "Julius told us what happened that night. What I wanna know is how did my cuz end up dead after y'all left there?"

He cut his eyes at Mayhem and asked, "Is this the nigga that was with y'all that night?"

"Fuck you wanna know who I am for?" Mayhem quickly spoke up.

Tank shot him a reprimanding look but it was too late. Doobie spun toward him with his hand automatically going to his waist but Mayhem's banger was already halfway out.

Tank quickly stepped between them. "Y'all niggas need to chill the fuck out," he barked.

Mayhem and Doobie stared each other down with their hands wrapped around the butt of their tools.

"Yo, Doobie, let me holla at you and Kendrick," said Tank.

Doobie stepped off to hear what Tank had to say but he never took his eyes off of Mayhem or let his hand fall far away from his waist.

Mayhem slipped his shades on and leaned against the side of the car. Muthafuckas would be walking around Doobie's neighborhood with dude's picture on their t-shirts if he didn't fall the fuck back!

Ten feet away Tank tried to convince Doobie and Kendrick that he hadn't had anything to do with Peanut's murder. Looking from one to the other," he said, "Y'all know I loved Peanut like a brother and I'm still fucked up over what happened to him. But after those niggas jacked us that night we split up. I hit the streets tryna find out who they were. Peanut was supposed to be going home. Those niggas that robbed us must've followed him."

Kendrick nodded his head, he seemed to be buying Tank's explanation but Doobie remained suspicious.

"What about your round over there? Is that the nigga that was with y'all that night?" he asked again.

"Nah," Tank lied. "He ain't even from 'round here."

They talked back and forth a little longer then Tank and Kendrick half hugged. When Tank embraced Doobie he could feel the resistance. “I’ma fuck with y’all later,” Tank said, maintaining a friendly tone.

“Bet that,” said Kendrick.

Doobie didn’t respond at all. His gut told him that Tank was lying. As he watched him walk to his car he looked down at the image of Peanut that was imprinted on his shirt. *I’ma get to the truth cuz and if that nigga had anything to do with your death I’ma kill everything he loves.*

“Those niggas are going to be a problem,” said Tank as him and Mayhem drove away. The sound of his voice matched the worried look that was etched on his face.

Mayhem sparked a blunt, leaned back in his seat, and inhaled the smoke into his lungs. He took a deep breath enjoying the strong scent of the weed. Glancing over at Tank he replied, “Shawdy, the only problem is the one that don’t have a solution. If those niggas are feeling some type of way let’s put them on their asses.”

“We might have to.” Tank sighed. “Especially Doobie because I could tell that he didn’t believe me and he ain’t no ho. He’ll bust a nigga head with no remorse, ya heard me.”

“Fuck that nigga. Straight up. Let’s go see him tonight,” suggested Mayhem.

“Nah, I’ma wait and see how it plays out. But we’re going to see Julius’ bitch ass tonight.”

Mayhem allowed a smile to creep onto his face. He wanted Julius just as badly as Tank did.

They drove out to Tank’s crib where they tossed back some Ciroc and blazed some loud while continuing to plot tonight’s bloody escapade.

A short while later Tweety came home and started fussing. “Tank y’all gotta go smoke that shit outside. I’m not going to keep telling you that over and over.”

Tank pulled her down on his lap and tried to kiss her but Tweety turned her face away from him. "Baby, why are you always fussing?"

"Because you're always pissing me the fuck off," she spat as she got up and glared down at him.

Mayhem stood up and apologized for smoking in her house.

"It's not on you. Tank's disrespectful ass know I can't stand the smell of that shit." She glowered down at Tank in exasperation.

Mayhem walked out on the porch and finished smoking his blunt. He could hear Tweety in there going off, calling Tank every kind of muthafucka known to man. Tank wasn't saying shit and Mayhem didn't hear any furniture moving around.

As he walked to the car he couldn't help thinking that if that had been Keedy talking to Tank like that he would've knocked her upside the head.

Ten minutes later Tank came out of the house and slid behind the wheel.

"I'm surprised wifey didn't put you on punishment," Mayhem cracked.

Tank looked at him with a glare but Mayhem just laughed. "Nigga, who you scaring?" he clowned as Tank peeled off. "And slow ya ass down, those tires ain't do shit to you."

He was cracking up.

As they rode around from ward to ward and the day eroded into nightfall Tank's mood darkened with the sky. Mayhem was cool with that because it fit perfectly with the mission at hand.

It was time to boot up and go put a couple of bitch nigga's on their asses.

Chapter 19

Mayhem leaned forward and blasted the music. Hardcore rap always helped him get turnt up before he put in work.

Rick Ross came in with the intro:

They told me it's never too late for prayer
Well Lord! Pray for us niggas
Cause we ready to die for this shit

Mayhem nodded his head to that real shit as he pulled out his tool and slapped a dick in it. The extended clip assured him that he would have enough ammo for whatever they faced.

If I die tonight I pray I get buried in clean drawers
Line us all up, just bury me with my dawgs
I look to my left, I look to my right
All I see is my blood, all I see is my life
If it go down tonight, my nigga look out for momma
Been robbing my whole life, I gotta look out for karma

Mayhem rocked back and forth to the beat as adrenaline coursed through his body. He looked over and saw Tank pop another Molly. That made the fourth one he had popped but Mayhem wasn't concerned; every nigga that he had ever put in work with had a different way of finding their zone.

When they reached Julius' street it was 2AM and everything seemed quiet. Tank circled the block just to make sure the police weren't anywhere in the vicinity.

By the time they parked a couple houses away from Julius' spot they were both in a bloodthirsty mood. Mayhem grabbed his backpack off of the backseat and climbed out of the car. He closed the door quietly and strapped the knapsack on.

Tank came around the car amped up and bouncing on his toes. "Let's do this shit. Let's do this shit," he chanted, holding his pump waist high.

Mayhem slipped on his shades then tilted his head to the heavens and tapped his heart with a fist. If something went wrong he would join his mother before he would fold.

"Let's go," he said.

Together they moved up the street with fatalistic purpose in their strides. When they reached the house they crept to the backyard as quietly as mice.

Stepping up on the back porch, Mayhem held his banger down toward the ground but he gripped it tightly and he was ready to bring it up and let it sound off at the first thing that moved.

Behind him Tank's pump was cocked and locked. And those Mollies had his eyes wild with anticipation of bloodshed. Neither one of them was masked up which spelled something menacing for those inside.

Mayhem leaned forward and pressed his ear to the door. He could hear a faint sound of music coming from inside but there was no sound of movement going on.

Standing to the side of the door he lifted his foot and smashed the heel of his boot right below the lock. The back door gave and he heard the frame splinter but the lock held. A second powerful kick sent the door flying inwardly. It clanged loudly against the corner of the sink's counter.

Mayhem stepped through the door with his nerves on alert and his banger chest high. Tank was right on his heels, cranked so high he was running up Mayhem's back.

They moved to the front of the shotgun house with urgency, quickly glancing in every room that they passed to make sure that it was unoccupied. At the second door Mayhem paused and lifted his gun. A curtain moved from a breeze that blew in the window almost causing him to splatter its threads.

Realizing that it was nothing, Mayhem moved on silently waving for Tank to follow. Proceeding down the narrow carpeted hall they reached the den where they had sat in conference with Julius just a week ago.

A quick glance detected that the den was unoccupied. Across the hall the door to a bedroom. Mayhem looked to the floor and didn't see any light shining from under the bottom but he could hear Charlie Wilson crooning from some type of music system inside.

Mayhem looked at Tank and put a finger to his mouth, motioning for silence. He reached down and quietly turned the door knob and eased inside of the bedroom. It was pitch black but he could hear moans and bed springs over the song.

He ran his hand down the wall until he located the light switch. When he flicked it on the room lit up like a stage. Julius stopped in mid-stroke and looked over his shoulder. The girl underneath him looked up and screamed.

Kaboom!

Tank's pump roared without hesitation. The lamp beside the bed shattered. "Shut the fuck up!" he barked, stepping toward them with ill intent.

"Hey, man, what the fuck is this," cried Julius.

Mayhem stepped forward and put his fo-fifth to the back of his head. "Get on the floor, nigga, and if you make one country ass break I'ma spray your shit all over these walls."

"A'ight, my nigga." Julius climbed out of the bed and put his dick in the carpet.

Mayhem slapped him across the head with his steel to establish that he was not there to play any games.

"Ahh," Julius moaned. "Bruh, you don't have to do all of that. I'm not going to give you no problems."

"I know you're not. Because if you do I got a problem solver," taunted Mayhem, jabbing him in the back of the head with his tool.

Julius lied as still as a rug.

Mayhem put his knee in the nigga's back while he removed his backpack and pulled out the duct tape. "Gimme your hands," he ordered.

Julius submissively placed his hands behind his back and allowed himself to be bound with the tape. After securing his hands Mayhem taped his feet together. He slapped him across the head with that iron again and threatened to make him a new asshole if he dared to wiggle.

He turned around to toss the tape to Tank and saw that he had straddled the girl and was groping her. Mayhem shot up to his feet and snatched Tank off of her. “Hell no, nigga, you not doing that shit. Fuck is wrong with you?” he spat.

Tank started to protest but even high on those pills he could tell from the grimace on Mayhem’s mug that he would have to kill or be killed if he insisted.

He looked away from Mayhem to the crying girl. “Bitch, you ugly as fuck anyway,” he snarled. “Get your ass on the floor too!”

“Please,” she cried.

Tank hit her in the mouth with the butt of his pump dislodging one of her front teeth. Blood splattered down on the bed and she crumpled to the floor on her side.

“Utter another word bitch and you’ll get a new hairstyle,” Tank spat.

Shawdy balled up into a fetal position and whimpered.

Mayhem stood over Tank as he duct-taped the girl and slapped a strip across her mouth to muffle her cries. When he was done Mayhem pulled a blanket off of the bed and covered her nakedness.

Now the fun was about to begin.

They walked back over to Julius. Tank stood looking down at him while Mayhem pulled up a chair and took a seat. He went inside the duffel bag and methodically removed a sharp knife with a long handle, and a pair of heavy duty pliers.

Lying on his stomach completely restrained, Julius’ heart pounded. He looked up at Mayhem with fear in his eyes.

Mayhem smiled down at him maniacally. “I call this my confession kit,” he said.

Julius’ whole body began shaking. He could see in Mayhem’s eyes that he was facing a killah that had no mercy for a perceived enemy. Still he pled for his life.

Mayhem looked at his man and asked sarcastically, "Who is this nigga talking to? You?"

"He ain't talking to me," Tank chuckled.

Mayhem hunched his shoulders. "Maybe he's praying," he smirked.

"All I'm asking y'all to do is hear me out," cried Julius. "I know why y'all are here but I didn't have nothin' to do with y'all getting robbed. I put that on my life."

Mayhem and Tank looked at each other and laughed. Fuck was he talking about, he didn't have a life anymore.

"Tank, you been knowing me all your life. You know I don't rock like that," Julius went on in a voice that had lost all of its bass.

"I don't know shit," refuted Tank.

Julius quickly deduced that they simply didn't believe him. "Look, man, I didn't do that shit but I'll give you back the money and whatever else y'all want. I got three birds here and a hundred thousand dollars. Y'all can have it all," he bartered.

Tank's eyes lit up. "Where the shit at?" he demanded.

When Julius told them where they could find the stash Mayhem tossed Tank the duffel bag. Tank caught it and hurried across the hall to the den.

Mayhem tapped his foot on the hard wood floor and silently stared at Julius as they waited for Tank to return with the loot.

Julius begged Mayhem to believe him. "Youngun', why would I do something like that in my own front yard, right where I lay my head? Man, I swear I had nothin' to do with that shit."

Mayhem remained silent. Julius wished he could see his eyes so he could read whether or not he was still going to kill him, but those sinister looking shades concealed the windows to his soul.

Tank returned with the duffel bag filled with loot and the three bricks that Julius had promised he would find. He walked over to Mayhem and let him peer inside.

Mayhem stood up with his ratchet in one hand and the pliers in the other.

"What you 'bout to do?" whined Julius. "I gave y'all way more than y'all lost."

"That satisfies him but I want mine in blood," spat Mayhem.

"Tank!" Julius cried out. "Man, don't let your round kill me over something I had nothin' to do with. Please don't do me like this."

Mayhem shook his head as he watched Julius weep. "Nigga, be twenty-one 'bout it. Admit what you done and die like a man!" he spat.

"But I didn't do that shit," Julius balled.

Mayhem couldn't take seeing a grown ass nigga turn bitch so he aimed his gun down at Julius and ended his sobs.

Blocka! Blocka!

Julius head jerked to the side and blood ran down from his temple. A third shot fired at point blank range caused a puddle of blood to form underneath his head.

Tank looked on puzzled as Mayhem rolled Julius over onto his back and straddled his chest.

Mayhem sat his banger down on the floor beside him, rolled Julius over and waved the pliers over his head. Then he pulled Julius mouth open and felt inside. Nodding his head up and down he stuck the pliers in Julius mouth and uttered, "Fuck make you think you can set me up to be robbed and not have to pay with your life?"

Julius couldn't answer, of course, he was on his way to see the Lord.

Mayhem clamped the pliers on Julius back tooth and began twisting, turning, pulling, grunting and sweating.

Tank looked down at him confused. "Yo, son, what the fuck you doing?" he asked.

Mayhem yanked so hard he fell backwards onto his back. But he had accomplished his mission. He got on his feet and held the bloody pliers up to Tank's face.

Tank saw that there was a tooth clamped in the jaws of the large pliers. He looked at Mayhem questioningly.

Mayhem said, "Nigga was too stupid to have a mutha-fuckin' wisdom tooth in his mouth, shawdy."

Tank's eyes bulged. He looked at Mayhem thinking, *this fool is throwed all the way off.*

"Let's go," Mayhem said as casually as if they were leaving the mall. He was disappointed that Larron hadn't been there but they could get his punk ass later.

Mayhem gathered up his tools and headed for the door.

"What about lil' mama?" asked Tank.

Mayhem continued out of the room without answering so Tank made the decision. He walked around the bed and leveled his pump down at her.

She looked up at him, shaking her head no, but her silent plea was rejected.

"Ugly ass bitch," Tank spat. I didn't wanna fuck you no way!"

Kaboom!

Chapter 20

Mayhem and Tank split the loot evenly and this time when they sold the work no one stepped out of the shadows and laid them down. They divvied up the money from the three bricks and added their shares to their banks.

Mayhem sold his truck to a chop shop and after a lady that Tank knew hooked him up with a false identity—complete with a driver's license, social security card, and a voter's registration—he went and dropped sixty-five racks on a brand new Corvette Stingray Coupe.

The sleek sports car was as black as Mayhem's skin tone and as fast as his trigger finger. The soft leather seats reminded him of his mother's comforting embrace and the high-tech sound system made every song sound like he was at a live concert.

A'nyah was sweating his upgraded swag like a too tight tank top. Mayhem still wasn't a fan of hers because she viewed niggas as trophies. He regretted that his name was one of many on her thong.

He had to give her props though, because her schedule stayed full. She didn't just rely on trick money, she worked at Verizon and could afford to pay her own bills if niggas acted up. But when it came to sex and relationships, A'nyah had the mindset of a man. She could fuck with no attachments at all.

Listening to her handle dudes on the phone like they were nothin' but lames, often had Mayhem shaking his head. A nigga would take her out, wine and dine her, and after the date she would come straight home and try to hop in his bed.

That shit didn't sit well with Mayhem at all. Some nights were harder than others to resist her because she was sexy as a muthafucka but she reminded Mayhem of Dream's punk ass so much his dick would shrivel up every time she tried to tempt him.

"If you get your mind off of Keedy you might be able to appreciate a real bitch, ya heard me. I just don't understand the attraction," A'nyah said out of frustration one night.

Mayhem didn't admit that his mind was on Keedy but his actions spoke loud.

He had spent the past two days getting things ready for her return home from the hospital and the energy he put into it clearly defined how he felt about her.

A'nyah wasn't fooled. She told herself that she was just going to sit back and observe because when Tank found out, that was when the shit was going to get real.

Mayhem walked into the lobby of University hospital holding a few shopping bags in one hand and several balloons in the other. He walked to the counter and requested his pass then moved to the elevators. When he stepped off on the fifth floor and walked down the hall towards Keedy's room he could feel the excitement pulsing through his veins.

As he pushed the door to her room open a slight calm came over him when he saw her standing by the window looking out of the blinds.

"Hey, you," he said as he approached where she stood.

Keedy turned in his direction and gave him a slight smile. "Hey, Mayhem. Thanks for coming," she said in a soft tone as she lowered her head.

His gaze settled on her face; there was still discoloration underneath her eyes and her left cheek remained slightly puffy. Mayhem swallowed the anger that tried to override his excitement. "No problem, shawdy, you know I got you," he said as he moved to the bed and sat the bags down.

Keedy looked up at the balloons and her heart skipped a beat at his gesture of kindness but the feeling quickly subsided as the sharp pain in her jaw stole her few seconds of joy.

Mayhem felt the same sting but in his chest as he watched her struggle with her emotions.

"I got you a few things," he said as he reached inside of the bag and pulled out a pair of light blue Escada jeans and a red Gucci shirt and placed them on the bed. “You know I had to cop that hotness for you,” he said then pulled a pair of Christian Louboutin sandals from the other bag and placed them next to the outfit.

The high end labels were way beyond anything she could’ve afforded to purchase for herself and she knew that they must’ve cost him a grip.

“You didn’t have to do that.” She walked over to the bed and picked up the items taking them into her hands.

“I know. But I wanted to do something to make you feel a little better.” He looked down at the side of her bruised face.

“Thank you,” she said a little above a whisper as tears welled up in the corners of her eyes and slowly broke free.

Mayhem reached out and caught them with the back of his hand. Keedy placed both of her hands on his and they stood there saying nothing but feeling so much more.

Keedy stroked the back of his hand with her thumbs. Mayhem smiled so beautifully she wanted to trace his mouth with her fingers and plaster his smile onto her face.

She reached up and touched the scar over his brow. “It healed nicely,” she observed.

“Thanks to Nurse Keedy,” he said affectionately.

Keedy lowered her head but Mayhem put a finger under her chin and lifted her gaze. “What? You don’t like looking at me or something?” he asked, being facetious. “Am I really that jacked up?” His deep baritone was therapy for her soul.

“No, Mayhem, you’re beautiful,” she said. This time she didn’t lower her stare.

Their eyes bore softly into each other’s as time stood still and words became unnecessary. Mayhem started to kiss her and Keedy desperately wanted him to but nothing happened.

Mayhem broke the silence. “Go get changed so we can get up outta here. We got some sunshine to catch.”

“Okay,” Keedy said on short breath as she tore her eyes away from that tasty looking black licorice that could warm her heart every time with a single word. She picked up the clothes and the shoe box and headed to the bathroom.

When she came out Mayhem was posted up in the chair with a small box in his hand. His eyes roamed over her frame checking out how perfectly the jeans hugged her curves. *Shawdy a star*, he said to himself.

Keedy placed her clothes in the bags and grabbed her balloons by the strings.

Mayhem rose to his feet and extended his arm passing her the small leather case.

Keedy popped it open and removed the black Gucci Aviator shades and slid them on her face. She felt like she could now face the world.

"I'm ready."

"Let's roll out, shawdy." Mayhem put on his shades and extended his elbow out to her.

Keedy rested her hand on him as he led the way. When they reached his new whip Keedy lowered her shades and looked at him questioningly.

"I had to cop something nice to pick a queen up in," he replied as he opened her door for her.

Keedy felt so special.

The car ride felt wonderful, Mayhem let the top back on his whip and the wind blew through her hair while the sun kissed her skin. Miguel played from the system enhancing the mood.

But the closer they got to her house the more anxiety began to take over her feelings. Mayhem looked over at her as she stared out at the passing scenery, taking deep breaths ever so often. His mind projected on what was causing her discomfort.

"If it's Tank you're worried about he won't be there. He's out of town," he said. Tank had taken Tweety on vacation to the Virgin Islands. "And even if he was there I wouldn't let him put his hands on you again. Not in my presence," added Mayhem.

Keedy didn't know whether to feel comforted or frightened by his assurance of protection. The last thing she wanted to do was cause blood to be shed over her. She wasn't worth that and Tank had proven that he would let his gun clap before he would let her go.

Keedy's mind flashed back to when her cousin had tried to defend her from Tank's fists at a club.

Tank had wet him up and warned, "Next time stay the fuck out of mine. I own this bitch. She ain't going nowhere."

And true enough Keedy hadn't gone anywhere. When her cousin found out that she was still fuckin' with Tank he vowed to never come to her rescue again.

"What you thinking about, shawdy?" asked Mayhem, bringing her back to the present.

"Nothing, I'm good," she replied as she tried to force a smile.

Mayhem reached over and took her hand in his. "Don't worry I got you. If you can keep him off of your mind, I can definitely keep him off your ass. Believe me, shawdy, he can't fuck with this."

Mayhem, I don't want to cause anyone to get hurt."

He thought that he heard uncertainty in her heart about her feelings for Tank so he retreated a bit. I'm not gonna interfere with y'all relationship but I'm not gonna let him hurt you again."

"There is no relationship anymore," she said in a tone that lacked conviction.

Mayhem didn't let that discourage him, he understood the mindset of a battered woman better than most.

When they pulled up to her apartment Keedy got a sinking feeling in her stomach. That night's events played strongly in her mind and the physical and emotional pain took over her movements. Mayhem stood with the car door open and hand extended but it seemed that Keedy was looking right through him.

"You ready?" he said, breaking her train of thought.

"As ready as I'm going to be." she reached for his hand and stepped out of the vehicle.

When they approached her apartment Keedy paused again and her legs trembled. The sound of Tank's voice as he attacked her echoed in her mind. She stopped to try to gather herself when she felt her knees began to give.

Mayhem reached out to her then lifted her into his arms. "I got you, baby girl."

Keedy put her arms around his neck as he ascended the steps.

Mayhem carried her to the door then placed her on her feet. Keedy pulled her keys from her purse and stuck it in the lock. Her hand shook as she turned it. Mayhem placed his hand on top of hers to assist her.

"You can do it. Just take your time."

Keedy took a deep breath then pushed the door open.

"Surprise!" roared through the room causing her to jump.

Keedy looked around at all the smiling faces, assortment of pink and white balloons and several bouquets of pink and white roses and tears began to roll down her face. She brought her hands to her eyes in an attempt to catch a few.

"Aww. Keedy," A'nyah said as she came to her and wrapped her arms around her tightly.

Lenika and Kim joined her and they stood in a group embrace. Someone put on the music and yelled out, "Welcome home. Let's celebrate."

At least a dozen of her friends and clients were there. They all came up to her one by one and hugged her closely. When the last girl let her go she was so overwhelmed with emotion she could hardly see through her tears.

With a newfound confidence she removed her shades and caught her tears. She stood there unashamed of her battered appearance. Yes she had been beaten but she was not going to be defeated, she decided.

"This is the last time any of you will see me looking like this," Keedy announced.

"Whoot whoot!" Lenika yelled, pumping her fist in the air and dancing her little skinny butt around.

"Yessss," chimed Kim, she could not stand Tank's trifling ass, he had tried to push up on her once but she wasn't having it.

Keedy turned to Mayhem and gave him a big smile and mouthed, "Thank you." This was the nicest thing any man had ever done for her.

"You're welcome, beautiful," he mouthed back.

It was no big deal to him but his gesture meant more than he knew. He not only began to repair Keedy, he had just earned her full loyalty, something she vowed to never give another man. But she could see he was not like every other nigga and she was going to prove to him that she was not like every other woman.

Mayhem took a seat and watched as Keedy began to let down her guard and enjoy what he set up for her. She was healing and doing that for her was also curing parts of him.

"I don't get any thanks, bitch?" A'nyah said, half-joking but feeling a bit jealous.

"Aww, of course you do *hunti.*" Keedy gave her another big hug. Thank you so much."

"Whatever, bitch."

The room erupted in laughter.

As the evening went on Mayhem took joy in seeing Keedy interact with her girls. Lenika was funny as hell and Kim was sweet as apple pie. The others were a myriad of personalities that kept the party live while the wine and finger foods that had been sat out disappeared.

They all tossed compliments his way and commented on his obvious affection for Keedy. They seemed very happy for her. But out the corner of his eye Mayhem detected hater vibes emanating off of A'nyah.

When the hour grew later the guests bid them goodbye. Lenika was the last to leave. "Are you okay to drive?" asked Mayhem. She had drank more than the others.

"Yep," she assured him. Before leaving she pulled him aside and issued a stern warning. "You better be good to my girl."

"I got you," Mayhem promised.

When the door closed behind her. Mayhem turned around to find Keedy already cleaning up. "Nah, shawdy this is your day. I'ma take care of all of that," he said, taking the empty wine glasses out of her hand.

Feeling giddy and reborn, Keedy wrapped her arms around his waist. "Thank you again," she whispered, rising on her tippy toes and placing a kiss on his cheek.

If Mayhem hadn't been holding wine glasses, he would've palmed her butt and laid claim on her.

Rising from the sofa, A'nyah cleared her throat breaking the heat that had begun to brew with Mayhem and Keedy. She walked up to them and pulled Keedy away saying, "Gurl, let him clean up. I got some tea for you fresh out the kettle."

A'nyah drug Keedy to her room and told her something that crushed her heart and erased whatever thoughts she had about Mayhem being different from other niggas.

As Keedy went to her room and locked the door, A'nyah laid across her bed satisfied with the salt that she had deviously sprinkled.

Chapter 21

Mayhem finished cleaning up and sat in the living room blazing a blunt, expecting Keedy and A'nyah to return. An hour passed and then two, but still neither of them came back to join him. He checked his wrist and saw that it was past midnight. A'nyah had to work in the morning so he figured that she had probably gone to bed, but he couldn't figure out why Keedy hadn't rejoined him or at least came to say goodnight.

When he went to check on her, he found her bedroom door closed. A pang of disappointment traveled from his heart to his head; he had looked forward to a few minutes of conversation with her before turning in.

Just as quickly as the letdown resonated in his mind, Mayhem pushed it aside and checked himself for being inconsiderate. Keedy was probably tired, and the wine mixed with whatever medication that she had been taking had probably knocked her out. It was all good, he would see her in the morning.

"Goodnight, shawdy," he mouthed as if she could read his lips through the door.

Anxious for morning to come Mayhem turned and went to his room. The sooner he went to sleep the sooner the sun would rise and he would get to see his diamond in the rough.

Damn, I'm becoming softer than pudding. Keedy had his G on time out, he admitted to himself with a chuckle as he undressed and climbed in bed.

Like a little kid anticipating Christmas morning, Mayhem found it hard to sleep. Laying in the dark with his eyes wide open he fondly recalled Keedy's smile when she stepped in the door and her friends screamed *surprise*. That moment had been priceless. Mayhem would've emptied his safe to ensure that shawdy would smile like that forever. But, of course, he knew that with a girl like Keedy money meant nothing.

Love and appreciation which he had in abundance were the only things that would assure her happiness. Mayhem cursed fate for not introducing them into each other's lives under better circumstances. She was his boy's woman and even though Tank didn't really want her, Mayhem was a principled nigga, he would not cross his dawg.

He contemplated stepping to Tank and asking his blessing, but how could he fix his grill to ask his mans' permission to get with *his* girl. The thought of that seemed mad wrong so he stashed it in a place that read *Do not enter.*

As his eyelids grew heavy Mayhem resigned himself to caring about Keedy and making her smile strictly as a platonic friend.

Keedy couldn't sleep either. The *tea* that A'nyah spilled to her caused her stomach to ache with disappointment and her glass heart to shatter into a cobweb of broken hopes.

She had been a fool to think that Mayhem was any different than the next nigga. He had visited her in the hospital in the daytime, treating her like she was special, and then went back to the apartment and fucked A'nyah night after night.

How could he do that shit to her? Keedy asked the mirror as she sat on the edge of the bed and stared at her reflection.

A tear escaped her eye, cascaded down her puffy face, and dripped onto her jeans—the jeans that *he* had bought. Now that she knew he fucked her girl, the things that he had given her felt like a thousand snakes crawling over her body.

Keedy shot up off of the bed and snatched the shirt over her head and slung it in the corner. She kicked those high priced shoes off of her feet with so much force they clattered against the wall leaving scuff marks as they fell to the floor one by one.

A sob threatened to come out of Keedy's mouth as she unbuttoned the jeans and wiggled out of them. She was so tired of crying over men, but Mayhem wasn't even her dude so she swallowed that emotion and quickly replaced it with an *I don't give a fuck* attitude.

Still she didn't want nothing on her body that he had purchased. How dare he think that he could buy her with gifts. *Did he really think he was going to have some Sister Wives shit going on up in here?* Keedy said to herself as she struggled to get out of the skin-tight jeans.

Filled with frustration, Keedy released a scream then sat down on the floor and pulled the jeans over her heels. "Fuck, niggas," she said as she balled the jeans up and damn near threw her arm out of socket slinging them across the room.

Keedy stood up to her feet and walked into the bathroom to shower and get her mind right. Twenty minutes later when she crawled into bed and closed her eyes, she vowed that when she opened them in the morning she would be a cold, heartless bitch just like A'nyah since that's what Mayhem craved.

Keedy slept fretfully so when a sliver of sun peeked through her blinds bright and early the next morning, she quickly awakened. After rising out of bed and going through her morning routine in the bathroom, she stepped into a pair of sweats and pulled on a loose fitting t-shirt.

Out of the corner of her eye she saw the Escada jeans and the other designer things Mayhem had bought her thrown haphazardly around the room. The sight of them began to stir her emotions all over again but she was determined to be a brand new bitch today. She dared the muthafuckin' tears to fall.

It surprised Keedy that she was actually able to close the floodgates. Feeling much stronger she gathered up the discarded items and placed them inside a bag that she pulled out of her closet. She would take them to the dumpster later.

As she opened her bedroom door to step out she was startled backwards, Mayhem was standing there with his knuckles in the air. "You scared me," she said, refusing to look him in the eye.

"My bad, shawdy. I was just about to knock. You good this morning?"

"I'm fine."

He looked at her curiously because her response sounded clipped. "Oh, I cleaned up your bedroom," he remembered. "So if you can't find something just ask and I'll tell you where I put it."

"No problem," she replied and brushed right past him.

Mayhem reached out and grabbed her arm, gently turning her to face him. "Hold up lil' mama. Do I detect a problem between us?" he asked.

"Not at all." She removed his hand off of her arm, twirled around, and headed for the kitchen.

A short while later Keedy stood over the stove making eggs over easy, cheese grits, smoked sausages and buttermilk biscuits. The mouthwatering aromas brought Mayhem out of the back and he posted up against the counter with a gift wrapped object in his hand.

Keedy pretended not to notice his presence until his voice commanded her attention. "Damn, that smells good, shawdy. What you hooking up?" he asked licking his full lips.

She called off the menu without so much as glancing in his direction.

Mayhem felt the frost coming off of her reply. There was nothing slow about him except his love-making so he figured correctly that A'nyah had put some fuckery in the game. He wanted to dispel it without getting into any he said/she said foolishness so he tried to make Keedy smile. "I got a present for you, baby girl. You wanna open it when you're done."

"My hands are full."

"Duh, I said when you're done," he teased.

Keedy didn't respond and she still hadn't made eye contact. Mayhem let that bounce right off of his chest. "A'ight, I'll just have to open it for you."

Mayhem untied the little bow that was wrapped around the gift then he carefully removed the gift paper and held up a replica of the lamp of hers that he had broken. He had browsed dozens of stores to find it. "What you know 'bout dat?" he smiled.

"Thank you, sir." She barely glanced his way.

"Whoa nah," he replied using a New Orleans expression that he had picked up from Tank. "We not gon' do it like this." He sat the lamp on the counter top and stepped towards her.

Keedy's hand shot up like a bright red stop sign. "Don't Mayhem," she warned. Her voice was low and as coarse as a Brillo pad.

Mayhem stopped and looked at her for a long time while Keedy went back to preparing breakfast as if he was simply part of the furniture. She turned the fire off under the eggs and began setting the table. "Are you eating?" she asked as she set the table.

"If you don't mind."

Keedy cut her eyes at him. "Don't do me that," she warned.

They sat down at the kitchen table and ate in silence. The mood hovering over them made the food taste bland on both of their tongues. Keedy chewed mechanically while Mayhem forked his grits from side to side on the plate, staring at her.

She glanced down at a whole sausage and the image that formed in her mind was one of Mayhem's dick going in and out of A'nyah. Keedy covered her mouth with her hand as her food threatened to come up.

"You a'ight, shawdy?" Mayhem put a hand on her wrist.

Keedy slowly lowered her eyes and the fire coming out of them singed his fingers.

That was it! Mayhem had had enough. He let the fork fall from his hand and clatter onto the plate. Then he reached across the table and lifted Keedy's gaze with a finger under her chin, forcing eye contact. "Shawdy, I'm not no beat around the bush type nigga. Nah mean?" he said. "Let's set this shit out on the table and talk about it."

“There’s nothing to talk about.” She removed his hand off of her, pushed back from the table, and stood up carrying her plate to the sink.

She expected Mayhem to get up and follow her and *demand* that they talk. When he didn’t it reconfirmed that he was a dog just like Tank and the rest.

Keedy was so angry she dropped the whole plate in the trash can. “Ugh!” she exclaimed in frustration. She bent down to pick up a biscuit that had fallen on the floor and her hand brushed up against a smoked sausage. She jerked her hand back as if it was actually Mayhem’s dirty dick and when she cleaned up she left the sausage right in the middle of the goddamn floor.

After drying her hands with paper towels and tossing them in the trash can, Keedy headed out of the kitchen. She wanted to get away from Mayhem quickly before she cracked him over the head with a skillet.

Mayhem hadn’t spoken a word in the past ten minutes. He waited until Keedy came by the table then he stood up and blocked her path. “You not going nowhere until we talk, shawdy,” he took charge.

“Move Mayhem,” she said.

“Nah, I’m not moving lil’ mama. I’m ten toes down. You gon’ have to hear me out unless you plan on going *through* me to get past.” He was rooted in his spot looking down at her from under those thick eyebrows.

Keedy folded her arms across her chest and breathed through her nose. *This man can’t be serious! Like we have something to talk about.* She tapped her foot on the floor indicating that whatever he was about to say would go in one ear and out of the other.

Mayhem wasn’t deterred though, he cut straight to the chase. “I know A’nyah been in your ear, but let me tell you how that shit really went down ‘cause I know she put some gas on it.”

"You don't owe me an explanation about what you do," she interrupted. "If you and A'nyah want to fuck until the cows come home. I. Don't. Fuckin'. Care." She looked at him through cold eyes and added, "As long as y'all wash my sheets."

Her words wounded him because he could see in her eyes that she was hurt. He put his hands on her shoulders and tried to hold her stare but Keedy turned her head to hide the tears that had begun to well up in her eyes.

"Baby—" The affectionate name slipped out before Mayhem realized but it felt right so he continued without recanting it. "I want you to care."

"Well, I don't. And quit touching me." She knocked his hands off of her.

Mayhem tilted his head to the side. "Is it really like that?" he asked.

"Yea," she replied without hesitation. And when he implored her with his eyes to take the knife out of his chest, the new, tougher, Keedy drove it deeper. "I'm Tank's woman anyway," she forced out. "I feel that you and I have gotten a little too close lately and it's time for me to fall back."

Her words slammed into Mayhem's chest with the force of an iron fist. His G had always been one thousand and he had thought that no one besides his daughter could fuck with his heart, but Keedy had just proved him wrong. He didn't know why he felt so strongly for her but he damn sure did. Her declaration was an affront to his feelings but he tucked that shit like a boss and refused to let it show.

Mayhem swallowed his spit and flashed her a resilient smile. "I feel you baby girl and I can respect that. I'll fall back too." He turned and began clearing his dishes off the table.

Keedy tried to go to her room but her legs wouldn't move. Damn, it was difficult to play hard. Out of the corner of her eye she caught a glimpse of the lamp on the counter. What other man would've been so thoughtful? she asked herself.

None.

She was still glued to her spot when Mayhem finished placing the dishes in the washer. When he walked past her on his way out of the kitchen she reached out to grab his waist but he stepped lively and her hands came back empty.

A sharp pain jolted through her heart and her legs felt weak. She placed her palms against the wall to steady her balance as the proof of her escalating love for that thuggish ass nigga slid down her face.

A few minutes later, Keedy found herself in the living room sitting on the sofa with her head down in her hands. Why did I do that? she questioned her sanity. Professing a commitment to Tank that she didn't feel just so Mayhem would be hurt like she was hurting wasn't right.

Keedy wished she didn't give a fuck how Mayhem might be feeling, but she did care. More than she could bring herself to tell him. *But he can't care about me if he fucked her.*

In a way Keedy felt relieved. Now she would never have to divulge her shameful secrets to him. But that didn't truly stop the pain because deeper than that lied a burgeoning love that urged her to give that man a chance to explain. The turmoil going on in her mind caused her head to pound and she reached up to massage her temples.

Mayhem came out freshly dressed in jeans, crisp G Nikes, and an Atlanta Falcons' t-shirt. A Falcons' fitted cap was turned backwards on his head and a new pair of black shades trimmed in platinum hid his eyes. A black duffel bag was thrown over his shoulder. He said nothing to Keedy as he walked past her and left out of the door.

Keedy unconsciously rose up off of the sofa and went to the window. She watched him get into his whip and drive off. She didn't know if he would ever return and that felt like her whole world had come to an abrupt end. The tough facade that she had effected when he was there melted away and the tears that slid down her face and into her mouth tasted just like the defeat that she had known all of her life.

Chapter 22

Mayhem drove aimlessly around the city for hours until he ended up in a suite at the W Hotel downtown off of Canal Street on Poydras, alone with an ounce of loud, two boxes of Swishers, a couple of po boys and some crawfish pasta.

Once his eyes were slanted and the munchies kicked in he put a serious hurting on the food. Then he blazed another Swisher filled with that goodness and laid across the bed with his hands behind his head. Keedy was heavy on his mind. Mayhem couldn't believe she had spat that hot shit to him.

There was no doubt in his mind that shawdy was in her feelings because of whatever A'nyah had told her about that night. He was certain that she hadn't told it like it happened but that still didn't lessen the sting of Keedy's words to him. *I'm Tank's woman anyway. I feel that you and I have gotten a little too close lately and it's time for me to fall back.*

"I heard that hot shit," Mayhem muttered. Keeping it trill with a female never seemed to pay off. Sometimes he wished that he could dog them out like the average muthafucka did, but what he had watched his mother go through just wouldn't allow him to mistreat a woman.

But I'ma have to get rid of my cape because they take that shit for a weakness, he lectured himself. Dream had been the same way. When they first met Mayhem had to smash a nigga that refused to let her go. He had done it more to free her from ol' boy's handcuffs than to win her heart but they had ended up together. Mayhem treated her like he had wanted a man to treat his mother but Dream never really appreciated it.

He hated to put Keedy in the same category with ungrateful chicks like his baby mama but today had opened his eyes to the uncensored truth. No matter what he might have wished Keedy still belonged to his mans. So, yea, he was going to fall the fuck back too.

Mayhem got so high he started tripping. The face of each and every man that he had ever murked came floating across the ceiling in such visual clarity that he grabbed his ratchet off the nightstand, gripped it with both hands, and aimed it at the ghosts. If one of those muthafuckas descended down from the ceiling an inch, he was emptying his clip.

Mayhem blinked his eyes a couple of times and the faces of those that he had slayed were gone, replaced by an image of his mother when she had died in his arms. He squeezed his eyes tightly and kept them closed until the vision vanished from his thoughts and sleep set in on his weary mind.

When he awoke and looked out of the window nightfall had cast its shadow over the city. He sparked a fat one then hopped in and out of the shower, changed into a fresh 'fit and went somewhere that would surely ease his mind.

The strip club She She's on Chef Menteur Hwy was off the meat rack. Big Money niggas was popping bottles and strippers were popping pussy. The music thumped and phat asses and perfect siliconed titties twerked and bounced to the beat.

Mayhem was playing a table in the corner of VIP, being entertained by Seduction, a thick black-bone with a pussy and ass so fat her thong looked like colored dental floss on all of that body. From behind his dark shades Mayhem watched her bend over, grab her ankles, and give him a look into paradise. In the background *Round of Applause* by Waka Flocka Flame drummed loud and clear.

Mayhem grabbed his bottle of Patron around the neck, lifted it to his mouth and took a few swigs as Seduction made one luscious chocolate booty cheek jiggle at a time. He took the bottle from his mouth and said, "Do that shit, shawdy."

Seduction dropped it to the floor then brought it back up and wiggled that glorious ass in his face. She made her oiled booty cheeks clap together a few times then she raised up, slowly turned around, and straddled Mayhem's lap.

Mayhem's grown man stood up stiff and strong. "Ooooh," moaned Seduction when she felt all of that steel pressing up against her thigh. She leaned forward and blew softly into his ear as she began grinding on his lap.

She dry humped on the wood until Mayhem felt like he was about to bust a nut in his pants but he was way too smooth to go out like that. He took a deep breath and summoned his gangsta to the forefront. He didn't have to call far because that G Mack shit flowed through his veins in abundance. "Turn around. Let me see your best asset," he directed.

Seduction lifted her leg all the way up over his head giving him a clear shot at the pinkness inside of her plump phatty as she spun around on his lap and began gyrating with her back to him. Her ass was a nigga's dream and she knew how to make the muthafucka act up. Her cheeks clapped together like a pair of hands. She reached back and pulled them apart showing him what a stack or two would get him. But Mayhem was nobody's trick and those bands that she was twerking for had cost him his soul so she would have to do way more than pop pussy to get her hands on his trap. He did, however, reward her with a couple of Franklins when the erotic performance ended with the record.

"Thanks, sweetie," she said. "Would you like a private dance elsewhere?" asked Seduction as she stood up and made her pussy breathe in and out.

He knew what she was soliciting and for a fraction of a second he started to take her up on her offer, but deep inside Mayhem wasn't the type of nigga that enjoyed casual sex. He was way too passionate in bed to share it with just any broad. "Nah, I'm good," he declined. "Thanks for the dance, lil' mama."

"Okay, boo, with your sexy ass," she remarked before moving on to an awaiting customer.

Mayhem smiled, readjusted his shades and leaned back with the chair against the wall just watching and thinking. While a smorgasbord of ass sashayed back and forth across his line of vision Mayhem's mind was on Keedy. He wondered if she was thinking about him at all and if maybe she regretted any of what she had said.

Fall the fuck back he reminded himself once again. Keedy had a nigga going through some thangs. An anger as thick as phlegm rose up in his throat and Mayhem dismissed everything from his mental periphery except what came naturally.

All around him dudes were flossing hard, popping bottles and bands, and rocking jewels that had cost a ghetto fortune. Mayhem watched them with an intensity that made him the prolific predator that he was. He was rolling dolo so he dismissed the cats that were crewed up, knowing that one gun against that many was a fool's move.

He sipped bubbly and tuned his radar in on a short squatty dude who sat a few tables away. The chubby nigga had dope-boy written all over him. Three girls was dancing for him at once and he had a stack of loot on the table in front of him. After several songs his trap money had been seriously depleted. Mayhem watched the dude pick up the remainder and count it as the ladies moved on to the next trick. That was enough for him to conclude that ol' boy wasn't a boss. A nigga that was paid didn't count their bands because it could never run out anyway.

Mayhem snorted. He started to go over to the fronting ass chump and pop two in his head for wasting his time, but he remembered that he had left his strap in his whip. Keedy flashed across his mind again as he scoured VIP for a worthy victim. The anger that she had caused him was going to cost a nigga his muthafuckin' life tonight.

His visage remained blank as his eyes locked in on a duo of potential marks that were caking with two strippers to his immediate left. Both of those niggas were rocking mad platinum and as he studied them inconspicuously, their swags screamed *official to the bone*.

Mayhem slid down in his seat and zoomed in on them like an infrared beam. Ideally, he would've preferred to stalk a single victim but since his gunplay was twice as potent as the next man's he didn't feel that he was at a disadvantage. He watched as they drank bottles of Patron like that shit was tap water.

Later, he waved a cute little redbone over to his table and broke bread with her to give him a couple of lap dances. But she was just a prop; Mayhem's full attention was on his targets. He watched as one of them got up and followed a stripper out of VIP, probably going to get more than a table dance. That was good because a nigga that had just busted a nut and was full of Patron should be nice and relaxed.

"You're not paying me any attention," noticed Lil' Red as she came up from twerking it hard, straddling Mayhem's lap.

"Maybe not but I'm *paying* you so hush and continue doing what you do," he checked her.

Unfettered, she reached for his shades. "Boo, let me take these off so—"

"Leave my shit alone," he growled, already morphing into the beast that would soon be all up in those niggas' chests.

Roughly admonished, Lil' Red dropped her hand and stepped to her business without enthusiasm. When the song came to an end Mayhem tipped her properly and the smile returned to her cute, dimpled face.

Shawdy loved herself a hard ass nigga and she sensed that Mayhem was granite. As she got up from his lap and tucked the money in her garter belt she looked down at him and ran her tongue around her lips. "This is what I want to do to you," she propositioned over the music.

"Some other time," he replied, rising up and heading for the door without glancing back.

Play time had come to a screeching halt, in the blink of an eye Mayhem was back on that 187 shit. Watching a nigga's blood run out on the pavement and driving off with their cheddar would be the perfect anecdote for his morose mood.

Chapter 23

Mayhem sat parked across the street from the strip club patiently waiting for his quarry to emerge from inside. A few other tempting marks crossed his vision as he watched the exit with a keen eye but his mind was resolute.

Like a lion stalking wildebeest he sat low and quietly, primed to pounce on his prey and eat heartily. On his lap was his toolie with a dick jammed in it, cocked and locked, and ready to go *Boc! Boc! Boc!*

Dmx's *I Can Feel It* played from the whip's stereo at a low decibel as Mayhem rocked back and forth and fingered his fo-fifth. Time became irrelevant because there was no way that his targets would spend the night up in that bitch; sooner or later they would come out and take that final ride to meet their Maker.

No more than forty-five minutes elapsed before Mayhem spotted the partners surface from inside the club. He slid further down in his seat and peered at them over the top of the steering wheel. They went to the parking lot and climbed into a black 2014 Escalade RWD Platinum. Mayhem knew that those trucks started out at eighty bands coming off the lot so those niggas had to be getting to some real cake.

He let them drive past him then he pulled off at a slow rate of speed so that he wouldn't draw their attention. It was almost two o'clock in the morning so traffic was sparse. Mayhem followed from an unnoticeable distance, waiting on a prime opportunity to strike.

His predatory instincts kicked in when the truck turned onto a dark side street. The neighborhood looked nice but he had no reservations about turning it into a crime scene. When he saw the SUV park at the curb in front of a ranch style home he hit his lights and parked about five houses down.

Lowering his shades to the bridge of his nose, he saw the driver hop out and casually walk up on the porch. A few seconds later a door came open and the dude went inside.

Now it was one on one—him against the dude waiting in the car— and the nigga didn't stand a muthafuckin' chance as far as he was concerned.

As Mayhem exited his whip he quickly glanced to the sky, summoning his mother to watch over him. He walked briskly up the street with his banger down at his side. When he reached the Escalade he wasted no movement or time and he gave no warning. He stopped at the front passenger door, raised his arm, and let that hammer bang.

Blocka! Blocka! Blocka! Blocka!

The rapid fire gunshots clapped like thunder; the window imploded in a spray of glass and the boy's skull and brains splattered all over the front seat.

Mayhem ran around to the other side of the truck and ducked down. A few seconds later the door to the house swung open and the dead boy's partner stepped out on the porch with a ratchet in his hand. The echo of the gunshots had him on full alert but from where he stood everything looked still.

"Lil' Rip! Lil' Rip!" he called out his round's name.

When he didn't get a reply he trotted down the stairs and towards the truck with his head on a swivel and a firm grip on his tool. As he approached the passenger door even in the darkness he could make out that the window was missing. "What the fuck," he exclaimed as he stepped closer.

Sticking his head inside the shattered window he saw his man slumped over. In a panic he snatched the door open and dropped his banger as he leaned in and half lifted his dawg into his arms. "Bruh! What the fuck happened, bruh?" he cried to a corpse.

Mayhem sprung up with fatal intentions. From outside the passenger door he aimed his fo-fifth through the window and turned the block red hot.

Blocka! Blocka! Blocka! Blocka! Blocka! Blocka!

The second boy's whole face got annihilated as four of the six shots hit him square in the mug. His head snapped back like a dangling tree limb caught in a gusting wind and his body slid halfway out of the vehicle.

Mayhem looked up and thought he saw a figure in the doorway of the house. He aimed his gun in that direction and made it whistle. Bullets whizzed past the shadow's head. A feminine scream followed and the woman scrambled inside.

Mayhem moved with the quickness! He rifled those nigga's pockets and snatched their jewelry. A quick search of the truck netted him a Crown Royal bag filled with loot. Now it was time to vanish before those boys in blue showed up and forced him to turn all the way up.

Smiling at his own audaciousness, Mayhem trotted back to his car and got in the wind.

Back at the hotel Mayhem dumped the loot out on the bed. He had two platinum chains with icy pieces, a Rolex, a couple of diamond rings and a total of thirty racks. For that two people had lost their lives.

After showering and blowing a fat blunt Mayhem sat on the bed looking over his ill-gotten gains. For the first time since he grabbed that steel and started laying fools down he felt remorse. He hadn't really robbed and killed for the money this time, he had done it because he was seething inside and the kill always soothed his anger. Not this time though.

A double homicide and he still didn't feel any better. He had to get a grip on himself because he was doing some very reckless shit. A nigga on the run couldn't survive unless he stayed low-key, jacking muthafuckas with no mask was wild as hell.

What Mayhem really wanted to do was go pop A'nyah's shit starting ass in the head with the rest of the bullets in his clip. He quickly rebuffed that idea. *It ain't even that serious,* he told himself to quiet the beast within before it demanded to roar.

If Keedy was a real chick, she would've asked his version before flipping out. Mayhem ran a hand down his face and sighed heavily; he was really on one. Shit, Keedy wasn't even his shawdy. *So why am I concerned about what the fuck she think?* he asked himself.

Mayhem knew the answer to his own question no matter how hard her tried to deny it. He twisted up some more of that gas and smoked until he was so high he no longer felt the pain of missing her.

Keedy felt like she had lost her best friend. Three days had passed since Mayhem left and she hadn't eaten a bite. She had barely gotten out of bed to wash her butt or brush her teeth. It was pitiful how she was pining over a man that she had only known a short time, add to that they had never been intimate with one another and he was her man's road dawg.

Logic told her that they could never be together anyway so get over it, but her heart was notorious for ignoring reason. She would've given anything to be able to take back the words that she had hurled at him out of pain.

Sitting on the sofa sewing a weave cap, Keedy kept watching the door hoping that by the force of her will Mayhem would return today. But as the hours crept by excruciatingly slow she began to lose hope. Her phone rang jarring her out of a deep thought. She looked down at the number praying it would be him and when she realized that it wasn't she answered, "Hello," in the driest of tones.

"What's good, bitch? I need you to do my hair, I got this lil' dip I'm tryna get with this weekend and you know I gots to be on point from head to toe," said Lenika, full of energy as usual.

Her excitement made Keedy feel worse. "Nik Nik, I'm really not in the mood to do hair," she said, rubbing her temple to relieve some stress.

"Umm, well you need to get in the damn mood because my shit is jacked up. C'mon, girl, I need you—you know I got you."

"It's not about the money," Keedy explained as she leaned forward and took a drink from her bottled water that was sitting on a coaster on the table.

"Please," Lenika whined. "You better not be over there crying in your pillow over Tank's bogus ass. That nigga ain't worth two pennies rubbed together."

"No, this is not about Tank." She screwed the top back on the bottle and sat it back down on the table as she waited for her girl to pry.

True to her noisy nature, Lenika replied, "Well spill the tea, ho. Because the only time you're ever feeling down is when some nigga is throwing you shade."

"Really, Nik Nik?" she said, shaking her head. "Is that what you think of me?"

"Hell, yea," laughed Lenika. "And why are you being so extra? I swear your ass be doing the most. Stop being dramatic and tell me what's wrong, boo."

"No, because you'll just laugh at me and I'm so not in the mood." Keedy was just talking, she was dying to share her feelings with someone. She would've preferred to talk about Mayhem with Kim instead of Lenika because Lenika's lips could get loose.

"I swear I won't laugh," pledged Lenika. She had a feeling that she already knew who this was about. She just wanted to hear her girl confess.

"Okay," agreed Keedy. She folded her legs up under her and sighed. Then she unburdened her heart.

When she was done Lenika screamed and bounced up and down in her seat. "I knew it! I knew it! Girl go 'head and tell the truth, you hit that didn't you?" She was laughing like crazy. "Yea, you got that dick."

"I did not!"

"Yes, you did! How was it? C'mon, bitch. I want details. But first I wanna know how big it is. That nigga look like he's packing something that will come straight out a bitch's back." She went on and on, making up her own details along the way.

"Nik Nik, will you stop!" Keedy interrupted her. "I have not slept with Mayhem. I just miss his friendship. He's the only man that has ever sat and talked to me and really listened."

"Bitch, miss me with the b.s. okay? Your ass is not tripping over some damn conversation or some dick you ain't never had. You probably got some while you were in the hospital. And that's why Mayhem threw you a welcome home party 'cause you sucked that dick real good. Yea, you did that shit, ho!" Lenika burst out laughing again.

Keedy couldn't help but join in, her girl was silly as hell, and no matter how strongly she denied fucking Mayhem, Lenika still didn't believe her. They laughed and talked for a good hour.

"So are you going to do my hair or what, bitch?" asked Lenika after the hilarity died down.

"Yea," Keedy responded. "Now get off my phone."

"Bye, ho."

"Bye." Keedy hung up the phone shaking her head. No matter how bad things got Lenika had a way of brightening her mood.

Feeling a little better, but still missing Mayhem's company, Keedy got up off the couch and went to shower and fix her hair. When she was done she pulled on a pair of shorts and a halter then went to fix herself something to eat.

As Keedy came down the hall, headed to the kitchen, she was diverted by a knock on the door. With no idea who it could be she went to answer it with a lump in her chest, praying that it was Mayhem. She pranced up to the door, stood on her tippy toes, and placed her eye to the peephole.

When she saw his thuggishly handsome face, she let out an excited scream. In the next instant, she covered her mouth in embarrassment. After taking a deep breath to calm her racing heart, Keedy unlocked the door and opened it to let Mayhem in.

They stood looking at each other with a hunger that neither one of them could no longer deny. *Take me into your arms and kiss me nigga*, Keedy urged with her eyes.

When Mayhem's mouth opened, she thought it was to cover hers and thrust his tongue inside. She closed her eyes and waited nervously to taste it. But there was no lip locking in the cards, instead the words that came out of his mouth shattered her fragile heart into a thousand tiny pieces.

"I came to get the rest of my things," he said.

Chapter 24

Keedy felt dizzy as she watched Mayhem head to the back of the apartment to retrieve the remainder of his clothes and whatever else he had there. She barely had the strength to close the door but managed to summon it from somewhere.

Her eyes were already red-rimmed from crying so they burned at the first appearance of tears. Every nigga that had come into her life had made her cry but this was so much different than the others. She knew that it was foolish because Mayhem was not hers, but a girl's heart paid absolutely no attention to logic. Hell, she didn't even miss the muthafucka that laid claims on her.

She tried desperately to fight the impulse to run back to the bedroom and plead with him not to leave because begging had never made the others stay. It had only delayed their exit and left her feeling like a goddamn fool in the end. But in her heart of hearts she knew that Mayhem was different. Underneath that thuggish demeanor was a loving man. She couldn't be wrong about that, she told herself as she recalled how he had set at her bedside and fed her with such tenderness.

Fight for that man's friendship shouted her whole inner being. It didn't take much convincing because as sad as it was to admit to herself, he was the only sunshine in her dark world. Keedy took a few deep breaths then commanded her legs to obey her heart. When she got to Mayhem's room he was just sitting his safe down at the foot of the bed. She looked down at her hands and saw that they were trembling. If he rejected her she would die on the spot.

Mayhem looked up and saw her staring at him from the doorway but he didn't comment on her presence. Keedy's hope eroded when he continued on as if she wasn't even there. She had to be the dumbest bitch in the world for thinking that a nigga like him would give two fucks about a duck like her.

She tried to force herself to just turn around and go in her room and let him pack and leave before she embarrassed herself, but it was like her feet were glued to the floor. She stood there unable to move or speak, wringing her hands with her eyes casted downward.

Mayhem finished gathering his things. When he was done he turned to her and saw a sadness on her face that mirrored what he felt inside. Part of him wanted to unpack, sit down and pour his heart out to her and make her give him a chance to explain what had really happened with A'nyah. But what did it really matter? he asked himself.

They could never be. Even if Tank wasn't in the picture he was on the run and eventually the long arms of the law would find him. When that fateful day came he was going out with his gun blazing and with no regrets. Matters of the heart was the last thing he needed on his mind when those boys came for him and he went out screaming fuck the world.

Both of them had every reason to just keep their mouths shut and let theirs be a story of two people that passed through each other's lives like a blip in the sky. But the unspoken energy between them would not allow their tongues to be still.

Mayhem sat down on the edge of the bed and ran his hand down his face. He looked up from his seated position and asked, "You wanna talk, shawdy?"

Keedy's head moved up and down.

"Why you still standing over there then? Come in and have a seat," said Mayhem.

"I don't want to bother you," she squeaked.

"It's no bother. This is your house anyway and I wanna talk to you before I bounce."

Keedy moved forward with steps so timid it made him want to take her in his arms and tell her that it was okay to step with confidence.

Mayhem reached out and guided her to a spot on the bed right beside him. "You okay?" he asked softly.

"Yes," she replied with her hands folded on her lap.

He looked over at her and took her hands in his. "Loosen up, baby girl, we're good."

Keedy lifted her head and replied, "Are you sure?"

"Yea, shawdy," he assured her. "Ain't no reason for us not to be. You did good by me, allowing me to lay my head here for a minute. For that you'll always be my slick partna."

It wasn't exactly what she wanted to hear but it elicited a little smile.

Mayhem put her hand to his mouth and kissed her knuckles. Keedy's heart fluttered. "Can I tell you what really happened between me and your girl—the truth?" he asked.

"You don't have to, Mayhem. I was wrong for getting upset."

"Were you?" He lifted her chin up and their eyes locked into each other's. Keedy's emotions were going crazy, he had such a powerful effect over her she had to cut her eyes away from him to keep from throwing her arms around his neck and telling him it didn't even matter.

"Yes, I was wrong," she forced herself to say.

Mayhem chuckled because he could feel what she felt. "Whatever, big head," he teased.

"Yours is not all that little," she dared.

Mayhem laughed hard at her comeback and Keedy let out a little giggle herself. With that the mood quickly lightened. They joked back and forth for a minute then Mayhem steered the conversation back to what had transpired with him and A'nyah.

Keedy listened to his explanation and although it would've sounded like a bold-faced lie coming from any other man, she could tell that he was being honest.

When Mayhem was done explaining he didn't ask if she believed him because the truth didn't require pounding into anyone's head. He just said, "If A'nyah told you anything different, it's a lie."

"I believe you, Mayhem," she said.

"Good. Because there's only one woman living here that I desire and that's you. I know it can't be but I wanted you to know it," he emphasized with a deeper bass in his voice than normally.

Keedy felt special for the first time in her life. She smiled but quickly covered it with her hand.

"Fa real, shawdy? You gon' really act like Celie on a nigga?" he joked as he gently removed her hand from over her mouth.

"Oooh, I owe you for that one," she feigned and slapped his arm.

"Ah, shawdy." Mayhem grabbed his bicep and fell back on the bed, faking serious injury. Before long he had Keedy laughing from the depths of her soul.

"You are so dramatic," she said, shaking her head at his clowning.

Mayhem sat up and fished his phone out of his pocket. He turned it in his hand and aimed it at Keedy's face.

Click. He took her picture before she could object.

"Mayhem!" she cried. "Why did you do that?"

"I'll show you why in a minute," he answered. He downloaded the photo to his gallery then enlarged it and held it up for her to see. "Who is that beautiful girl with that million dollar smile?" he asked.

Keedy blushed and covered her face with both hands. Mayhem stood up then held his hands out to her. "Hey, you," he said.

Keedy peeked over her fingers than placed both hands in his. He pulled her to her feet and led her over to the mirror. Standing behind her, he tenderly moved a strand of hair out of her face so that they could see her full reflection. The swelling was completely gone from her face and her eyes were radiant. "Now tell me why you would ever hide all of that beauty and sexiness?" he asked.

Keedy naturally dropped her head but Mayhem put two long fingers under her chin and slowly lifted her gaze. He nuzzled his nose in her hair and whispered, "Keedy, you're beautiful. Don't you see what I see?"

"No," she answered honestly. "I'm not beautiful, Mayhem. You don't have to lie to make me feel good."

"What?" Mayhem turned her around so that she was facing him. He looked deeply into her sad eyes and spoke to her soul. "Why do you put yourself down, baby girl? I'm not lying to you, you're more beautiful than words can express. And when you smile you melt a nigga's heart. Straight like that."

Unaccustomed to receiving compliments Keedy dropped her head. "No, shawdy," he said softly but with firmness. "Hold your lead up, beautiful, and look me in the eyes."

"I can't," she mumbled shyly.

He leaned in and placed an assuring kiss on her forehead. "Yes you can. C'mon, let me see those gorgeous brown eyes."

Keedy's head came up slowly. Her nervousness caused her eyelashes to bat but Mayhem didn't mind, it made her look even prettier. He had never seen such an attractive girl with such low self-esteem. Normally a chick with her looks thought that they were all of that.

Mayhem turned her back around so that she was looking at her reflection in the mirror again. He pointed out the sexiness of her mouth, the cuteness of the one dimple in her right cheek, the mystery that danced in her light brown eyes and the smoothness of skin.

"But I'm ugly inside," she said.

That rocked Mayhem. He turned her back around and wrapped his arms around her, pulling her into his chest. "Don't say that about yourself, Keedy," he said with a tenderness that belied his gangsta. "And don't ever allow nare muthafucka put that in your head," he went on.

"There are things you don't know," she said regretfully. "Things in my past—"

She left the rest dangling in the air but Mayhem jumped right in. "Things that don't matter," he finished the sentence for her. He didn't care about what was in her past, she was beautiful inside and out as she stood before him now so the rest was irrelevant. "Keedy, not one person that ever walked this earth is perfect. Your past is your past. Don't let it define you," he encouraged.

Those were the words she had always hoped to hear a man say to her. She wrapped her arms around him, laid her head against his chest, and enjoyed the feel of his body pressed against hers. Her heart beat a love song and her center moistened. "Mayhem," she called his name with a hunger that had gone unfulfilled her entire life.

"Yes, beautiful," he answered as he stroked the side of her face.

"Please don't go. I like having you here."

Before he could reply they heard voices coming down the hallway. Keedy's eyes shot open and she stepped away from Mayhem a split second before A'nyah peeked her head in the room.

"What y'all doing?" She looked at them with suspicion. Kim peered over her shoulder smiling from ear to ear. She winked an eye at Keedy and grabbed A'nyah by the arm, trying to pull her blocking ass out of the room but that wasn't happening.

A'nyah snatched away and planted herself firmly between Mayhem and Keedy. "I know y'all ain't doing Tank like that," she accused.

Mayhem wasn't sweating that shit but Keedy went into a panic stricken denial. The mere mention of Tank's name sent fear racing through her heart. "We were just talking, that's all. So don't go making it more than what it was."

"Un huh. I bet," said A'nyah disbelievingly. She trained her eyes on Mayhem and opened her mouth to question him but he made her check that shit at the gate.

"Shawdy, you better sit your ass down somewhere," he said before she could utter a single word. He didn't hit women but he knew how to put a bird ass bitch in her place.

A'nyah shot him the evil eye and turned and walked out of the room.

Kim let A'nyah walk past her then she pointed at her back and mouthed, "Hater in the house."

Mayhem and Keedy both smiled.

"Y'all look cute together," she added in a whisper before going to join A'nyah in the living room.

Mayhem closed the door then turned and took Keedy's hands in his. "Shawdy, I'm not even gonna front," he said, looking into her eyes. "I want you in a way that I've never wanted any other woman in my life but there's a right way to do things. Do you understand what I'm saying?"

"Yes, Mayhem." She looked up at him with love and admiration in her eyes.

Mayhem let one of her hands slip from his grasp. He put two of his finger to his lips, kissed them, and then he softly pressed them against her luscious lips. Keedy unconsciously ran her tongue across his fingers. She longed to taste him.

Mayhem wanted her too but he didn't want to do it in a way that compromised her self-respect or his principles. He lifted her hand to his mouth and kissed the back of it. "Gon' out there with your girls, shawdy, before A'nyah run tell some shit that ain't even happen. I don't want things to get crazy around here. I'ma unpack and holla at you later, a'ight?"

"Okay," Keedy agreed with a smile so wide it almost slid off the side of her face.

As she opened the door and left out of the room her heart beat with a happiness that she wasn't quite sure she deserved.

Chapter 25

Mayhem unpacked his things then went out on the balcony and put some weed smoke up in the air. His mind went back and forth on what would be the respectful way to step to Tank and tell him that he was really feeling Keedy. He considered various approaches but most went against his get-down; he wasn't a "tiptoe" type nigga so any anything less than looking a man in his eyes and keeping it real wasn't an option.

The one thing he refused to do was creep with another nigga's shawdy, especially his dawg's. He also needed to know that when Keedy and Tank were face to face she would still be able to stand there and make the same choice.

Mayhem knew without a doubt that Tank's initial reaction would be wild but he was going to do everything in his power not to let that shit escalate into beef. Because at the end of the day he hadn't tried to do him dirty. A nigga couldn't choose who he fell in love with, that shit was predestined.

Over the next few days, Mayhem and Keedy spent every waking moment together. They hit the malls and shopped with no regard to price tags. When Keedy objected to the lavish spending, Mayhem silenced her with a peck on the lips. "Chill, shawdy, I got this. We only live once and when it's our time to go we can't take none of it with us," he told her. He wanted her to know what it was like to have a man who would give her anything she wanted because that is what she truly deserved.

That night Keedy fell asleep looking at all of the outfits that Mayhem had bought her. The gifts were nice but what had truly touched her heart was his patience in going into a dozen or more stores with her and allowing her to take her time selecting exactly what she wanted. When she tried on different things he showed sincere interest in how well they looked on her; when she had trouble deciding between one pair of shoes or another Mayhem purchased both. Tender moments like that had Keedy floating on a cloud.

While she closed her eyes and dreamed peacefully, Mayhem was still up in his room thinking of other special things he could do to put a smile on her face. He used his cell phone to go online and plan a romantic rendezvous for them the next day.

The next morning Keedy cooked Mayhem breakfast and moved around the apartment with newly found pep. A'nyah noticed her exuberance and knew exactly why she was so upbeat. Jealousy shot from her eyes although she tried her best to hide it. Through clenched teeth she bid them goodbye and headed off to work.

"She's going to start trouble," Keedy feared.

Mayhem looked up from his plate. "Don't worry about her. I can handle any trouble that comes our way," he said confidently.

Comforted by his assurances, Keedy pushed all feelings of trepidation out of her mind. Later, she left to do a sew in for a client that lived across the canal. While away she and Mayhem texted back and forth like high school sweethearts that couldn't stand being apart. The hours crept by at a snail's pace then finally Keedy was back home.

Mayhem met her at the door with a smile and a long hug then he rushed her to get ready for the evening he had planned for them.

"Where are we going, baby?" she asked, feeling exited.

"You'll see" is all he would divulge as he nudged her toward her room to shower and change into a fresh outfit

Dressed in a beautiful D&G floral brocade sun dress and wedge sandals, Keedy looked marvelous as she stepped out for the evening on Mayhem's arm. Forever thuggin', Mayhem rocked jeans, a T-shirt, and some fresh J's.

As he held the car door open for her he commented on how lovely she smelled. "Aww thank you, bay-bae," she beamed. "You're so sweet."

Mayhem flashed her that thuggish smile before carefully closing her door. He dapped around to the other side of the car and climbed behind the wheel and made the roof disappear.

Keedy tuned the radio to Q93 and Jay Z's *On The Run* became the background music as Mayhem programmed the GPS on his cell phone to direct him to the French Quarters. Driving off he looked over at Keedy affectionately. She was dancing in her seat, singing along with the song.

Who wants that perfect love story anyway, anyway?
Cliché, cliché, cliché, cliché
Who wants that hero love that saves the day, anyway?
Cliché, cliché, cliché, cliché
What about the bad guy goes good, yeah?
And the missing love that's misunderstood, yeah?
Black hour glass, our glass
Toast to clichés in a dark past
Toast to clichés in a dark past

The cool evening breeze blew through Keedy's hair as she slid on her big movie star shades and continued to bounce her shoulder up and down. She was really feeling herself and she owed it all to Mayhem.

She reached over and rubbed his arm. "Thank you," she said above the music. There was no need to explain, Mayhem understood perfectly. He placed his hand on top of hers, allowing his touch to stand as his reply.

They shared light conversation until they reached Jackson Square on the bank of the Mississippi River. With undeterred determination Mayhem found a place to park in the busy tourist area. Holding hands, he and Keedy walked up and down around the square enjoying the sight of the different performers up and down the street.

They stopped and watched three black boys perform a badass tap dance routine that left Mayhem shaking his head in amazement. He tipped them generously and led Keedy further up the square. Passing what he thought was a statue painted black and gold, Mayhem reached out to touch the hat on its head.

"Noooo," Keedy cried out in laughter and pulled his arm down. "You can't be touching him."

"Why not? It ain't nothin' but a statue," he replied as they stood staring.

"You're so crazy. That's not a statue, it's a mime," she said, laughing harder.

"A what?" he looked from her to the mime and back.

"A pantomime, baby?"

"Fuck is that?" Mayhem cocked his head to the side.

It tickled Keedy that he didn't know what a mime was. Just when she was about to explain the mime began moving and gesturing. Mayhem jumped and his hand went to his waist. "What the fuck?" he gritted

"No, Mayhem don't." Keedy held onto his arm with both hands until he let it fall to his side. She was cracking up but Mayhem was eyeing the mime like he wanted to do something to that muthafucka.

The mime silently acted out an apology and went to his knees to beg Mayhem's acceptance. The pleading faces he made were mad funny. Before long Mayhem was laughing as hard add Keedy.

"Yo, this shit is wild, shawdy," he said.

"He's good ain't he, baby?" She clung on to Mayhem's arm with her body pressed to his side.

"Yea, he's fi' but he almost got wet the fuck up." Mayhem went in his pocket and dropped a Franklin in the mime's collector. His generosity made Keedy love him all that much more.

The mime gestured a sincere "thank you" and Mayhem nodded his head. The money was nothin' it came easily and that's how he spent it.

They moved from the mime to an artist that sketched a beautiful portrait of Keedy and after that they took a romantic horse and carriage ride around the French Quarters enjoying the historic sights. Mayhem had no idea what he was looking at but Keedy was smiling and that's what mattered most to him.

After the carriage ride they enjoyed beignets and coffee at the world-famous Café Du Monde. The food was delicious and their conversation was even better. Mayhem put all his cards out on the table. He told her about Dream and Brandi and the situation that forced him to leave.

"I don't care about any of that, Mayhem. I just want to be with you," she professed.

He reached across the table and stroked her face. "You sure, shawdy? Because one day they're gonna come for me and I refuse to ever go back to jail. Straight up! I'ma make them carry me away in a bag. If you ain't built for that then let's just leave this as a friendship because my story ain't gonna end pretty."

"Pretty is for some other bitch," she stated, staring him in the eye. "I've had it ugly all of my life. I've been talked about, dogged out by family, friends—and let's not even talk about men. You saw how Tank did me."

Mayhem nodded his head sympathetically and Keedy continued. "I don't care if you're on the run, I'll go wherever you go. I don't care if it's to Alaska just give a bitch a sled and an igloo and I'm there. And when it's your time to go, I'll gladly die by your side because I was already dying inside before you came into my life."

"Hush, shawdy, before you witness a thug cry," he said with a sexy little smirk on his face.

"I'm serious, bay-bae. I know we haven't known each other very long but I love you, Mayhem. I wouldn't have a reason to live if you're gone."

"Damn, you got a G all choked up in this bitch." He let go of her hands, grabbed a napkin and dabbed at his eyes demonstratively.

Keedy reached across the table and playfully smacked his hand. "Stop. You play too much." The laughter in her voice matched the smile on her face. Mayhem leaned across the table and tasted her lips.

He sat back in his chair and looked at her lovingly. He didn't know how much time they would have together before his troubles caught up with him and he chucked his middle finger up in the air and went out in a blaze of gun smoke. Whether it was a minute or a day, a month or some years, he was gonna make their time together a true love story, he promised. "But first I gotta step to Tank like a man and let him know the deal because I'm not with no cruddy shit," he explained.

Keedy respected that although she feared the outcome. She also feared that what she was holding inside would end their story before they turned the next page but she had to reveal it to him and let him decide if he still wanted her. That was the right thing to do. "Mayhem, before we go any further I have something to tell you," she said cautiously.

He picked up his glass of water, took a sip, and sat it back down on the table. "What's up, baby girl?" he asked, looking up at her.

Keedy took a deep breath in a futile effort to slow her heart beat. Her palms sweated and her throat became dry as she tried to formulate the words in her head before letting them fall from her tongue. This was the moment of truth and his reaction to what she was about to disclose would either make her or break her. "Um—uh—um."

Mayhem reached across the table and held her hand. "Just say it, shawdy. Nothin' will change what I feel for you," he promised.

Keedy tried to force the words out of her mouth but her tongue wouldn't cooperate. She dropped her head in shame and stared into her empty bowl. Mayhem didn't have a clue as to what had her so troubled. He stroked the back of her hand and tried to reassure her that whatever it was, he would love her nevertheless. "Just spit it out, beautiful. It's okay," he soothed.

"I'm ashamed." Her voice was so low he could hardly hear her.

Mayhem stood up, carried his chair around to her side of the table and sat down beside her. He wrapped her in his arms and held her.

The power of his embrace gave Keedy the courage to open up all the way to him. "Mayhem, I've been with a lot of men," she said as her voice began to crack with emotion. "More than I care to admit." Tears welled up in her eyes and trickled down her face.

"Shawdy, I don't care nothin' about your past. I already told you that," he said.

"It's more than that, Mayhem."

"Baby just tell me what it is and we'll deal with it. I'ma be your nigga no matter what."

"That's what you say now but you're not going to want me after I tell you this." Now the tears were flowing like water.

Mayhem leaned down and tried to kiss Keedy's tears away but there were a flood of them. He held her tighter, oblivious to the stares of the other patrons around them. "Shawdy, my love is a rock," he whispered to her. "No matter what, it's gonna remain unchanged. I'm not those other niggas. I'll weather any storm with you. Just trust me."

Keedy had nothing to lose at this point so she decided to sit her heaviest burden on his lap and see if his love was as solid as he proclaimed. She wiped her tears with her hand and asked him for a glass of water.

Mayhem held his glass to her mouth while she took a few small sips to wet her throat.

"I'm okay now. Thank you," she said as she sat up straight, ready to face the gate of her heart. Mayhem straightened up too as he patiently waited for her to speak.

Once she had gathered herself Keedy blurted it right out before she lost the courage to do so. "I have herpes. Now you can tell me that you don't want my trifling ass. I promise I won't be mad."

This time Keedy didn't lower her gaze. She looked him right in the eyes and waited for him to crush her heart. She was so used to that. What she wasn't used to was the response that she got from him.

"C'mere shawdy," he said as he reached out and pulled her back into his arms. "Did you really think that was gon' change anything? You're right here." He tapped his heart with his fist. "And that's where you gon' stay *Til My Casket Drops*."

"But—"

"But nothin'." He silenced her with a kiss. "I know all about herpes. My baby mama has it. We're good. We can deal with that."

"Do you have it too?" she asked.

"Nah, but I have you and that's all that matters."

"Yes it is," she replied as the tears began to pour from her eyes again.

Mayhem gave her a little tongue this time. Keedy wrapped her arms around his neck and tried to make the kiss last forever. When their lips came unglued she was out of breath and in heaven.

They concluded the evening with dinner at Copeland's Cheesecake Bistro on St. Charles Ave. Keedy couldn't remember ever having a better time. But if life had taught her one thing it was that happiness was not meant to last.

When they arrived back at the apartment her worst fear came to roost.

Tank was parked outside, leaned against the hood of his truck with his gun down at his side.

"Oh, shit!" Keedy gasped.

All hell was about to break loose.

Chapter 26

Mayhem pulled in next to Tank's whip, threw his Corvette in park, killed the engine and the headlights. He looked over at Keedy, she had her arms wrapped around her shoulders and she was trembling so bad her teeth rattled. He put a hand on her knee and spoke protectively. "Stay in the car. Let me get out and talk to this nigga."

"Mayhem, I don't want anyone to get hurt over me." Her voice shook with fright.

"It's gon' be a'ight, shawdy," he said calmly.

"No it's not, Tank is crazy. Please Mayhem can we just pull off," she begged of him.

"You know I can't do that, baby girl." He didn't wanna get into no gunplay with his mans but his G was too official to run from it.

Mayhem unfolded his body from out of the whip and closed the door. He walked around the front of the car and stepped to his boy in a non-confrontational tone. "Sup, shawdy? When you get back?" he asked.

"I got back when I did," shot Tank with his face balled up.

Mayhem licked his lips and chuckled. His eyes traveled from Tank's knitted brow down to his hand and back up to his face. "Sup, bruh? Why you mean muggin' with ya toolie out?"

"Why you riding around lamping with my bitch?" spat Tank.

"Oh, so that's how you gon' step to me?" Mayhem questioned.

"Fuck you mean, nigga? I let you lay your head at my bitch house and you fuckin' this ho behind my back? That's some foul ass shit." Tank's jaw twitched as jealousy coursed through his blood hot and explosive.

"Bruh, I don't even get down like that. Who told you that shit? That ratchet ass bitch A'nyah? She just a hater, fam."

"Whatever, my nigga," Tank scoffed. "This ain't even about you. I'm about to show this lil' bitch who the fuck she belongs to."

"You trippin', dawg. The shit ain't that serious. Me and shawdy just went to The Square, walked around and grabbed something to eat. But you don't care nothin' about her no way so why you wanna take it there?"

Tank wasn't trying to hear none of that. A'nyah had already blown things all out of proportion. "It's serious to me. I own that ho," he spat. "Punk ass bitch must think I'm something to play with!" He stepped up to the passenger door and banged on the window so hard with his gun that it cracked.

Keedy cowered down on the floor with her hands over her head. Tank pressed his face to the window. "You gon' get out or make me snatch you up out this bitch?" he threatened.

Mayhem was prepared to kill or die to protect Keedy. He whipped out and stepped right up to the back of Tank's neck. "Leave her alone, man. Shawdy ain't did nothin'. If you just gotta squabble, bring that shit to me."

Tank's head snapped around but he didn't do nothin' stupid because he felt that steel pressed against his head and he knew that Mayhem's gun didn't bluff. "Nigga, you're *my* round. I put in work for you and you gonna let this nothin' ass, dick sucking ho come between our friendship?" he challenged, but Mayhem's love for Keedy was rock solid.

"Bruh, just let your gun fall to the ground then we can talk like men," Mayhem said calmly.

Tank's chest heaved in and out as he tried to decide how he could reverse the tables on Mayhem and leave him and that bitch face down.

Killahs understood the minds of other killahs so Mayhem could read Tank's thoughts as if they were his own. He gripped his banger with both hands and widened his stance. "Don't make me do it, shawdy," he pleaded. "Fa real, bruh. I don't wanna take it there. I'm not tryna chump you but you're not in your right mind right now. Just drop your strap and we can talk 'bout this."

Tank hesitated then he reluctantly let his toolie clatter to the ground. Mayhem kicked it underneath the car then checked Tank's waist for a backup. Satisfied that he was disarmed he removed his gun from the back of Tank's head.

A neighbor pulled up, parked a couple of spaces down from where they stood, and climbed out of his Durango. He glanced in their direction but continued on inside his apartment without comment.

Tank turned around breathing fire. He stared at Mayhem with contempt thick enough to strangle him. "You're going out like a straight sucka over a bitch that has fucked every nigga from here to Biloxi, Mississippi," he exaggerated.

Ignoring the insult, Mayhem said, "Bruh I just want you to know that Keedy and I haven't slept together but we are feeling each other. Shawdy don't mean nothin' to you but she's a diamond to me so just let her go."

"Let her tell me she wanna be with you, ya heard me," said Tank.

"I can do that," agreed Mayhem, nodding his head up and down as he stepped around him and peered inside the car.

When he saw Keedy balled up on the floor visions of his mother flashed in his mind and the rage that bubbled in his veins was hotter than an inferno. It took every ounce of restraint he could muster to keep from spinning around and blowing Tank's whole muthafuckin' head off.

Mayhem tapped on the window and called Keedy's name. Hearing his voice she uncovered her head and peeked up.

"Get out of the car shawdy and tell this man what time it is. It's okay I'm right here."

Standing to the side of Mayhem, Tank was bristling. As soon as that lil' bitch got out of the car he was gonna knock her on her ass. If she thought a nigga could keep him off of her ass she had life fucked up.

"Keedy, open the door and get out. It's all good, shawdy," Mayhem repeated as softly as if he was speaking to an abused child.

Keedy was shaking all over as she pulled herself up off of the floor of the car. A wet spot stained her pants from when Tank had cracked the window. She had been so frightened she peed on herself.

She looked out of the window and saw Tank glaring inside the car at her. Even with Mayhem close by Keedy was scared to death. She had to reach deep down inside of herself to a place that she hadn't known existed to find the courage to get out of the car. When she got out her knees were shaking so bad she had to lean against Mayhem to keep from falling down.

Tank instantly snapped. "Bitch bring your muthafuckin' ass over here," he raged. His mouth was crooked and his eyes were flaming red. At the terrifying sound of his angry command Keedy ducked behind Mayhem. "I'm giving you two seconds to c'mere then I'm coming to get you. I don't give a fuck if Jesus is protecting you," Tank threatened.

Keedy was afraid to move and afraid not to. She thought for sure he was about to shoot her dead and she would've been right had Tank still been strapped.

Tank's anger rose to the top of his head when Keedy didn't come to him. He clenched his fist and tried to step around Mayhem to get to her. Mayhem's hand came up gripping that thang. "Don't get ya dome exploded," he warned.

Tank froze in his spot and scowled at him. "Pussy got you turning against ya peoples, huh?"

"My *peoples* don't beat on women," Mayhem drew the line. He reached back and took ahold of Keedy's arm, pulling her in front of him so that she could face Tank's coward ass once and for all. "Shawdy, tell this man that you no longer wanna fuck with him," he prompted.

Keedy uttered it softly. Tank misread her fear for indecisiveness. Pouncing on that, he switched tactics. "Baby, we been to hell and back together but I still love you. I lose my temper sometimes but I'ma do better, ya heard me. Gon' tell this muthafucka who you belong to so he can stay the fuck outta our business before I act the fuck up."

Keedy took a deep breath while Tank looked at Mayhem and stuck his chest out. But it quickly deflated when she made her decision. "I don't want to be with you anymore, Tank. I'm in love with Mayhem. Please let me go."

Tank's smirk melted off of his ugly face. "What the fuck did you just say," he barked, trying to intimidate her.

"Look him in the eye and say it loud, shawdy, so he don't get it confused," Mayhem cut in. "Trust me, he don't want no trouble 'cause I live for that twenty-fo' muthafuckin' seven."

Keedy wrapped her arms around Mayhem's waist. Feeling protected, she looked up at Tank without fear in her eyes. "I don't want you anymore. Mayhem is my man now. Please leave me alone," she said loud and clear.

Tank's mouth curled up. He balled his fist up and drew his hand back ready to black her muthafuckin' eye.

Mayhem quickly raised his gun and aimed it at the center of Tank's forehead. "Nigga, I wish the fuck you would," he snarled.

Tank let his arm fall down to his side and he unclenched his fist, but the look he gave them said that it was not over. Had he been just a random nigga, Mayhem would have stretched him out on the pavement right then and there, fuck letting him walk away and come back for revenge. But they had been partners; he was hoping that Tank would let the shit go once he cooled off.

Mayhem wasn't a fool though, he understood that the friendship was dead. He didn't give a fuck because he despised niggas that beat on women anyway. "Fam, I know how you get down," he said with his ratchet still pointed at Tank's thinker. "I'm warning you not to come for me. Just let it go and move on or I'ma be your worst nightmare. Test this shit if you want to," he cautioned.

Tank gave him a cold stare then turned and hopped in his truck. As he drove off with his wheels spinning Mayhem had a feeling in his gut that the next time they crossed paths only one of them would live to tell about it.

He waited until Tank's tail lights faded away then he looked down at Keedy and said, "Let's go pack all of your stuff. I don't want you here if he comes back."

"Okay, but first I'm about to go in here and get a piece of this bitch's ass. I might be afraid of a man but I'll mop the floor with a cute bitch like A'nyah."

Mayhem couldn't help but smile as he followed her up the walk. He had to walk fast to keep up with her because Keedy was itching to beat a bitch down.

Chapter 27

Mayhem and Keedy unloaded the last of their things out of both cars and carried them up to the suite that they had rented at Loews Hotel in the Garden District. As soon as they sat the bags down Keedy unpacked some toiletries and night clothes and rushed to the shower to freshen up.

When she came out of the bathroom in panties and a short sleeping shirt trying to display her little hips, Mayhem was stretched out across the bed calling zzz's. She sat down next to him and moistened her skin with Amber Romance. The seductive fragrance of her body cream quickly brought Mayhem out of his sleep.

He sat up and kissed the back of her neck. "I didn't know a woman could fight so well and smell so good," he kidded.

Keedy giggled, he had been teasing her ever since they left the apartment. "I told you cute bitches can't fight but I give her credit for trying," she said.

Mayhem laughed. "It did her no good to try, you tore her ass up. You were beating her so bad I wanted to pull you off of her."

"Humph. I wish you would have!" She turned and gave him the side eye. "That ass kicking was long overdue. All of that shit she be talking and her ass can't fight a lick."

Mayhem smiled at her newfound spunk. He got up off of the bed and raised her arm above her head. "And the winner by knockout and still," he elongated the last word, "lightweight champion of the world—Keedy the Two Fisted Pretty Assassin."

Keedy bounced up off the bed and fired a couple of quick punches at an imaginary target. Mayhem was loving that shit. He threw his hand up in surrender as if to say he wanted no parts of her. It felt good to see her come out of her shell.

She stepped closer to him bobbing and weaving on her tiptoes. Mayhem pulled her in his arms and kissed her passionately.

"What is that for?" she asked when he broke their tongue lock.

"That's called a *just because* kiss," he said. "Now let me go get up under this water so we can go to bed." He let go of her and headed to the shower.

"Mayhem," Keedy called out. He stopped and turned around to see what she wanted. "Don't just stand under the water," she said, "You gotta wash."

He smiled. "Oh you got jokes."

Keedy stuck her tongue out at him. "I love you though," she sang.

"Love you, too, shawdy." And even though everything between them had happened so fast he knew that their love for each other was destined to be one of a kind.

While Mayhem showered, Keedy unpacked the rest of her cosmetics and a couple changes of clothes for both of them. She stacked her perfumes neatly on the dresser then sat down on the bed, reached over to the lamp on the nightstand and dimmed the light.

A short while later, Mayhem came out of the bathroom with a towel wrapped around his waist and beads of water on his sculpted chest and shoulders. Keedy handed him a pair of boxers that she had already laid out for him.

"Thanks." He leaned down and kissed her lips.

"You're welcome, my king," she said sweetly.

"I like that sound of that," he replied as he let the towel fall to the floor and stepped into his underwear.

Keedy's eyes were as huge as quarters. *Damn. He's going to tear my stuff up.*

"What you staring at?" Mayhem teased.

"Nothing," she giggled and lifted her eyes from his dick.

"I hear you but I don't believe you." He reached down and pulled her up into a hug, allowing her to get a feel of what had her eyes bulging. His hands slid down her back and cupped her ass.

Keedy felt short of breath. Their mouths joined together naturally and she sucked on his tongue. The heat thermometer in her panties shot through the roof.

Mayhem released her just when it was getting good. She gave him the side eye again and said, "If you keep that up I'm going to start thinking you're scared of me."

"Never that, baby girl." He took her hand and brought it down below his waist. Placing it firmly on his long, thick shaft, he said, "You're the one who better be scared."

Keedy sucked in her breath because now that she'd had a feel of that thing she was afraid that he would rip her coochie in two. "You ain't right," she laughed to disguise her nervousness.

"Don't get scared now," he said, peeping her game.

She didn't offer a comeback because he had pulled her card. "I'ma have a drink. You want something?" he asked.

"Yes, I will have whatever you're having," she replied as she reached for the remote and turned on the television.

Mayhem went to the bar on the other side of the suite and perused the selections. Settling on a Brandy, he grabbed two glasses. He threw in some ice and poured the Grand Marnier over it. When he returned with their drinks Keedy had gotten out of bed and was sitting on the sofa with her feet up on the table.

"One fifty," he said.

"What does that mean?" she asked with a wrinkled brow.

"Half the rent of the room, you all kicked back like you're at home up in here."

"You always talking junk." She gave him a little push as he sat down next to her placing the glasses on the table.

"You know I'm just playing, baby girl."

They toasted to being together then tasted their drinks. "You missed your calling," she complimented. "You would've made a pretty good bartender."

"Only for you." Mayhem sat his drink down and looked into her eyes.

Keedy followed her king's lead, placing her drink down beside his. He leaned over taking her face into his hands then he took what he wanted.

Keedy melted to his touch enjoying the taste of his sweet lips. Out of nowhere her fear of loving and then being hurt crept up and stole some of the pleasure from his touch. She pulled back slowly looking at him with a low gaze.

"What's wrong?" he asked.

"Nothing," she stated shyly, shaking her head from side to side.

"Are you afraid to let me love you?"

"I'm not afraid to let you love me. I am afraid of what will happen after I let you love me." She turned away from him staring down at the carpet.

Mayhem reached out and placed his finger under her chin, turning her back in his direction.

Keedy looked in his eyes and tears formed in hers. She had been down this road many times and each time it ended in disaster. She knew he was not like the other men she had dealt with, however, she would always find out a man's true intentions the hard way. And as if he was reading her mind he spoke what her heart felt.

"I'm not going to hurt you, baby. You don't have to be afraid of me." Mayhem attempted to put her worries to rest.

"I'm not afraid of you. I'm afraid of being broken any more than I already am." She blinked and warm tears slid down her cheeks.

Mayhem could feel her pain. He knew that a woman like her needed actions because promises had always been broken.

"I know what to do with your heart. But I'm not going to tell you, I'ma show you." He leaned in and kissed her lips.

Keedy let out a soft moan as his tongue slid across hers. Slowly he pushed her back on the couch continuing to taste her sweet lips.

"Let me have you, baby." His baritone caressed her eardrum while his hand slid up her shirt gently caressing her breast.

Keedy's body began to heat up as he positioned himself between her legs. She quickly placed her hand on his as he ran his hand down her quivering body.

"Baby, wait," she whispered.

"I can't," he said, lowering his head and placing his warm mouth over her breast.

Keedy slightly arched her back as the tip of his tongue tickled her nipple. Surges of electricity moved through her body and stronger moans left her lips as his mouth and hands moved as if her body was screaming out instructions.

"Are you okay to do this?" he whispered.

She knew what he was asking. "I believe so," she said. She was currently receiving treatment and she hadn't had an outbreak in a long time but she could never be one hundred percent sure. "Let me protect you, baby," she whispered. "Just in case."

Mayhem shook his head no. It was his vow of unconditional love. Whatever she was going through he would gladly share her burdens.

"Please, Mayhem," she insisted but he covered her mouth with his and silenced her protest.

Mayhem slid his hands down into her panties. Her wetness coated his fingertip as he moved it between her lips. He brought his finger to her clit and circled it slowly, staring down into her eyes and enjoying the pleasure written all over her face.

Keedy watched the strength in his eyes as he played knowingly with her clit bringing her to the point of no return. When she felt his dick stiffen against her leg she knew there was no turning back. The combination of love and fear took over her emotions as she felt her pussy began to contract. Keedy reached up and grabbed the back of his neck with one hand and his wrist with the other.

"Move your hand baby and come for me." His firm deep tone left no room for any protest.

"Ahhh." she moaned as she twitched beneath him.

"Sss. That's it baby come for me." He circled faster, causing her legs to tremble.

Keedy had never come with a man in any way but she wanted desperately to give him what he wanted. She closed her eyes and tried to let go of the mental blocks that denied her that pleasure.

Mayhem's fingers was skilled and determined. It circled her clit with the same results as if she was doing it with her own hand. Keedy inhaled sharply when she felt a little bolt of lightning shoot to the tip of her pearl.

"Come for me, baby," he whispered. "Wet my hand with your juices."

The combination of his voice and his persistent touch caused her to cry out as she felt an orgasm begin to brew.

Mayhem continued caressing her clit as he slid two fingers on his other hand inside of her slippery lips and found that spot that took her flying over the edge. "Oh, god," Keedy screamed out in ecstasy as her juices exploded and coated his fingers.

Mayhem waited until her legs stopped shaking then he rose to his knees and slid her panties all the way off. He dropped them on the floor and reached inside of his boxers. As he pulled his dick from its enclosure he stared down at Keedy with anticipation of how good it was about to feel pushing in and out of her tight wet pussy.

Keedy's eyes slightly widened as he stroked his thickness in his hand. Leaning in he placed soft kisses up her stomach then nibbled gently on her nipples.

Keedy felt the warmth of her juices welcome the tip of his dick as he placed it to her opening. She closed her eyes and gripped his back with the tips of her fingers as he bit into her neck and pushed in slowly.

"Baby," she cried out as he gave her short strokes breaking down her tightness.

"Yes," he answered, pushing deep and stroking long.

"Not too deep, baby." She pulled back each time his dick hit the bottom.

"Don't run, shawdy. Throw that pussy back at me," he said on heavy breath, pulling back a little as his pipe bounced from wall to wall.

Keedy held on rotating her hips and gripping firmly around his thickness with every muscle. Mayhem placed his mouth on hers and kissed her profoundly, then he stroked even deeper.

Keedy's head spun; she felt like she was floating. There was no turning back from here. She vowed to allow him to heal her soul. And with every slippery stroke he was fixing all of her broken parts. Her mind raced with emotion as her pussy released sticky passion all over is dick. Keedy gripped her legs on his waist and the flood of emotion rose to her tongue and escaped her lips.

"I love you, Mayhem," she panted in his ear.

"I love too," he confessed, picking up speed ready to release the pressure rising within.

Keedy clawed his back and cried out for him to flood her with his powerful, hot essence. Mayhem pushed in deeper and let his seed explore her womb.

Keedy brought her lips to his and for the first time she savored more than a kiss, she tasted love.

Chapter 28

In the weeks that followed, their love was like a whirlwind. Everyday Mayhem found a new way to make Keedy's heart flutter. He spoiled her with daily gifts and never-ending affection.

Keedy was floating on a cloud. She looked around the suite at the vases filled with roses and the dozens of shopping bags from their latest excursion to the mall. As she walked around the room straightening up, a card that Mayhem had given her earlier caught her eye.

She walked over to the table where it sat, picked the card up and began re-reading the words again. Her eyes teared up as she read the postscript that Mayhem had added.

Baby, thank you for making every moment we're together the best times of a nigga's life. Because of you if this world comes to an end tomorrow I will go with a smile on my face.

I love you, shawdy.

Keedy held the card to her chest as a tear slid slowly down her face. He was everything that she had ever hoped and prayed for.

"What you doing, shawdy?" asked Mayhem, walking up behind her with his a blunt hanging out of the corner of his mouth.

Keedy sat the card back down on the table and tried to wipe her tears before turning around, but another tear streaked down her face just as she turned and looked up into her man's eyes.

Mayhem took the blunt out of his mouth and stared at his woman with a questioning look. "What's wrong, baby?" he asked.

She wrapped her arms around his waist and laid her head against his chest. "Nothing. I was just thinking about how much I love you," she said in a whisper.

"I love you too, baby girl. Now stop crying, you know your tears break a nigga's heart. Fuck around and have me boo-hooing right along with you," he kidded.

"Be quiet, Mayhem," she giggled. "You're so silly. They're happy tears."

"Happy tears?" He looked down at her feigning confusion. "That's an oxychloride, ain't it?"

Keedy looked up at him and burst out laughing. "You mean *oxymoron.* I know you used the wrong word purposely, Mayhem." She was sure of that because underneath his thuggism he was quite intelligent. "You play too much," she said, smiling at him.

"An oxymoron? Fuck is that?" He scrunched his face up. "You mean like a big ass dumb muthafucka?" He spread his arms out questioningly. "Ox? Moron?" he clowned.

Keedy was cracking up. Mayhem continued his charade until she had tears running down her face. He put the blunt out in an ashtray on the table and pulled her into his arms. "Now that's that shit I like," he said. "Damn, you're pretty as fuck when you smile."

"Humph." She drew back and looked up at him with her lip curled dramatically. "Are you trying to say I'm not pretty all of the time, sir?" she joshed.

Now it was Mayhem who was laughing. Keedy tickled his sides. "Stop, shawdy," he cried as he grabbed at her wrist and tried to squirm away.

"Let me find out your gangsta ass is ticklish," Keedy smiled devilishly. She held her fingers up like weapons and stepped toward him.

Mayhem slowly backed away from her until he ran out of room and fell back on the bed. "I got that ass now," she exulted.

She pounced on him, straddling his waist. "A'ight, shawdy, you got that." He raised his arms above his head in surrender.

"Nigga, please. Don't do me," she laughed. "Ain't no mercy."

Mayhem welcomed the tigress that his love had brought out of Keedy and he absolutely loved when she talked shit. Keedy began tickling him until he was laughing and squirming like a bitch.

Mayhem cried out for her to stop. "Please, shawdy," he begged. "I'll take you to the mall and let you buy that bitch out," he bartered.

"Nope." She shook her head and continued tickling him. "You already did that."

"A'ight, what you want?" he laughed. "I'll give you whatever."

Keedy stopped, put her finger in the corner of her mouth, and looked down at him impishly. "Did you say whatever, sir?"

"Yea. Whatever you want. Just name it, lil' mama, and you got it," he promised.

Keedy lowered her eyes and began moving her finger in and out of her mouth very erotically. "Hmm. I wanna taste it?" she said. Her voice was husky with naughtiness.

"Taste what?" Mayhem replied, fucking with her.

Keedy reached down and grabbed that dick. "Nigga, you know what I mean. Don't make me take this shit."

"You ain't gotta take nothin', it's already yours.

"Let me get my shit then," she said as she slid down his body and unbuckled his pants. Now it was her turn to fuck with him. In a wet, sloppy way.

She freed his dick then looked at it hungrily. It was already swelling in her hand and she hadn't even spat on the Mic yet.

Keedy stroked it up and down enjoying the elongated effect that her touch inspired. She put it against her skin and rubbed it all over her face then she licked the head, savoring the taste of his pre-cum. "Umm," she moaned.

Mayhem licked his lips too. She looked sexy as fuck working her tongue. “Do that shit, shawdy,” he rasped.

“I’ma do it, baby. And I’ma do it hella good,” she said as she took him deeper into the warmth of her mouth and slurped on his dick noisily.

Mayhem’s whole foot curled up. He grabbed a handful of her hair and bit down on his lip. Keedy slid his pipe out of her mouth and looked up at him. “If you pull my tracks out I’m going to beat you,” she joked.

Mayhem let out a little laugh, she was funny as hell but right now he wanted to touch her tonsils. He guided her head back down to his throbbing muscle.

Keedy took him back inside of her mouth and began bobbing her head up and down, stroking him with both hands as she fucked his dick with her throat.

She looked up to see Mayhem’s eyes closed. *Hell no. I’m not having that.* “Open your eyes, bay-bae, and watch your girl act a fool on this sweet dick,” she muttered.

Mayhem opened his eyes just in time to see her dribble spit all over his hard meat and lick it right back off. “You like the way I suck this muthafucka?” she asked as she wet it up again.

“Hell yea.”

Keedy lowered her gaze and released the freak in her. “Talk nasty to me then. Make me know that you like it, nigga.” She slapped his wood across her face then covered it with her mouth and slowly took him inside inch by glorious inch.

“Sss.” Mayhem moaned. “Suck your nigga’s dick, shawdy. Get that shit in. Make me burst down your throat.”

Mayhem’s words turned Keedy the fuck on. Her pussy started moaning and her tonsils begged to be coated with his seed. She re-gripped the dick and put her head game down something serious. “Nut in my mouth,” she mumbled around a mouth full of pipe.

Mayhem’s hips came up off the bed in rhythm with the up and down movements of Keedy’s head. He gripped the back of her head and fed her all nine thick inches. She worked her throat muscles with no restraint.

Mayhem was moaning but he wasn't nutting. Keedy spat his dick out and looked at him with a purpose. She rose up, pulled her shirt over her head, and slung it on the floor. "Nigga, you must think I'm playing with you. You're about to give me that nut."

This time when she stepped to her business she could not be denied. She sucked Mayhem to the back of her throat and held him there until he rewarded her with what she wanted.

Mayhem sat with his back against the headboard smoking a blunt as he watched Keedy move around the room spraying air freshener. "Bae, you're going to get us put out," she said.

"Fuck that. We're lamping. A muthafucka come up here talking shit, I'ma put something hot in their chest." He hit the blunt again and blew a fresh cloud of smoke to the ceiling.

Keedy looked at him, sucked her teeth, and threw her hands on her hips. "Good head make a nigga real bold," she cracked.

"You ain't talking 'bout nothin, shawdy," he chuckled. "Come hit this shit." He held the Swisher out to her.

"I'm talking about a lot. You know I put it on you. That's why you're lying there without a worry in the world." She smiled as she went and sat down beside him.

Keedy accepted the blunt and put it to her lips. She wasn't a heavy smoker so a couple of hits had her above the clouds.

"Look at my baby," Mayhem teased, "all chinky-eyed."

"It's your fault." Keedy pushed his shoulder. "Got me sitting here high as hell with my titties out."

"Them ain't your titties, they're mine." Mayhem lifted up and cupped her breasts in his hands

"Oh, yea?" she moaned. "What else is yours?"

"I'm 'bout to show you," he said as he laid her down and finished undressing her.

"You ain't talkin' 'bout nothin'," Keedy mocked.

"We're about to see." He dropped her pants to the floor, stood up, and stepped out of his clothes.

He got back in bed and pushed her legs open with his knees. "I bet I make you scream my name," he vowed as he stroked himself to full length.

"I bet you can't," she challenged, knowing who would win.

Mayhem didn't say nothing. He was about to show her ass. He entered her slowly and slid in deep. When he touched bottom Keedy sunk her nails in his back and whimpered.

"Talk that shit now," he said as he began punishing that pussy.

A half an hour later when he mercifully lightened his stroke and filled her with his cum, the whole floor knew his name.

Chapter 29

While Keedy slept with her thumb in her mouth, thoroughly satiated. Mayhem opened his safe and did a quick estimate of his bank. The bands were dwindling. They would be alright for a while but alright wasn't good enough—until Jesus called him home he wanted to give her the best that life had to offer.

Mayhem closed the door to the safe and grabbed his black robbing gear out of the back of the closet. He carried it in the bathroom with him and booted up. After reloading his extra clip, he slid it in his waist next to his fo-fifth.

He grabbed a Nine off of the sink and carried it in the bedroom with him to awake Keedy.

Keedy woke up smiling. In her dream Mayhem had just slid five carats on her finger. She rubbed sleep from her eyes and looked up to see him standing over her, dressed in all black, and holding a gun out to her.

Alarmed, Keedy sat straight up and came fully awake. "Baby, what's going on?" she asked, praying that his trouble back in Atlanta hadn't caught up to them.

"It ain't nothin'. I'm about to hit the streets and eat off of a muthafucka. But I want you to be safe while I'm gone," he explained.

Keedy looked down at the gun as if it was a serpent. Mayhem saw the fear in her eyes. He sat down next to her on the bed and put a comforting hand on her knee.

"Shawdy, don't freeze up on me," he said gently. "I showed you how to use it the other day. I don't believe that nigga knows where we're resting at. But if he comes through that door while I'm gone you blast his ass right back out of that muthafucka. You hear me?"

She nodded her head up and down and accepted the banger from him. Mayhem watched her to see what she would do. He smiled proudly when she turned the Nine over, ejected the clip, checked its rounds, and then clacked it back in.

"Go 'head and house one in the chamber," he instructed. "When it's time to bust you don't wanna have to click-clack. You just wanna aim it and make that bitch pop off."

"Okay, baby." She did as he instructed then looked up.

"Now remember," Mayhem coached. "All head shots. Nothin' to the body 'cause he could be wearing a vest."

Keedy listened intently. She knew what to do but she wasn't sure that she could actually squeeze the trigger and take a person's life even if it was Tank's dirty ass.

When she said that to Mayhem, a frown came across his face. It was the very first time Keedy had ever seen him unhappy with her. "I'm sorry," she quickly apologized.

"You don't have to be sorry." He leaned over and kissed her softly on the lips. "If you don't think you can do it I'll just never leave you by yourself. It's all good."

His words were touching but Keedy could still see the disappointment on his face. She closed her eyes and briefly relived all of the unwarranted, merciless ass kickings Tank had given her. She shivered as she recalled the last one; it had left her hospitalized and in a pamper. Her mouth tightened at the awful memory and then her eyes opened, red and fiery. Staring straight into Mayhem's eyes, she said, "Baby, I *can* kill that muthafucka, kick back, and then get chinky-eyed."

Mayhem smiled. "Shawdy bad," he said. He tapped her chin with his fist then stood up to leave.

Keedy reached out and grabbed ahold of his pants leg. When Mayhem turned around, she sat the gun down and stood up and hugged his waist.

"Sup, shawdy?" he asked.

"Bay-bae, you don't have to rob for me. I make good money doing hair. I can take care of both of us," she said.

"Guess what, baby girl?" He stole a quick kiss before she could respond. Then he looked her in the eyes and stated,

"Real niggas don't let their woman take care of them. The man is the provider—let me *provide*."

"But—"

Mayhem put a finger to his lips gesturing her to hush. "You ain't talking 'bout nothin'," he said.

He kissed her again then left out of the door to go make a muthafucka kiss life goodbye.

Keedy sat on the couch with the Nine firmly in her grip. She was prepared to light a spark in Tank's ass if he came to that door. But her mind wasn't really on Tank. She was worried about her boo.

Mayhem had been gone for over two hours and panic was beginning to set in on her. Time moved painstakingly slow but Keedy's heart beat fast. Her man was out there all alone, stalking the streets for a lick so that he could give her things that she really didn't want or need. Money, Gucci bags, and all the designer clothes in the world wouldn't be able to repair her heart if something had happened to him.

Keedy glanced at the television. It was on mute but she had it tuned to the local news station, hoping that she wouldn't see a report that would snuff out her life. That's exactly what would happen if Mayhem was in a body bag; they might as well get hers ready too because there was no way she could go on without him.

She knew that the chance of him being in jail was zero—when he said that he would go out letting his toolie spit Keedy absolutely believed him. The only way they would get her nigga behind bars was if they imprisoned his corpse.

Keedy managed to smile through her brimming tears as she recalled the cocky look on Mayhem's face whenever he talked about how he envisioned his final day. She just hoped it wasn't tonight.

I should've gone with him and popped my tool at his side like a real bitch, she chastised herself.

Her worry turned into to anger at herself. *No thorough ass bitch would let her man rock alone.*

She jumped up off the couch and began getting suited and booted. She was hitting the streets to find her nigga and if a muthafucka had him faded, she was going to turn the block into a fireworks display.

Keedy laced up her G Nikes, pulled on a hoodie, and tucked her Nine. As she grabbed her keys and raced for the door, she heard movement right outside in the hallway.

"Fuck!" She snatched her tool out just in case it was Tank. She was the wrong bitch to try right now.

As she watched the door knob slowly being turned, Keedy gripped the Nine with both hands and widened her stance just like Mayhem had taught her. She slid her finger on the trigger and gritted her teeth. *Come on in muthafucka and watch me treat you like target practice.*

The door slowly swung inward and Mayhem stepped inside the room. He stopped and stared at Keedy. She had that thang pointed dead between his eyes.

He smiled at his sexy ass protégé. She was on muthafuckin' point! "Honey, I'm home," he sang playfully. "And look what I brought you." He held up a shoe bag full of loot.

Keedy let out a scream. She cared nothing about what was in the bag, she was just happy that he had made it back, safely and in one piece. She dropped the gun and ran and jumped in his arms, covering his face with wet kisses.

Mayhem gave Keedy the whole bag of money for herself and he would not allow her to turn it down. He hopped in the shower, soaped up, and then let the water rinse his latest victim's blood off of him.

He smiled at how easy it was to catch a muthafucka slipping. All he'd done was go to a strip club and case out a fool that was flashing his bands. Once he'd identified his mark it was just a matter of patience.

This time he had been able to follow his victim home and creep him as he went inside. The idiot had bucked on the robbery and now he was on a cold slab in the morgue. The funny thing was that Mayhem had gotten the nigga's stash anyway because his terrified woman hadn't made the mistake of testing his gun.

Because she had been very cooperative Mayhem had left some stacks behind. He had also left her duct-taped but he hadn't left her with any extra holes in her head.

"That's my good deed for today," he said aloud then chuckled at his own sarcasm.

After showering and changing into some fresh gear, Mayhem took Keedy out for a late-night breakfast at Waffle House. They sat next to each other in a booth and enjoyed the homemade waffles and a fresh brewed coffee.

That quickly became their ritual as over the next few weeks Mayhem hit the strip clubs hard at night and became a baller's worst nightmare.

Chapter 30

Keedy led Kim and Lenika on a full tour of her and Mayhem's new condo. Every room was laced. Mayhem had laid mad niggas on their asses to provide Keedy with the most exquisite furniture.

Returning downstairs to the kitchen, Kim remarked, "Girl, please tell me your secret. I need to know what you did to get Mayhem so sprung so I can do the same thing to my stingy ass man."

"That ho probably let him fuck her in the ass and licked his booty hole," Lenika broke in, clowning as usual.

"Don't do me," said Keedy. "If that shit worked your little skinny ass would've been had a man."

"Okayyyy," Kim laughed. She and Keedy slapped hands at Lenika's expense.

Lenika raised her arms over her head and twerked her itty bitty booty. "Bad girl, I never made love, I never did it. But I sure know how to fuck," she sang.

Keedy grabbed a butter knife out of the top drawer and playfully jabbed it at her. "I swear if I hear you sing that shit again I'm going to stab you straight through the heart. Every time I hear that song it reminds me of that bitch, A'nyah. That was her anthem."

"Yep," confirmed Kim as she climbed up on a stool at the island.

"Dang, that's my shit," said Lenika. She sat beside Kim and started punching the air playfully. "Keedy, tell us again how you kicked that bitch's ass. That was cray," she laughed. "Man, I wish I would've been there to see it."

"Let's go over there and jump that ho," said Kim.

"Hell yea." Lenika hopped down and started shadow boxing.

"Nik Nik, sit your skinny tail down before you break a bone," Keedy teased.

Lenika frowned her face up and huffed theatrically then climbed back up on the stool. She grabbed the banana out of the fruit bowl and gave it some head.

"Bitch, you *stoopid,*" laughed Kim.

Lenika continued acting up until Keedy and Kim were in stitches. "Nik Nik, if you don't quit clowning, I'll never get started on y'all hair," Keedy warned. "And I promise you when my baby gets home y'all ho's getting up out of here. Because I'm getting me some of that *act right* as soon as he walks through the door."

Lenika settled down and Keedy went to work. She hooked Kim up with a $400 Brazilian weave and some claw nails. Then it was Lenika's turn in the chair. She got some box braids.

Mayhem came home just as Keedy was finishing up. He handed her a dozen pink roses and gave her a deep kiss. He spoke to her company then went upstairs.

Kim and Lenika commented on how Keedy's face lit up as soon as Mayhem walked in the room. "I'm so happy for you, girl. You deserve it more than anyone," said Kim.

"I'm jelly, bitch," added Lenika.

Keedy knew that she was just playing. She hugged her girls then hurried their asses out of the door.

When she got upstairs Mayhem was just coming out of the shower with a towel wrapped around his waist. Keedy walked up to him, snatched the towel off, and jumped his bones.

Laying in Mayhem's arms that night, Keedy's world seemed perfect. The only thing missing was the acceptance of the woman that had brought her into this world.

Keedy and her mother had a tumultuous relationship. Every time she thought about it she became sad. Mayhem noticed that she had become quiet. He asked what was wrong.

"Nothing," she said.

Mayhem knew that when she said that it usually meant the opposite. He turned over on his side, facing her, and pulled her closer into his chest. "Talk to me, shawdy. Whatever is wrong you know I'll help make it right," he said.

"I miss my mother, but I know if we go to see her it's going to turn into a disaster."

She had told Mayhem all about their fractured relationship so he understood the pain and apprehension that resonated in her voice. Mayhem would've traded his soul to have his mother back so he strongly encouraged Keedy to let go of the past and patch things up with her mom.

"You only get one mother," he reflected painfully as he stroked Keedy's cheek. "Cherish her while she's around because in the blink of an eye she can be gone."

Keedy looked at him and blinked back tears. *God, I don't know what I did to deserve this man, but thank you for bringing him to me.*

She scooted as close to Mayhem as she could get and fell asleep in his strong arms.

Chapter 31

Keedy stood at her dresser putting on her jewelry and contemplating the visit that she was about to have with her mother. In the past, her thirst for her mother's approval had always left her longing because the woman refused to forgive her mistakes.

Keedy didn't feel good about this visit but she told herself that she had to try. She wanted her mother to meet Mayhem and see that she had finally found a man who truly loved her.

"You a'ight, shawdy?" Mayhem asked as he came up behind her.

"Yes. I'm fine. Just preparing for the worst and praying for the best." She looked up in the mirror and enjoyed the warmth in his eyes as their gazes locked.

"I'ma be right there with you. Just take it one step at a time," he comforted, kissing her on the shoulder.

"Thank you so much. Your support means so much to me."

Mayhem gave her a smile that tickled her stomach. "You ready to go?"

"Yes, my king." Keedy grabbed her things and they headed to the car.

The ride was comfortable and uneasy at the same time. Mayhem's optimism was uplifting but Keedy's reservations remained right below the surface. As they pulled up in front of the small two bedroom house, Keedy prayed that her mother would be happy to see her and wouldn't send her home in tears like she normally did.

Mayhem parked and hurried around the car to open Keedy's door for her.

"Thank you, baby." Her voice quivered with nervousness.

Mayhem kissed her cheek and placed her hand on his elbow. "It's gon' go fine," he assured.

They walked quickly up the several cement steps moving upward to the porch. Keedy took a deep breath and rang the bell. Each second ticked by like hours as she waited.

The door knob turned slightly before she heard her mother's unmistakable high-pitched voice. "Who is it?"

"It's me, Ma," Keedy yelled back.

When the door sprung open her mom stood with a hand on her hip and the other one firmly on the door panel. Her eyes roamed over Mayhem and Keedy.

Keedy forced a smile to calm her nerves but it only hardened her mother's cold stare.

Keedy cleared her throat. "Ma, can we come in?"

"You're here now so I guess so," she said, moving to the side leaving them little space to pass.

"Mommy, this is Mayhem. Mayhem this is my mother, Mrs. Duplessis."

Mayhem extended his hand towards her. Mrs. Duplessis put her hand out, expecting him to shake it. Mayhem surprised her when he brought it to his mouth and planted a single kiss on it.

"Oh, you found one with manners," she jabbed at Keedy's past choices of men.

Mayhem looked down at the frown trying to creep across his boo's face. "Keedy is teaching me how to be a gentlemen," he said, giving her a comforting smile.

Keedy smiled back then looked over at her mother whose unwelcoming digestion hadn't changed.

"Y'all can come have a seat," she said with a creased brow.

Keedy and Mayhem reluctantly moved to the couch and sat down. Mayhem rubbed her back then folded his hands in his lap.

"So what brings you this way?" Mary asked putting fire to the end of her cigarette then inhaled deep.

"I haven't seen you in months plus I wanted you to meet Mayhem."

"Who in the hell named their child that?" She gave him a tight eye glare.

The remark was an affront to the woman whose memory Mayhem held dearest but he respectfully replied, "It's just a nickname that I got as a little boy."

"Drugs and murder I guess."

Mayhem just smiled and held his tongue.

"That's the type she likes. Niggas who will give their life over bullshit, waste money and whip her ass." She turned to scrutinize at Keedy.

"Mommy he's not like that, He is very respectful and he loves me," Keedy spoke up in Mayhem's defense.

"Don't worry, just stick around and he'll show his true colors. Those are the only type you attract." She sat back, taking another long pull on the nicotine.

Keedy couldn't take anymore. "Why do you hate me?" she asked as she fought back the tears that were ready to flow.

"I don't hate you. I'm just never proud of you. You turn up on my doorstep with different men you claim to love and within weeks your back is beaten out and your heart is broken." She stared at Keedy and the tension between them caused the tears to flow down Keedy's face.

"Mommy I'm trying. But how can I change and you won't let me forget my mistakes?"

"A mistake is one. After that, that shit is on purpose. I'm convinced they switched babies on me when you were born because your ass is too loose to have come out of me."

Mayhem stood up; he had had enough. Out of respect that he had for all mothers he held his tongue but the fire in him would not let him hold it much longer if they didn't get the fuck out of there. He looked down at Keedy and held out his hand. "You ready to go, baby?"

Keedy stood up with a heavy heart. She looked at her mother with conflicted love in her eyes. But what came out of her mouth was what resided in her heart. "I love you, Ma, no matter what. Regardless of how you treat me I will always love you and I am here if you need me."

"I won't ever need you for anything," spat Mrs. Duplessis. She looked from Keedy to Mayhem and warned, "You better watch her around your friends. She's real free with her cookie."

"I'm good. You make sure to take care of yourself," Mayhem uttered through pursed lips.

Mrs. Duplessis sucked her teeth. "You have a good day. And, oh yea, get you some condoms. Her apple is rotten," she chuckled. "She didn't tell you?"

Keedy gasped.

Her mother looked at her unperturbed.

"You are so miserable," Keedy spat. She moved past Mayhem before she broke the promise she made to herself and knock her mother's head off.

Mayhem watched Keedy run out of the door. When it clanged behind her, he glared down at her mother. "You didn't have to embarrass her. She's not asking for nothing but your love. And for your information, she told me everything there is to know about her and my love for is unwavering."

"You're a fool then," she derided him. "Because you're in love with a whore."

Mayhem was appalled that a mother could be so malicious towards her only child. Her cold-heartedness infuriated him. He snatched his gun off his waist and put it to her head as his nostrils flared and his chest heaved up and down.

Mrs. Duplessis was so frightened her scream came out silent. Mayhem saw the same fear in her eyes that he'd seen in his mother's before she was killed. He eased his finger off of the trigger and lowered the gun to his side.

"Get on your knees tonight and thank an angel for sparing your life," he gritted. Then he turned and went outside to the car to comfort his woman.

Chapter 32

In the days following the disastrous visit with her mother, Keedy sunk into a state of depression that Mayhem couldn't seem to lift her up out of. For three days she hardly uttered a word or ate a bite. Mayhem didn't once leave the house, he was by her side 24/7 trying to brighten her spirits by reassuring her that nothing that her mother had said could weaken his love and respect for her.

"Shawdy, what I feel for you ain't painted on me, it's *inside* me and can't nothing wash it off," he reaffirmed not only with words but also by his actions.

If Keedy didn't close her eyes Mayhem didn't shut his either. When she cried in the middle of the night he was right there to hold her in his arms and wipe away her tears.

"Bae, as long as there's breath in my body you will never be alone or unloved," he whispered as he rocked her back to sleep.

Mayhem's love was powerful but Keedy's mother's rejection cut deeply and her mood remained dour. Mayhem spent hours each day trying to find a way to put a smile back on his girl's face, but nothing seemed to work or last very long. At wits end Mayhem scrolled through Keedy's phone and found Kim and Lenika's phone numbers. He figured that with their help he could get her up and smiling again.

It didn't take but one call and Keedy's besties were ringing the doorbell. As usual Lenika came through the door upbeat and full of playful energy while Kim trailed behind her with a gift wrapped box in her hand for Keedy.

"She's lying over there on the couch." Mayhem pointed across the living room.

It didn't take long before Lenika had Keedy perked up. Keedy's smile widened further when Kim handed her a surprise. She unwrapped it and found a batch of homemade pralines candies inside. She was all teeth, she grinned so hard.

"My favorite," she beamed as she stood up and joined her girls in a group hug.

Peeking over Kim's shoulder, she saw Mayhem smiling from across the room. "Thank you, baby. I love you so much," she said.

"I love you, too," Mayhem called back.

"I love you more." Keedy's words reflected in her eyes.

"O-M-G! Y'all so damn extra," Lenika intoned.

"Hater!" Keedy and Kim chimed.

Lenika made a funny face and the three of them erupted in laughter. She turned to Keedy and said, "Seriously, bitch, you need to get up and do something to your head. Over here looking like Moses with titties."

"Shut the hell up!" Keedy took a playful swing at her.

"You do look like a Haitian refugee," Kim cracked.

Lenika fell down on the couch laughing and holding her stomach. Keedy took off for the stairs as they continued to go in on her like only best friends could. When Mayhem told them to leave his girl alone, Lenika replied, "Oh, you can get it too. Standing over there with those ashy ass lips, looking like Pookie from New Jack City."

Mayhem cracked a little smile and hurried upstairs with his boo before Lenika went Comedy Central on their asses.

An hour later when they descended the stairs, Keedy was back on her A-game. She had pulled her hair up into what was called a 'Messy bun' and the light makeup that she wore accentuated her strong features.

Keedy's orange and white Juicy Couture fitted top hugged her perky titties as her white stretch pants clung to her hips while her matching Christian Louboutin wedged sandals showcased her pretty toes.

"That's my bitch!" exclaimed Lenika, happy to see that her swag was back.

"You killin' 'em, girl," added Kim. To her, Mayhem had been a godsend to Keedy. As Kim looked in his eyes she had absolutely no doubt that he adored her friend.

Mayhem complimented Keedy with his usual gear: jeans, fresh t-shirt, a pair of Jays, and a Colgate smile. His swag was nine milli.

"Look at y'all," Kim gushed. "Y'all look so cute."

"Thank you," said Keedy sincerely.

Lenika asked where they were going.

"I'm taking everybody out to eat then we're going to the casino and break those muthafuckas," announced Mayhem.

Lenika cheesed and started twisting her butt. "Whoot! Whoot!" she belted.

"No, we don't want to intrude on y'all night out," said Kim, giving Lenika an admonishing stare.

Lenika almost knocked her to the floor, covering her mouth with her hand, "Bitch, will you shut the hell up? Damn!"

Kim wrestled away from her and continued to decline the invitation, but Mayhem wouldn't accept *no* for an answer.

Kim acquiesced, Lenika rejoiced, and Keedy stepped out that night feeling both bold and beautiful on her man's arm.

After dinner at Houston's on St. Charles Ave. they went downtown to Harrah's Casino. Before getting out of the car. Mayhem slid his fo-fifth under the seat and fought off the paranoia that came with going anyplace unarmed.

Kim and Lenika had rode separately, but managed to park not too far from Mayhem. Both ladies were ready to hit the casino hard. Mayhem discretely broke them off a band apiece and wished them luck. Keedy blushed at her man's generosity.

Once inside, Lenika took off for the slot machines while Kim made a beeline for the Roulette Wheel. It was Keedy's first time visiting a casino so she deferred to Mayhem.

"C'mon, shawdy," he said, leading her by the hand. "We're going to the Black Jack table and rope these sonuva bitches."

A couple of hours later, Mayhem and Keedy had thousands of dollars' worth of hundred dollar chips stacked up in front of them. As the dealer reshuffled the cards other less fortunate players looked at them with envy.

"Shawdy, you're my good luck charm," Mayhem leaned over and placed a kiss on Keedy's lips. When he pulled back he was wearing some of her orange lipstick.

Keedy looked at him and giggled, then she picked a napkin up off of the felt covered table and wiped Mayhem's mouth.

"Bae, I have to go to the ladies room," she said in a whisper.

"A'ight. I'ma go cash in these chips. Meet me at the cashier's counter over there," he said, pointing.

"Okay." She slid off of the stool and headed to the restroom, looking over her shoulders to see if she could spot either of her girls, but there were too many bodies moving to and fro.

Stepping out, Keedy looked around trying to regain her sense of direction. She couldn't remember if the cashier's counter that she was supposed to meet Mayhem by was to her left or right. She glanced around for something familiar but saw nothing. "Oh, well," she hunched her shoulders and sighed, then took off to her right.

As Keedy weaved her way past patrons and cocktail waitresses moving about in a hurried manner, her eyes darted side to side in search of the designated spot where she hoped Mayhem would be, waiting for her.

Suddenly, she stopped dead in her tracks as her eyes came to rest on the last two people on Earth that she would've ever expected to see together.

Tank and A'nyah stood around a craps table hugged up like happy newlyweds. Keedy couldn't help but recall the many times A'nyah had called her a goddamn fool for fucking with Tank and the dozens of times Tank had blasted A'nyah, calling her a gold-digging ho. Keedy wasn't mad, though. A'nyah was more than welcome to the ass whoopings and black eyes if that's what *she* wanted. However, Keedy was good without his abusive ass because it would take a thousand Tanks to make just one Mayhem!

As Keedy tried to move past them without being noticed she turned and bumped dead into Tank's cousin, Breeze. "Whoa nah," he said as he stepped back, balancing a drink in his hand.

"Excuse me," said Keedy as she glanced up at his big-headed ass and tried to keep moving.

Breeze stepped in her path, blocking her way.

"Slow down, lil' mama," he slurred. "Damn, you're looking good. Holla at your boy since you and cuz don't kick it no mo'. We can get together and go half on a baby. Tank told me that you got that wet shit."

"Get the fuck out of my way," Keedy hissed.

"Fuck you talkin' to?" Breeze drew his free hand back ready to slap Keedy's lips crooked. As he tried to bring his palm forward he felt a powerful hand lock around his wrist and then his arm twist behind his back.

"Nigga, you must wanna take your last breath," Mayhem gritted on the side of his face. He locked his forearm around Breeze's neck and applied pressure to his windpipe, cutting off his breath.

When Mayhem released him, Breeze fell to the floor spilling his drink. The commotion caused heads to turn in their direction. Tank ran over and helped Breeze up off of the floor. A second later a little pot-bellied nigga ran up and started wolfing. It was a three on one but Mayhem wasn't fazed. He moved Keedy behind him and told them to come on with the business!

Security rushed over before the first punch could be thrown and while they were quieting Tank and his peoples down, Mayhem zeroed in the chain and medallion that hung around Breeze's neck. It was a platinum piece of the state of

Louisiana. "The Boot" was written across the bottom of the state in blue diamonds and red rubies.

As Mayhem's mouth tightened into a slash across his face, he lifted his eyes. Tank was watching him closely and when their gazes met he knew that his betrayal had been exposed.

"It is what it is, nigga," Tank smirked. "Now straighten it."

Breeze and his pregnant looking brother both recognized Mayhem's face now. Breeze held the medallion up and boasted, "I'm from that CTC, 'cross tha canal, baby boy. I get it how I live."

Mayhem eyed all three of those niggas with contempt as he contained the fury that exploded in his gut. He knew that none of them were strapped, including himself, so all they were doing was posturing. With security around them in heavy numbers wasn't nothing poppin' off but those bitch niggas' mouths.

Keedy tugged Mayhem's sleeve. "Baby, let's go," she said.

A'nyah peeked her head around Tank. "Yea, bitch, you better get somewhere before I get in your ass," she fronted.

Keedy didn't even respond, she had already proven that she could whoop that trick's ass without breaking a sweat.

As Mayhem backed away maintaining a visage cold enough to freeze lava, Tank threw his arms around his two cousins and shouted, "Welcome to the Boot." The three of them laughed like hyenas.

He who laughs last laughs longest, Mayhem told himself as he turned away from them and led his woman to search for her girls.

Chapter 33

"You know what, baby? That doesn't even surprise me," Keedy remarked after Mayhem told her everything that had happened with Peanut. "Tank ain't shit, but that's how those dudes are from that way. Those grimy ass niggas will cross out their own blood," she shook her head at Tank's betrayal.

Seated on the sofa next to her, Mayhem leaned forward and picked up his glass of Henny. He took a shot to the head, sat it back down on the table and then let out a long sigh. Keedy rubbed his arm in an attempt to calm the storm in his head.

"I killed Peanut and Julius for nothin'," Mayhem regretfully recounted. "And all this time the muthafuckas that set me up to get jacked was the one I least suspected. But God has a way of showing us the truth."

Mayhem leaned back on the couch and stared up at the ceiling. "It wasn't a coincidence that we bumped into that nigga tonight," he continued. "Had I not seen his people rockin' Peanut's chain I would've never known the truth. And I would still be hunting Julius' mans, Larron."

Keedy stared into her man's face as she listened to him reflect. The pain of Tank's deception was evident in Mayhem's voice. He sat forward and gulped down another shot of Hen Dog as the robbery replayed in his mind as clearly as if he was watching a movie. He called forth the descriptions of the jackers that he had stored in his mind.

"Breeze is the nigga that slapped me with the gun and kicked me in the face," he uttered aloud. "And that rollie pollie nigga was with them too."

"That's Breeze's brother, Bump," intoned Keedy. "They're Tank's first cousins and they're foul just like him."

Mayhem nodded his head. He tried to describe the fourth dude that was with them that night, but the description drew a blank in Keedy's mind. After a pause Mayhem said, "Well, Tank and his cousins are food enough! This time they fucked with the wrong nigga, shawdy." The hardness in his eyes underlined his statement.

"Baby, I know where Breeze and Bump live. I can show you if you want me to," offered Keedy.

"Nah, baby girl. I'm not involving you in this. This is man's business."

"Mayhem, if I'm your *ride or die* let me ride," she strongly insisted.

"No, shawdy," he rejected.

"Why not?" she questioned him with vigor.

"I got this," Mayhem replied just as vigorously.

Undeterred, Keedy got up and straddled his lap. Gently putting her arms around his neck and clasping her hands together, she stared at him. Forcing him to look into her eyes, "Mayhem, you don't get it do you?" she asked rhetorically. "If you're worried about me getting killed, let me go ahead and put some real shit out there for you to ponder." Keedy leaned closer and brushed her soft lips up against his. When she continued her voice was low but strong with sincerity. "Mayhem, I was already dead before you rescued me and gave me life, and if anything was to happen to you I would not want to live on," she declared. "So if I'm going to die, baby, let it be at your side."

Mayhem felt that shit all in his chest. He put a hand behind her head, bringing their mouths together, allowing their tongues to become one, in sync with their hearts. When he pulled back he licked his lips savoring her sweet taste as his dark eyes held hers captive. "Shawdy, that's some real shit you just said and I feel you. But you know I can't put you in harm's way. I didn't come into your—"

"Mayhem, I'm going to stop you right there, baby." Keedy cut him off. She readjusted herself on his lap and squinted her eyes at him. "Do you remember when you asked me to let you love me?" she asked.

"Yea, shawdy."

"I was afraid to because my entire life niggas had stomped all over my heart. But I decided to give my love one last time because I believed in you." Keedy pressed her finger into his chest.

Mayhem stroked her face with the side of his hand and opened his mouth to speak but Keedy silenced him.

"No, let me finish," she said softly and then went on. "Baby, I'm all in—hook, line, and sinker. Ain't no turning back or playing the sideline for me. I'm going to ride with you until the wheels fall off and if that cost me my life, so be it."

"Shawdy, you don't understand," he protested.

"I understand perfectly well," she insisted as she removed her arms from around Mayhem's neck. Still holding eye contact, she took his hand and placed it over her heart. "You feel that?"

Mayhem nodded *yes*.

"That's all yours. Without you it would stop beating. Now, you promised me that you would never deny me anything that my heart desired. Isn't that what you said?" Keedy put him on the spot.

"Yes, that's what I said," Mayhem was forced to admit.

"Well, my heart wishes to ride by your side," she said. "No matter the outcome. So, what's your answer?"

Mayhem didn't respond for a good while. He and Keedy just stared into each other's eyes with a love for one another that eclipsed the greatest hood love ever known. Keedy leaned forward and kissed his lips. "I'm waiting on your answer, sir," she said just above a whisper.

Mayhem swallowed his spit then gently lifted her off of his lap and sat her down on the sofa. He stood up and grabbed the bottle of Henny around the neck and knocked down a huge swig as he began pacing back and forth in front of her. He contemplated hard before he spoke, "You would have to learn how to be cold. I'm not talkin' about busting at a nigga from a distance. You would have to get real close and put a muthafucka on his ass."

Keedy looked up at him and watched him wear out the carpet. Slowly she allowed a smile to creep onto her face. Mayhem stopped and glared down at her.

"What's so fuckin' funny, shawdy?" That was the first time he had ever hardened his voice at her, but Keedy knew that it was nerves not anger.

"I'm sorry, baby." Keedy rose to her feet, wrapped her arms around her nigga's waist, and laid her head against his chest.

Mayhem relaxed in her embrace, then kissed the top of her head. "Shawdy, if I lose you I'm never gon' forgive myself," he uttered on strained breath.

Keedy looked up into his moist eyes and tried to comfort his soul. "Your enemies are my enemies, Mayhem," she pledged wholeheartedly. "Teach me how to help you erase them."

Mayhem released a heavy sigh as he reluctantly gave into her dangerous request. "Okay, shawdy," he conceded, hoping he wasn't making the wrong decision.

Excitedly, Keedy grabbed him around the neck and jumped into his arms, wrapping her legs around Mayhem's waist. He lifted around her ass and opened his mouth to receive her tongue. Their kiss began as a flame but quickly erupted into a wildfire. Their breathing grew heavy, their hands got busy, and their clothes began flying off. As Mayhem laid her down on the sofa and placed himself between her thighs, teaching her to bust a gun was temporarily put on hold while Mayhem went deep, deep, deeper inside of her hot, slippery heaven until he bust his own *nine*.

Two weeks later…

Mayhem and Keedy sat parked across from the Bottom Line on N. Claiborne Ave. in his whip waiting patiently for Breeze and Bump to emerge from inside of the nightclub.

Fantasia played from the radio as Mayhem kept his vision trained on the door of the club. In the passenger seat, Keedy bounced her shoulders to the beat of the song and hummed along. Her lax demeanor had Mayhem's nerves as frazzled as a worn out wool blanket. He leaned forward and turned the music off. Keedy cut her eyes at him but said nothing.

"Shawdy, this is not a game," he said with slight irritation coating his statement.

"Baby, I know. You've told me that five times already," Keedy replied.

On edge about her accompanying him, he instructed, "Check your gun again. Make sure that it's already click-clacked and that the safety is off."

"Mayhem, I've already checked it twice."

"Well, check it a third time," he drilled.

Keedy sighed and then did as he ordered. After assuring that the Glock .50 was ready to spit, she slid it back between her legs and stared out of the window.

"Don't forget, you're following my lead. If there's not many people around when they come out of the club we'll smash them right then and there but don't you move until I do," Mayhem repeated himself for the umpteenth time.

"And don't get so close up on him or he might grab my hand. Aim at his chest to give myself a bigger target. Keep firing until he hits the ground, then hit him in the head with at least two shots. If a witness comes out of the club don't look them directly in the eye but don't look away either. Walk back to the car at a normal pace," Keedy recited the rest of what he was about to repeat.

Mayhem could hear the annoyance in her tone, but he would rather she be peeved than dead. "Shawdy, I'm just tryna make sure that there's no mistakes. Really, I don't know why I let you talk me into bringing you along with me on this."

"Oh-em-gee, Mayhem," she groaned. "Please, hush. You're making *me* nervous," she leaned forward and turned the music back on.

When Mayhem turned it back off Keedy tightened her hoodie around her face, grabbed her gun from between her legs, and jumped out of the car, slamming the door behind her. She shoved the Glock inside of the front pocket of her hoodie and went and sat on the hood of the car.

Mayhem stared at her through the windshield and drummed his fingers on the steering wheel as he tortured himself for giving into Keedy's demand.

Fuck am I doing? he asked himself. He was supposed to protect her not involve her in murder. Sure, he had spent the past two weeks training her to bust that toolie, but wetting up a tree was much different than dumping in a nigga's chest. There was no way to gauge how she would react to taking a life until the very moment she had to look a man in the eye and squeeze the trigger. Tonight wasn't target practice, it was the real deal.

Mayhem simply could not put his girl in harm's way. He appreciated her love and devotion, but his love for her outweighed any sense of duty Keedy might've felt she owed him. *Hell no*! he told himself. *There's levels to this shit.*

Out of the corner of her eye Keedy saw Mayhem coming around the front of the whip. She quickly hopped off of the hood, ran back around to the passenger door, slid back inside of the car and locked the doors. Mayhem came around to her side of the vehicle and tried to snatch the door open. Finding it locked, he rested his arms on top of the whip and glared down at her through the window.

Mayhem's mouth was moving, but Keedy had turned the music on to drown out his words. She felt he talked her to death, already.

"Shawdy, quit playing," he elevated his voice, then checked the area for unwanted attention.

Keedy refused to look at him. She stared straight ahead and rocked her shoulders to the sound of Kelly Rowland. It wasn't her intention to upset him, but she had to relax.

"Shawdy," Mayhem called out sharply, pressing his face against the glass.

Keedy looked at him and covered her ears with both hands, gesturing that she was not listening to him. Mayhem's lips kept moving as he demanded that she hit the locks, but Keedy just stared right past him.

"Baby, please, stop playing. This shit is not a game." The frustration in Mayhem's voice was sharp enough to cut through the glass window that separated them.

Keedy finally popped the locks and opened her door. Mayhem leaned in, ready to chastise her, but Keedy slid out of the car wearing an expression of stone on her face.

She looked at Mayhem and calmly stated, "Baby, when you get done fussing here comes Breeze and Bump crossing the street." She slid her ratchet out and held it behind her back.

Mayhem turned his head in the direction of the club and saw the brothers strolling toward them. He instantly flipped into G-mode, easing his banger off of his waist. "Get back in the car, shawdy. I got this," he said to ears that refused to obey.

When Mayhem glared down at Keedy she was locked in on Breeze and Bump. Now was not the time to argue so Mayhem begrudgingly accepted that his shawdy was about to catch a body. "Let's do this shit," he said through gritted teeth.

Keedy had to half trot to keep up with Mayhem as he stepped long and hard, quickly closing the distance between them and the unsuspecting pair.

"I'm following your lead, baby," reassured Keedy. Her voice quivered a bit and her palms became sweaty as the moment of truth rushed up on her. She swallowed hard and tightened her grip on her ratchet.

Breeze and his brother strolled casually toward Bump's '64 Impala. They were both full of Patron and looking forward to hitting up Passions Men Club on Downman Rd. and sweating some pussy before taking it in for the night. They were sharing a laugh over an incident that happened inside of the club between themselves and some chicks they knew from out of the St. Thomas project when the swift patter of feet caused them both to look back, curiously. They immediately froze in their spots when they saw the two hooded figures step up in their grills, mugging hard and brandishing heat.

Mayhem lowered his hoodie, then shoved his tool in Breeze's mouth. "Remember me, pussy boy?" he snarled, backing them up onto a dark side street.

Breeze instantly showed his panties. He threw his arms up and started snitching. "Bruh, that shit was on Tank. He set the whole thing up. We didn't even know who you were."

"Well, now you do."

Blocka! Blocka!

Mayhem hit him in the face with two quick shots. Blood, teeth, and skull went spraying up in the air as Breeze staggered back and hit the ground with a thud, landing on the steps of an abandoned house.

Beside him, Keedy held her toolie chest high in a firm two handed grip as she faced the moment of truth. Her throat felt dry and her heart pounded hard in her chest. Sweat moistened her palms and fear flashed in her eyes. Bump peeped the nervousness in her stance and made his move.

"Punk ass ho, you ain't built like me!" Bump growled, then lunged for her.

Keedy screamed and stepped backwards, and the gun went off accidentally, hitting him high in the chest. But the second shot was on purpose and so was the third, fourth, and fifth. The Glock jumped in her hand as it fired out death in rapid succession.

Bump's body hit the ground face first at Keedy's feet, and his blood leaked out from under the soles of her black Air Max's. Keedy looked down at his riddled body, horrified. She dropped her gun and covered her mouth with both hands to repress her scream.

Mayhem stood over Breeze, staring down at Peanut's chain that hung around his neck. It was a grave reminder that he had smashed Peanut for nothing. He couldn't give Peanut his life back so he did the next best thing—he sent them to join him.

Blocka! Blocka! Blocka!

Quickly glancing to his left, he saw Keedy frozen stiff by the bloody reality that was sprawled out crookedly at her feet. Bump's left leg twitched and Mayhem could hear him groaning. The dim light from a nearby street lamp illuminated the area allowing Mayhem to catch a glimpse of Keedy's Glock on the ground. He bent down, swooped it up, and forced it back into her grasp. Staring into her eyes, he grumbled, "You wanted to ride, now finish your business."

Keedy remained stock still.

Mayhem looked from her down to Bump who was trying in vain to crawl away. He took two quick strides and stood over him with his fo-fifth aimed down at the back of his head.

"Where you tryna go, sugar ass?" Mayhem taunted as he kicked him in the side.

Bump collapsed down onto his chest, coughing and gurgling blood. Feeling no sympathy, Mayhem used his foot to turn him over onto his back so that he could look death in the face and take his picture to the grave with him.

"Please don't kill me," Bump gurgled as blood leaked out of his mouth and onto the cold ground.

"You killed yourself when you left me alive, stupid muthafucka," spat Mayhem. He squeezed the trigger and splattered Bump's forehead.

Spinning quickly on his heels, Mayhem scanned the area as he stepped back over to Keedy and took ahold of her arm.

“Shawdy, let’s move out,” he said, leading her back to her whip.

A few onlookers stared in shock from the other side of the street but Mayhem and Keedy just kept it moving, avoiding eye contact.

As they hopped in the car and mashed out, leaving two bodies behind, their hearts were bonded by more than love and loyalty—murder had just been added to their pact.

Chapter 34

Tank took the news of his cousins' murder very hard. The three of them had been raised practically off of the same titty since Breeze and Bump's mother had taken custody of him at an early age.

"That bitch ass nigga," he uttered as he sat with his head down in his hands. No one had to tell him who had killed his peoples. Just from the way he was told they were gunned down, he knew that shit had Mayhem's get-down written all over it.

Tweety sat next to him on the edge of the bed, staring at him questioningly. He kept mumbling Mayhem's name saying how he was going to crush him!

"Tank what's going on? Why would Mayhem kill them?" she questioned.

Tank was too overwhelmed with grief to respond. He took a deep breath and a sob escaped his lips. Shit was really fucked up. First Peanut, now Bump and Breeze. He shook his head as the weight of his complicity in their deaths fell upon his slumped shoulders like a ten ton brick, causing the tears to flow down his face like a river. It wasn't supposed to go like that. When he planned the robbery with Bump and Breeze he never would have dreamed in his worst nightmare that it would lead to three of his peoples' death. *Damn! I told Breeze to get rid of that goddamn chain.*

"Tank, are you going to answer me? I asked you why would Mayhem kill Breeze and Bump? What did y'all do to him?" Tweety's accusatory tone boomed in his ear and pissed him the fuck off.

"Fuck you mean?" he snapped, lifting his head and staring at her through squinted eyes and a hard scowl. "We ain't do shit to the nigga," he lied.

Tweety scoffed. "Somebody had to do something to him. From what you said, it's not his MO to just run around killing for no damn reason."

"You don't fuckin' believe *me*?" he barked.

"Look, I know when your ass is lying," she shot back. "Let you tell it, you don't know what happened to Peanut. But that's not the word on the streets."

"Bitch! You think I give a fuck 'bout what people are saying? My cousins are—"

"Hol' up! Nigga, did you just call me a bitch?" she cut him off.

"That's what the fuck you heard," yelled Tank. This was the wrong time for her to test his manhood.

Tweety was that bitch, though. She pounced up off of the bed and glared down at him. "If I'm a bitch," she said acidly, "you're a bitch ass nigga."

Tank shot up off of the bed and grabbed her by the throat. "You know what? Your mouth is too muthafuckin' slick. I'm about to teach you some muthafuckin' respect." He slung Tweety down on the floor and backhanded her.

Whack!

Tweety was shocked. He'd never put his hands on her before. Angrily, she hopped to her feet to fight back, but Tank put her right back on her ass.

"Nigga, you wanna beat on a woman? Go fight a man! Fuck with Mayhem if you're so muthafuckin' bad. I bet you won't fuck with him 'cause he'll kill your punk ass," Tweety hurled insults from the floor.

Tank saw red! He grabbed Tweety by the hair and slammed his fist dead into her slick ass mouth. By the time his fury subsided, Tweety was curled up in a ball, whimpering.

Shanica was tugging on Tank's pants leg, screaming for him to leave her mommy alone. Her cries snapped Tank out of his violent trance. He looked down at his daughter's wet face and frightened eyes, then he looked over to Tweety. Her mouth was busted, her eye was swollen, and lumps were forming across her forehead.

Tank fell to his knees crying as he lifted her into his arms, muttering, "Baby, I'm sorry. I swear to God I didn't mean to do this shit."

As Tank stared through his tears into Tweety's bloodied and battered face, he placed the blame for his actions and torment squarely on the back of Mayhem.

He vowed to murder that nigga and his recycled bitch if it was the last thing he ever did.

Chapter 35

Mayhem wasn't the sole source of Tank's torment. Tank was finding out that when it rains, *it pours*. Tweety had sworn out a warrant against him for domestic abuse and Peanut's cousin, Doobie, was said to be hunting that ass night and day. After hearing that Breeze had been rocking Peanuts' chain when he got murked, Doobie put two and two together and was gunning for Tank's head. In addition to all of those things, A'nyah had begun throwing him shade.

Tank popped his fourth Molly in the past couple of hours as he drove around the city trying to formulate his next move. Muthafuckas had the game wrong if they thought they were going to run him in a hole.

Lil Wayne's *Tunechi's Back* thumped out of his speakers as he pulled up to a stop light alongside a silver Ford Expedition. When he looked over the driver of the SUV was mean mugging for no apparent reason.

Tank's fo-fo was already resting on his lap for easy access in case one of his adversaries rode up on him. He didn't know the fool that was grilling him from the Expedition, but the way he felt anybody could get it at any moment. Tank let the passenger window down, eased the toolie off of his lap, and pointed it at ol' boy. "Bruh, you must got a problem with your eyes," he shouted over the music.

Fear flashed in the man's eyes and he shouted out a plea. "Bruh, I don't want no problems."

"Well, turn ya muthafuckin' head, ya heard me."

Dude's head snapped forward and as soon as the light changed to green he mashed on the gas.

Soft ass clown, Tank said to himself as he pulled off at a moderate speed, bobbing his head to the hard beat of the song and feeling invincible on those Mollies.

Tank drove until he reached A'nyah's apartments, then he parked and climbed the steps up to her door. He knocked three times and waited for her to answer. A minute or so later the door swung open and she stood there with her hands on her hips and her mouth twisted up.

Tank didn't wait to be invited in. He barged right past her and took a seat on the sofa. "Excuse you," said A'nyah as she kept the door open, letting him know not to get comfortable. "Um, I'm about to get ready to meet a friend out for drinks." She shifted her weight from one foot to the other, displaying her impatience for him to kick rocks.

Tank lowered his brow and stared at her. She had on boy shorts and a baby tee. Her pussy print was as fat as her attitude was foul. Tank chuckled because just a couple of weeks ago she was all on his dick. "That's how you gon' try to handle me?" he asked in a disdainful tone.

A'nyah closed the door and walked over to where he sat so she could get his ass straight once and for all. She stopped dead in front of him and looked down at him with mad conceit in her posture. "Let me keep it all the way real with you. Your money nor your dick game is strong enough for my taste, so I'm going to keep it moving."

The sudden shift in her attitude toward him left Tank felling played. "What about the shoes and the bags I bought you and the money I gave you at the casino?" The questions came piling out like dirty laundry.

A'nyah twisted her neck and curled her lip. "I didn't ask you for any of that, you did it on your own," she reminded him.

"Your thirsty ass didn't turn it down either," he spat.

"Tsss. You can have that shit back. Trust, I got lines of niggas willing to replace that shit." A'nyah turned and walked to her bedroom. A couple of minutes later, she returned with the gifts that Tank had bought her still in their boxes. She tossed them at his feet and said, "There goes your shit back. Now lift your ass up off of my couch so I can go kick it with a real boss nigga."

"You're a cold ass bitch." Tank stood up.

“So I’ve been told.” A’nyah was unfazed by the intended slur. She smiled at him, then turned for the door to politely let his trifling ass out.

As soon as A’nyah stepped toward the door, Tank reached out and snatched her by the back of her head. “C’mere, bitch,” he gritted as he slipped his fo-fo out and put it to her temple.

“Let me fuckin’ go!”

Tank let go of her hair and cracked her over the head with the gun. A’nyah staggered but she didn’t fall. *Whack!* The second blow knocked her to her knees, then she crumpled on her side. Tank threw both hands high above his head and did the Ali shuffle. “Down goes Frazier! Down goes Frazier!” he chanted maniacally.

A’nyah whimpered as blood ran down her neck and soaked the back of her t-shirt. Tank looked menacingly down at her and showed no mercy. He grabbed a fist full of her hair and drug her back to her bedroom.

“Please, Tank,” she cried as she looked up and saw him unbuckling his pants.

“It’s too late to beg now.” He whipped his dick out. He now knew that A’nyah had only sexed him to spite Keedy and that shit deflated his ego.

Tank gnashed his teeth together as he stared in her face with unbridled rage. He reached down and snatched her up on her knees. Pressing his banger to A’nyah’s forehead, he commanded, “Open your mouth!”

Crying and trembling and woozy from the violent blows, A’nyah obeyed him meekly. Tank forced his engorged dick in her mouth and promptly took a piss down her throat. “Swallow it ho or I’ma leave you dead up in this bitch,” he threatened.

A’nyah gagged as the warm acidic liquid splashed against the back of her esophagus. The strong, foul taste caused the contents in her stomach to rise up in her mouth. Tank rammed his dick further down her throat and laughed insanely once he finished, watching her throw up all over the floor.

"Nasty ass bitch," he frowned, stroking his ramrod. "Clean that shit up then get naked and assume the position. I want you face down with that ass tooted up in the air, ya heard me. I'm gon' fuck you in that dookie chute tonight."

Just the thought of him anally assaulting her caused A'nyah to shake as she stood to her feet, sobbing. She used the wall to support her as she staggered to the bathroom with Tank right on her heels, threatening to puff out her wig if she didn't steady her step.

As they passed by Keedy's old room, memories of how he had left that fake ho sprawled on the floor with a dildo shoved up her ass flashed through his mind and made his dick jump.

An evil smile came across his face as an idea came to mind. He would spare A'nyah the punishment of the dildo but he was going to fuck the bitch in her nasty ass and leave her in the exact same spot that he had left Keedy.

Tank was on a roll.

Two days after he had savagely raped and beat A'nyah, he was primed to teach someone else a lesson about testing his get-down. But this time, the bitch he was stalking had a pair of balls.

As Doobie slid out of his whip and walked to the trunk to unload the groceries that he had just picked up from the store, he heard a menacing voice at his back.

"Chump ass nigga, you don't look for me, I look for you," gritted Tank.

Doobie knew who the voice belonged to. Just as he knew that he had got caught slipping. He tried to ease his hand under his shirt but it never quite made it.

Boc! Boc! Boc!

Tank watched Doobie's body lurch forward, then drop to the ground as blood and brains splashed across the back window of his whip.

He looked around and saw dozens of witnesses staring at him. The sun was glaring down with bright intensity clearly showing Tank's unmasked face, but he didn't give a fuck. He slid his hand in his pocket and brought out a Molly. He coolly popped it into his mouth and swallowed it dry. He smiled at the witnesses, chucked up the deuces, then casually strode to his whip with his two fingers still suspended in the air.

I ain't playing no games 'round this bitch, he said to himself as he drove off without a care in the world.

Chapter 36

"I know I shouldn't care, but I do," said Keedy. She had just heard the news from Kim that A'nyah was in ICU at Charity hospital.

Mayhem continued savoring the tender steak that Keedy had pan seared. He swallowed the succulent meat, then tasted the asparagus and baked potato. "Shawdy, you put your foot in this," he complemented.

"Thank you, bay-bae," Keedy smiled from across the kitchen table. She glanced down at her own medium-well sirloin and lost her appetite as visions of what Tank had done to A'nyah formed in her mind. She sat her fork down and closed her eyes. When she opened them Mayhem was staring at her, intently.

"Baby girl, you amaze me," he said in a tone that resonated pure admiration. "Most women would be celebrating right now."

"That's not how I am," she reaffirmed.

"I know. And that's not how I am either. Regardless to how spiteful A'nyah can be she didn't deserve what Tank did to her. If I ever catch up with him, I'ma make him pay for every woman he ever abused, especially you. That's on my mother's grave," he vowed.

Keedy saw a combination of sadness and tempered rage wash over Mayhem's face. She slid her chair back from the table, walked over to him, and wrapped her arms around his neck. She placed a kiss on the back of his head like he was a little tot and purred, "I love you so much."

Mayhem reached back and stroked her arm. "I love you too, shawdy," he replied.

Keedy just nestled her head against his and thanked the heavens, as she did every day, for bringing him to her. His gangsta turned her on, but it was his tenderness toward women that won her love.

Keedy thought back to the night she had clammed up after shooting Bump. She had expected Mayhem to go off on her once they got home. Instead, he had blamed himself for allowing her to ride with him in the first place. And when Keedy tearfully apologized for not being able to murder with no remorse, Mayhem had taken her in his arms and whispered, "You can do no wrong in my eyes, beautiful."

"Mayhem," she said now, "I want to go to the hospital with Kim and Lenika to see A'nyah. Is that okay with you?"

"Yea. But, I'm not letting you go alone."

"No. It will be the three of us," she restated.

"Nah, shawdy. I don't trust that. I'll go with you. Call your girls and tell them that we'll meet them there."

With Tank running around on the bullshit, there was no way Mayhem was letting Keedy out of his sight.

When they returned from the hospital, Keedy was in tears. Mayhem's eyes weren't exactly dry either, but the fury in his chest trumped all other emotions. Keedy and her girls hadn't been at A'nyah's bedside no more than ten minutes when she had a brain hemorrhage and slipped into a coma.

"That nigga gon' get got!" fumed Mayhem as he moved around the condo placing a ratchet in every room.

Keedy was at his side. She was supposed to pay attention to where he stashed the artillery, but everything was a blur to her. She could not conceive the prognosis that A'nyah was not expected to come out of the coma.

"He didn't have to do her dirty like that," she wept as she followed Mayhem back into their bedroom. "I hate him!" Keedy screamed as she crumpled down on the bed and her tears soaked the pillow.

Mayhem laid down next to his boo and tried to comfort her in his strong arms.

Keedy wept late into the night. The following evening she received that dreaded phone call from Kim—A'nyah was no longer in a coma.

She was dead.

Tank knew that it was over. He had seen his name and face splashed across the TV screen. Channel 4 News had made him out to be a psychopath, when the truth was the opposite—he was just a real nigga who spared no one that wronged him.

At least that's what he convinced himself of.

He popped a Molly as he slid a little bit further down in his seat and waited for his next victim to pull up in her driveway. He had already decided that he was going to do the slut dirty whether she disclosed the info he wanted or not.

An hour passed before he saw her pass by where he was parked down the street from her house. Adrenaline surged through his body as he sat up and grabbed his tool off of the passenger seat. Skilled as a creep artist, Tank eased out of his car and quietly closed the door. His all black gear blended in with the darkness that enveloped the quiet neighborhood on this moonless night.

Tank's Reebox soldiers barely made a sound as he moved quickly up the street. She had just placed the key in the side door and was pushing it open when he caught up to her and clamped his hand over her mouth from behind.

Thunk!

He cracked her over the back of the head with his steel and shoved her inside on the floor. He stepped inside the house and closed the door behind him. He knew that they were alone because he had watched her mother leave out just twenty minutes earlier.

She was lying on the floor, groaning with her hands on the back of her head. Warm, sticking blood coated her palms.

Lenika rolled over and looked up into the familiar face of her assailant. His eyes were wild and his smile was scary.

"I wanna know where that bitch and nigga live," demanded Tank. "Play games if you want to, and I'ma chop yo' lil' skinny ass up and leave you in the refrigerator like leftovers."

Lenika looked straight into his beedy eyes and spat, "Fuck you! I'm a real bitch!"

"Oh, yea?" Tank laughed as he unbuckled his pants.

By the time Tank left up out of there the entire kitchen floor was splattered with blood and semen. And every Tupperware dish in sight was filled with Lenika's remains.

Chapter 37

Keedy was cramping unusually bad. She had swallowed the last of the Motrin several hours ago and still the pain hadn't subsided. The cramping was so intense she was balled up on the living room sofa with her arms around one pillow and her knees clutching another.

Mayhem was afraid to touch her because every time he did Keedy would wince and curse. He paced the living like an expectant father. Each time Keedy groaned out in pain a sharp ache shot through his body and helplessness seized his heart.

Mayhem ran his hands through his closely cropped hair and sighed in frustration. "Baby, you want me to carry you upstairs?"

"Nooo," Keedy whined. The mere thought of being touched caused her to ache even harder.

"Shawdy, I'ma go to the store and get you some more medicine," said Mayhem.

"Okay," she moaned.

With much effort she gave him a short list of items to get, including tampons and pads. "If you'll be too embarrassed to buy them, I could probably have Nik Nik or Kim stop by to bring me some," offered Keedy.

"Shawdy, you ain't talkin' bout nothin'."

Keedy braved a smile. She loved to hear him say that.

"I'ma stop and grab us some hot plates, a'ight?" he said, wanting to assure that she would be alright until he returned.

"Yea. I'm going to just lay in this spot," she said.

"Can I give you a kiss before I go?"

"Of course, baby," Keedy brightened.

When their lips touched it was as if the pain magically went away. Keedy didn't dare move though—she knew that those suckers weren't going anywhere.

Mayhem picked her cell phone up off of the table and handed it to her. "Call me if you need me," he said.

"I will," she promised.

She forced a smiled on her face, but as soon as Mayhem left out of the door she cried out in agony. The cramps were back and they had brought their whole fucking family.

Tank was cramped up in a small, seedy motel room watching the morning news to see if Lenika's body had been discovered. There were no reports of it on the local stations, so he assumed that her mother hadn't returned home last night. That was the best news that he could've hoped for because it meant that Keedy didn't know that her tramp friend was dead, yet.

Tank popped two Mollies and grabbed Lenika's cell phone from off of the nightstand. After locating Keedy's new phone number in the contacts he sent her a text.

8:18AM: Hey bitch! What you doing?

8:19AM: Hey. Cramping like a MF!

8:20AM: That sucks. Where's Mayhem?

8:23AM: Gone to the store to get meds.

8:24AM: K. What's yo address? Ordering that new book by La'Tonya West for you.

Tank knew that Keedy was in love with the Side Chic series. As soon as the address popped up on the screen he sent a quick reply.

8:30AM: Thanx. I'm going to bring you some yakamein.

Another favorite he knew she loved.

Keedy texted back saying that Mayhem was picking up food as well. But Tank never read the response because he was already out of the door.

Keedy heard Lenika's familiar knock but without the usual loud mouthing. She started to yell, *Go away!* But knowing Lenika that would just invite her to bang harder.

Sighing, Keedy sat up gingerly and waited to see if the pain was going to course through her body and render her immobile. When nothing happened she rose to her feet, weakly. At the same time her phone rang in her hand. She glanced down at the screen and saw Kim's number flashing. She pressed the answer button and put the phone to her mouth, "Hold on a minute," she said. Kim was crying hysterically but Keedy didn't hear it, she'd already placed her cell down on the end table. "Hmmm," uttered Keedy and she headed to the door, walking slowly, with one hand over her stomach.

Keedy reached the door and disengaged the locks. Although she'd told Lenika that she didn't need any of her infamous yakamein, she knew her hard-headed friend was going to bring it anyway. Grimacing from the aches, Keedy opened the door and was met by Tank's fist.

Her back hit the floor and everything went black.

Chapter 38

Mayhem's mouth watered and his stomach growled loudly as he stood at the counter in the corner store, waiting his turn in line, ready to place his breakfast order. The delicious aroma that floated in the air of the store was enough to make Mayhem want to whip out and jack Big Mama, as the regulars called her, for the entire menu.

Mayhem chuckled as the vision flashed in his mental. A girl standing next to him gave him a little smile along with a lingering stare. She was a pretty brown skinned chick with a nice figure, but Mayhem's interest was only for Keedy. He looked away from the girl's flirtatious gaze as he wondered if Keedy was feeling better. He had already stopped by CVS and picked up the items that she asked him to get and as soon as he grabbed their food, he was going home to attend to his boo.

Just when Mayhem shoved his hands down in his pockets and moved up a space in line he felt his phone vibrate. Thinking that it was Keedy, Mayhem hurried to pull his cell out and answer the call. "Sup, shawdy? How you feeling?"

Dream's hysterical voice, not Keedy's, came through the phone. She was sobbing so hard Mayhem couldn't make out a word she was saying. He stepped out of line and turned his back to the others. "Dream, slow down. I can't understand you," he said, raising his voice in irritation. She repeated herself, but it still came out in starts and stops with loud sobs in between. Mayhem had to piece together what she had said, then he prayed that he hadn't heard her correctly. "Did you just say that Brandi got hit by a car?" he asked as fear choked off his breath.

"Yes!" Dream cried. "She's in critical condition. You need to come right away."

Mayhem's heart dropped to the floor. Whether it was her fault or not, he was so distraught and angry at Dream for letting something happen to his daughter. He hung up without saying goodbye. He dialed Keedy's number as he hurried out of the store. Her phone rang and rang and then the voicemail picked up. Mayhem hung up and redialed. Again, there was no answer.

As Mayhem started his whip and backed out of the parking space, he wondered why Keedy hadn't picked up, but his major concern was his daughter's health. He drove home with a heavy foot and an even heavier heart, unprepared for what he would encounter when he got there.

Chapter 39

Keedy's head was ringing and the taste of blood was thick in her mouth. As she tried to regain her senses she felt herself being snatched up off of the floor.

"Yea, bitch, I found your ass," roared Tank. His breath was hot on her face as he had yanked her inches toward his mouth. "Your boy can't save you now," he grabbed her by the throat and slammed her into the wall.

Keedy fell to the floor, then scrambled to her feet and bolted for the door, but Tank darted in her path, smiling like a crazed mad man.

She turned and raced for the stairs. Tank jumped over the coffee table and grabbed her from behind in a bear hug, lifting her clear off of her feet. Keedy kicked and screamed as he carried her over to the couch and slung her down. "Leave me the fuck alone, you bastard," she screamed through her busted lips.

"I'ma leave you alone," Tank pulled out his piece, "after I kill you. And after I slump your punk ass, I'ma wait on your pussy whipped ass nigga to return and then I'ma crush his ass too."

"Kill me then, I don't care!" She was done cowering to him.

"Oh, I am," he said. "But, I'm a do it my way. The same way I did your slick mouth friend."

Keedy thought that he was referring to A'nyah but Tank was talking about Lenika. He put the gun back in his waist-band and brought out a bloody knife—the same one he had used to dismember Lenika.

"You're weak, that's why you pick on women. I hate you!" Keedy spat a glob of blood dead in Tank's face.

He wiped it away, then licked it off of his hand.

Staring down at her with a twisted grin, Tank said, "Nah, I ain't weak, you're a weak bitch so that's how I treated you."

"Fuck you, Tank!"

“Nah, bruh, I’m about to *fuck you.*” He held the knife up and twirled it in his hand. The light from the lamp on the end table bounced off of the razor-edged blade. Tank grabbed the waist of Keedy’s sweats and snatched them down to her knees. “I’ma shove this knife so far up your ratchet pussy, it’s going to come out ya ass.”

Keedy’s eyes grew as big as saucers.

She tried to scoot away from him but Tank held on to her leg. She screamed, then kicked him hard in the face.

“Aaaahhh! You bitch!” he bristled, rubbing his eye. As Keedy tried to get up, her hand slipped under the cushion of the couch and came in contact with cold steel. It was one of the guns that Mayhem had stashed around the house. When Tank regained his full vision and scowled down at her, Keedy had that toolie pointed up at his chest, and the scowl on her face was harder than his.

“Fuck you gon’ do with that? Timid ass ho,” said Tank as he raised the sharp knife over his head ready to plunge it down into her chest.

“You’re the bitch. *Bitch*!” she gnarled as every single ass whooping that she had ever suffered from him zoomed through her mind in a stream of degradation and terror. A vision of a comatose A’nyah while in Intensive Care flashed before her eyes just as Tank began bringing the blade down with murderous intent. “You punk muthafucka!” Keedy screamed.

Boc! Boc! Boc! Boc!

The .357 roared as it spat hot revenge, loud and deathly. The weapon slipped from Tank’s hand and fell harmlessly on the floor a second before his body crashed down on top of Keedy’s. Blood poured from the holes in his chest and soaked the front of her Saints t-shirt. Keedy squirmed from underneath his weight, gun still in hand. Tears streamed down her face as she stood to her feet.

Lying face down on the sofa and bleeding profusely, Tank wheezed with every labored breath that he took.

"Keedy! Keedy!" Kim's frantic voice thundered through the cell phone. She never hung up from earlier. "Pick up the phone!"

Keedy faintly heard her name being yelled, but she couldn't focus on the location of the sound. She stood there in shock with the gun down at her side. Sweat dripped off of her forehead, and her chest heaved up and down. She looked down at the bastard who had caused her so much torment and shuddered.

As she turned her head away from the sight of him, Tank languidly rolled over on his back and reached for his waist.

Mayhem pulled up in front of his building. He parked and let out a long sigh as his daughter's condition weighed cripplingly on his heart. Before getting out of the car, he grabbed the CVS bags off of the passenger seat. His shoulders were slumped, however, his mind was still on point. Out of habit, he quickly scanned the area. He did a double-take when he thought that he spotted Tank's truck parked on the far end of the lot. *Fuck! Yea, that's him!*

Mayhem dropped the bags, snatched his banger off of his waist, and went flying toward the door. He kicked that muthafucka in and stepped inside with his teeth gritted, and his tool moving swiftly from left to right.

The loud bang of the door crashing against the wall startled Keedy. She spun around with her gun held high, and almost sent Mayhem flying back out the same way he came in, but with a chest full of lead to take with him. Once she realized that it was him, she dropped her gun and ran toward him crying.

Behind her, Tank had his fo-fo in hand. With struggle, he cocked the slide. The all too familiar sound alerted Mayhem. Looking over Keedy's shoulder, he saw Tank's arm come up. "Shawdy, watch out!" he yelled as he pushed Keedy to the floor just as Tank's banger popped off.

Blocka!

The single, errant shot lodged into the door frame. Tank's eyes blinked, and his hand shook as he tried to summon up enough strength to squeeze the trigger again.

"Oh, no, my nigga!" Mayhem scowled. "I warned you not to fuck with mine." Walking toward Tank, he sent heat that coward's way with every step.

Blocka! Blocka! Blocka!

"This was never what you wanted." *Blocka!* "Nigga, you ain't no real killah." *Blocka!* "This how you murk somethin'!"

Blocka! Blocka!

He stopped a foot from the sofa and looked down at the sorry dude that he had once considered a friend. Half of Tank's head was splattered across the back of the couch. "You victimized defenseless women," he snorted phlegm from within and spat on what remained of his face. "Weak, pussy bitch!" said Mayhem with no remorse.

He started to walk away, but then decided to kill that nigga again.

Blocka!

He shot him in the half of his head that was still intact. "Fuckin' with my, shawdy." Mayhem turned and held his arms out and Keedy rushed into his embrace.

"Keedy! Keedy!" Kim was still screaming her name at the top of her lungs.

Mayhem glanced down and realized where the voice was coming from. He grabbed the phone and put it to his ear but he only had time to tell Kim that Keedy was okay because the sound of the police sirens screamed in the distance.

They had to grab whatever they could and get in the wind.

Chapter 40

Keedy's cries filled the whole car as they drove to Atlanta in Mayhem's Corvette. After snatching up the money, guns, and a few clothes, they had barely peeled off before the cops arrived. As soon as they had gotten on the highway, Keedy had called Kim and the news that she received crushed her world.

Her Nik Nik was gone. Murdered was an understatement, she had been mutilated. Now she knew what Tank meant when he said, "*I'ma do it my way. The same way I did your slick mouth friend.*"

Keedy's shoulders rocked as painful sobs came from deep down in her soul. She had been crying for the past three hours and Mayhem could find no words to comfort her.

When they arrived in Atlanta, hours later, Mayhem rented a room at a motel on Fulton Industrial. Keedy was too weak with grief to walk, so he carried her up to their room on the second level. After undressing her and tucking her into bed, Mayhem went back down to the car to retrieve their things.

He sat up all night listening to Keedy weep, and with each heart-wrenching sob that emitted from her lips, a silent cry wailed in his heart. Mayhem couldn't help but think that if he had never come into Keedy's life, her friend would still be alive, and she wouldn't be a suspect in a murder. The anguish he felt over loving her so much, yet causing her so much tragedy, was like a stake through his heart.

Mayhem decided that he was going to free her of whatever burdens he could. Once he checked on Brandi, he was going to contact an attorney and have them to work out a deal. He would surrender peacefully, and admit full responsibility for everything, in exchange for Keedy's immunity. He knew that if he mentioned his plan to her, Keedy would not go along with it so he kept it to himself.

In the wee hours of the night, Keedy finally cried herself to sleep. Mayhem didn't close his eyes at all. He stayed up all night. Watching over his girl, and keeping an eye on the parking lot.

Dream had the audacity to have a funky attitude with Mayhem because he had brought Keedy to the hospital with him. When Mayhem made the introduction, Dream groveled, "I don't care to meet your little raggedy bitch."

Mayhem caught himself before he bopped her.

Keedy put a hand on his elbow, "Baby, don't let her upset you. Go on in there and see your daughter. I'll be right out here when you're done."

"Thanks, boo." He bent down and gave her a quick kiss on the lips, then headed in the children's ICU.

When Keedy looked up. Dream was giving her a cold, nasty look. After everything that Keedy had been through lately, she was the wrong one to beef with. She smiled at Dream sweetly, but the words that came out through her clenched teeth were anything but sugary. "Let me tell you something, *hunti*," she stretched out the word. "If you have a problem with me, step your pissy, yellow ass outside and I'll give you the business. *In that order!*"

Dream's mouth flew open and she started yapping. She snaked her neck and flung her arms around, talking shit, but her feet damn sure didn't move.

Keedy waited just outside of the door, itching for her to follow so she could punt that bitch like a football. But Dream didn't want none.

Little Brandi was heavily medicated. She had suffered two fractured legs, a broken arm and a bruised sternum along with minor scrapes and bruises. But as soon as she heard her daddy's voice, her eyes fluttered open and her face lit up.

Mayhem leaned over the bed rail and kissed his angel's forehead. "Hey, Daddy's girl," he whispered as he tucked a little Care Bear under the blanket with her.

The oxygen mask over Brandi's mouth prevented her from responding, but the love that flashed in her eyes warmed his heart. "Daddy is here, baby, and you're going to be just fine," he said tenderly.

Mayhem looked at his princess all bandaged up with casts on her small limbs. He had to bite down on his lip to contain his emotions. He blamed himself because had he been there, he would've thrown himself in front of that truck, sparing her.

Dream came in the room talking loudly about dumb shit that didn't matter. Their daughter was laid up in ICU, yet she was popping off. "You and that bum bitch out there can go back wherever the fuck y'all came from before I get in that ho's ass. Me and Brandi are good!"

The nurses turned and looked at her reproachfully. "Shhhh!" One of them sternly gestured her to silence.

Dream was about to go off on the woman. Mayhem saw the look in her eyes and tried to quiet the storm before it erupted.

"Let's just be concerned about Brandi," he whispered, placing a hand on her arm.

"Fuck you!" Dream knocked his hand off of her. "If you touch me again I'm going to ask them to have security escort you out of here."

Mayhem knew exactly what she was threatening to do. He looked at Dream and for the very first time he felt hatred toward her. He wanted to tell her that if she paid a fraction of the attention to their child as she did to those niggas she fucked with, his baby wouldn't be all broken up. But he didn't want to give her ammunition to create a scene.

He turned away from Dream and cooed to his daughter. "I love you so much, princess," he said. "Always remember that."

He lightly pressed his forehead against hers, and the tear that fell from his eye dripped onto her chubby cheek. When Brandi drifted back to sleep, Mayhem planted another kiss on her forehead and whispered, "Baby, please forgive Daddy for not being here to protect you. And know that I love you with every single fiber in my soul." He took a deep breath before adding, "Never, *ever* forget that."

Mayhem kissed Brandi's cheek, then turned to leave. He had an overwhelming feeling in his soul that this would be the last time he would ever see his little girl. He stopped at the door and turned back around to stare at her. His heart ached with a pain that was unlike any that he had ever known.

Mayhem cut his eyes in Dream's direction. She had her arms folded across her chest glaring at him hatefully. He stepped over to her and said, "Shawdy, like I've always told you, in spite of everything, you gave birth to my only child. I'm forever grateful to you for that if nothin' else. Please take better care of our baby."

"What? Oh, you're leaving and not coming back?" Dream cocked her head to the side and got real extra. "You don't care about *my* baby 'cause if you did, you wouldn't be leaving. What, that bitch don't want you to be here?"

Again the nurse indicated for her to lower her voice.

Mayhem couldn't believe that Dream would really go there. But he wasn't about to entertain her. "I'm very uncomfortable here right now," he spoke very low. "But you already know that if I feel safe, I'll be back to see my baby. If I don't return you'll know I'm in cuffs or a casket."

"Whateva," she hissed.

"Bye, shawdy." He looked at her with deep regret for whatever it was that wouldn't allow her to see that he only wanted the best for her and his seed.

On the way out of the door Mayhem stopped to confer with a nurse. What she told him relieved some of his concern—Brandi would be just fine in time.

"Thank you," he said with sincerity. Then he sent a silent *thank you* up to heaven before leaving out.

Back at the hotel, Keedy could tell that Mayhem was deeply troubled. He was unusually quiet and withdrawn. She assumed that he was simply worried about his daughter, but it was more than that.

Mayhem was trying to decide when and how he would turn himself in, but he needed to be able to say goodbye to Keedy properly before doing so. He just couldn't figure out how to do it without crushing her heart.

For the next two days they didn't leave the room. Mayhem wanted to go back to the hospital and visit Brandi again, but he felt strong trepidation every time he considered going. If he was arrested as opposed to having an attorney work out immunity for Keedy in exchange for his surrender, they wouldn't give Keedy a break. He couldn't risk having that happen, he told himself as he sat on the bed with his back against the headboard, contemplating.

Keedy came out of the bathroom with her hair freshly combed, and she was dressed to go out and get a little fresh air today. "Bae, let's go get something to eat, she suggested. "I always said that if I ever came to Atlanta I was going to *Gladys Knight's Chicken and Waffles* joint."

"Did you?" he replied matter-of-factly.

Keedy walked over and sat down on the edge of the bed. "You okay, bay-bae?" she rubbed his arm.

"Yea, I'm good, beautiful."

"No, you're not," she said, looking at him closely. "You haven't really slept since we've been here. I know you're worried about your daughter but there seems to be something else on your mind. Do you want to talk about it?"

"Nah. Really, baby girl, I'm straight," he maintained. But Keedy couldn't be fooled.

She took his face between her hands and read him like an open letter. "If you're worried about me, you don't need to be," she assured, staring into his eyes. "I'm where I wanna be, baby. As long as I'm with you I have no regrets. We're in this together, until the very end," she kissed him softly.

"You're a G," he smiled. But that didn't change what he was committed to do.

"I'm going to go out and get a few things. What can I bring you back?" she asked.

"I thought you wanted chicken and waffles?"

"We can do that another day, it's okay. Now let me do something for *you*. What would you like to eat?"

"Wendy's. But I'm gonna ride with you. I don't want you to go alone." He swung his legs over the side of the bed.

"No," she protested, passionately. "You're going to get some rest, sir. I got this."

Mayhem began to object, but Keedy put a finger to his lips, hushing him. She rose up on her tippy toes and gave him a reassuring kiss. "I'll be fine. I saw a Wendy's that's not too far from here."

"A'ight," Mayhem reluctantly agreed. But only because he needed a while alone.

Keedy picked her purse and her Nine up off of the nightstand then headed out.

As soon as she was gone Mayhem grabbed his phone and started searching for a lawyer to turn himself in to.

Chapter 41

It took several inquiries but finally Mayhem made contact with a reputable attorney that had represented him in the past. Without divulging Keedy's name, Mayhem began laying out the situation.

The lawyer listened intently. When Mayhem had put everything on the table, the man was honest with him. He didn't think a district attorney would be eager to grant Keedy full immunity, but he assured Mayhem that with his surrender and full confession, Keedy would be given leniency.

"Hell no!" Mayhem stood firm. "My girl walks or we can hold court in the streets. They don't want that," he warned.

They attorney couldn't promise anything but he agreed to make the inquiry on they're behalf. A retainer wasn't necessary because if he had a hand in surrendering Mayhem peacefully, the publicity alone would be invaluable. He gave Mayhem a day and a time to call him back and told him to be safe.

Mayhem hung up the phone and went to the window to watch for Keedy. Time passed at a turtle's pace. By the time she finally pulled up, he had been ready to go looking for her.

Mayhem held the door open for her as Keedy came in with other bags in addition to the fast food. She sat everything down on the small table and explained that she had stopped at Wal-Mart.

"Shawdy, I was starting to get worried. I was about to paint this city red," he said seriously.

Keedy smiled. "Calm down, sir. I told you I would be fine. Did you get some rest while I was gone?"

"Yea," he fibbed.

Keedy washed her hands, then set their food out on paper plates. She tore into her salad and her chicken sandwich but Mayhem only ate a couple of bites of his burger and fries.

Keedy saw that he was still feeling somewhat down. She didn't want to add to his stress by questioning him so she busied herself with cleaning up the room. After everything was in place she retreated to the bathroom to take a bubble bath.

Half an hour later, Keedy came out of the bathroom feeling relaxed. Now she had to do the same for her man.

Mayhem paced back and forth to the window with a gun in each hand. Keedy knew that he had a lot on his mind. She went up to him and hugged him from behind. "Baby, I ran you some bath water. Let your woman hook you up, it will help you relax."

Mayhem allowed her to lead him into the bathroom, then pamper him with a sponge bath. Her touch washed away the tension in his taut muscles and because he wanted her to remember their last days together fondly he allowed the stress to fade from his face.

Back in the bedroom area, Keedy turned the lights down in the room. She wanted to set the mood just right. She walked up behind him, wrapping her arms around his waist, squeezing him tightly. She ran her hands up and down his toned torso, enjoying the feel of his washboard stomach.

"Mayhem, we don't know how this is gonna end," she accepted. "But I do know how I want us to be at the end of this night. So, please, baby, just relax and let me take care of you tonight."

Keedy planted soft, wet kisses up and down his back, loving the smoothness of his dark skin. She ran her tongue down the center of his back, tasting the sweetness of him. "Baby, lay down," she guided him to the bed.

Mayhem folded his hands behind his head and watched her retrieve a candle from inside one of the Wal-Mart bags. After lighting it and placing it on the nightstand, Keedy slowly removed the black, lace teddy that she had slipped into.

Mayhem's eyes locked on that fat, sexy V between her thighs. He licked his lips slowly, anticipating her wetness on his tongue. He could smell her feminine desire as Keedy's pussy thumped to the beat of her heart. The fragrant essence of her core let itself be known as it filled the air around them.

Keedy crawled on the bed, removed the towel from around Mayhem's waist, and stared at his masculine asset as if seeing it for the very first time. Tonight she wanted him, needed him, like never before.

She straddled him and leaned down so that her aching nipples grazed across his pecs. "Umm," she moaned as electricity shot from her nipples to the very tip of her clit.

"What you gon' do, shawdy?" his voice was thick with need.

"I'm going to please my man," she whispered in his ear.

She planted soft kisses on his lips and then his neck where his mother's name was tatted. Mayhem cupped her ass in his hands and grind his dick against her moistened pussy.

"You want me, baby?" she asked needlessly.

"Bad," he confirmed what his rock hard pole indicated.

"I want you bad, too." She lightly traced her tongue over the three bullet scars on his stomach. She recalled the stories he told her behind each wound. Her boo was thugged the fuck out yet gentle, too. Damn, she loved him so much.

Her body was in accord with her heart. She felt her walls become wetter but she needed to hold out a few minutes more. She stopped her hips from moving and sat up, still straddling him with a knee on each side of his waist.

"Sup, my love?" he asked, thinking something was wrong.

Keedy put a finger over her mouth. "I have something I want to tell you," she said softly before heartfelt words of love began to pour from her lips. "Baby, you've held my heart in the palm of your hands since we first met. I don't know what tomorrow may bring, but I want to share whatever time we both have together. You complete me in ways I never believed a man ever would."

Tears filled Keedy's eyes as she recalled all of the heartbreak that she had gone through with other niggas, and how Mayhem had come in and erased all of the pain. "You made me smile when there was absolutely nothing to smile about," she continued. "No one ever loved me until you came into my life, and I'm so grateful for you, baby."

Mayhem couldn't remain quiet any longer. "I'm grateful for you, too, baby girl. You showed me that love and devotion still exist." He reached up and gently pulled her head down until their lips locked.

As usual, he took her breath away. Keedy giggled nervously. "It's crazy how you still make me tremble every time you touch me," she exhaled. "The air I breathe carries your scent throughout my being, even when you're away from me. And when you hold me in your arms and make sweet love to me I feel whole. That is when I'm at my fullest as a woman."

"Damn, that's deep, baby."

Keedy looked deeper into his eyes. "I love you, Mayhem. You have no idea how much. I vow my heart to you, my life to you. My world is not complete without you existing within it. Your love is everything that I need."

"That's exactly how I feel about you. Fa real. Life wasn't shit until you came in it, shawdy. You're my rib."

"I'm happy you feel that way." Keedy leaned over and grabbed something off the nightstand that she had purchased while out. It was a small box. She opened it slowly. "Mayhem, will you marry me and officially make me yours?" she asked as she brought out a gold wedding band.

Mayhem was overwhelmed by her proposal. He pulled her down to him and met her lips in a crushing kiss. A full minute passed before they came up for air. "Yes, I'll be honored to marry you," he said.

Keedy slid the band on his finger and then handed him a second box. This one contained the bride's ring set. Mayhem did not have to be coached.

He climbed out of bed and went down on bended knee, butt ass naked. Holding Keedy's hand in his, he looked up into her eyes and said. "Baby, never before has a woman made any man happier than you've made me. Every single day that you've been in my life you've given me a new reason to appreciate love. You are the most beautiful, intelligent, sexy woman that God ever created. Will you be my wife, Kedada Marie Duplessis?"

Keedy couldn't answer through her tears, so she nodded her head up and down. When she finally found her voice, she cried, "Yes, I'll gladly be your wife."

Mayhem slid both rings on her finger, then rose to his feet and pulled Keedy to hers. They wrapped their arms around each other and got lost in a long, passionate kiss.

This time Mayhem had to suck in oxygen. Keedy had taken *his* breath away. He licked his lips, savoring hers. "I now announce us husband and wife," he said.

Keedy took his hand and pulled him down on the bed. "Hurry," she panted, "your wife needs some of that honeymoon loving."

She opened her thighs to her husband, and when he entered into her, neither of them had a worry in the world.

Chapter 42

The *newlyweds* spent the majority of the next two days with their bodies intertwined. On the third day as he had done each day previously, Mayhem woke up and called the hospital to get an update on Brandi's condition. After being told that she was doing fine, he awoke his wife with a kiss.

Keedy came out of her sleep with the desire to feel him deep inside of her. She gave him that look that he had come to know well, and Mayhem gave her a whole lot of that morning *breakfast* that she loved to wake up to.

Keedy was singing *Loving You* by Minnie Riperton as she showered.

While she freshened up, Mayhem talked to his lawyer in a hushed tone. An agreement had been reached: if Mayhem turned himself in immediately and confessed to the murders that he had committed in Atlanta and New Orleans, the state of Louisiana would not pursue any charges against Keedy. "But you have to do it ASAP, the attorney stressed. "You can come to my office and I'll surrender you or I can come where you are.

"I need an hour or two," Mayhem negotiated. Fuck that, he was taking his wife to Gladys Knight's Chicken and Waffles, if it was the last thing he ever did as a free man.

"I'll be in court by then. You can surrender yourself to any peace officer and once you're booked I'll be to see you after I leave court. Be careful though because you're listed as armed and *very* dangerous. I'll have to surrender the young lady to New Orleans at a later time, but I assure you she will be released on her own recognizance."

Mayhem knew the lawyer to be a man of his word. "Okay," he agreed. "I'll turn myself in. Don't let me down. My girl walks, understand me?"

"Yes, you have my word."

Mayhem was just hanging up when Keedy came out of the shower. She had no reason to suspect him of anything so she didn't question who he was talking to.

After Mayhem showered and they both dressed, they drove to Gladys Knight's restaurant out in Lithonia, Georgia. Keedy was in a good mood, she bounced in her seat and sang along with every song that came on the radio.

Mayhem was contemplative. But he was at peace with the decision that he had reached.

When they arrived at the restaurant, it was Keedy who suggested that they order takeout. With nationwide warrants out for both of their arrests, she was not trying to chill in public.

"Hubby, I'm going to run in and get the food. You wait your handsome-self right here and don't you look at nare woman that passes by. You're a married man, now," she teased.

She leaned over and kissed him and then she put on her Chloe shades and went to see what all the fuss over Gladys Knight's waffles was about.

It was with a heavy heart that Mayhem watched Keedy walk away from the car. He knew that in just another hour or so, he would never hold her in his arms again. With all the murders that he planned to confess to in order to free her, he expected to be sentenced to death.

Mayhem was good with that, he would be a step closer to where his mother was. And once that needle went in his arm, he would be all the way there. He believed that God would open the pearly gates for him because the big G in the sky knew his heart.

But what would become of Keedy? he worried. She would be free, but would she ever find love and happiness again?

Mayhem didn't know the answer to that, but he was damn sure going to give his honey a chance.

As if it was a sign from above, a police cruiser pulled in the lot. Here was his chance to surrender peacefully and afford his wife with a new start in life. He wished he could kiss her lips just once more, but it was now or never.

Mayhem leaned forward and glanced through the restaurant's glass windows. Keedy was at the counter, but her head was turned away from him. He blew her a kiss anyway.

I love you, shawdy. Stay beautiful and live your life.

Mayhem took the strap off of his waist and placed it on the floorboard, disarming himself. He looked up to see the lone cop standing outside the cruiser smoking a cigarette.

Time to put your money where your mouth is.

Keedy waited patiently for her order to be filled. When the counter person finally handed her *her* food, the aroma made her want to sample those blueberry waffles and chicken wings right on the spot. She pressed her nose against the bag and inhaled the deliciousness.

She couldn't wait to share the meal with Mayhem; she was going to hand feed him like an itty bitty baby. *Yea, that's what I'm gonna do.*

Keedy felt all giddy inside. She turned to the door with excitement that immediately vanished when she looked outside and saw Mayhem engaged in a conversation with a policeman. Panic filled her chest. She could not allow him to get arrested or it would all be over!

Keedy dropped her order and slid her hand inside her oversized bag. Her heart pounded as she moved quickly to the door.

She stepped out into the lot with a single purpose.

When she was within three feet of Mayhem and the cop, the po po turned his head in her direction and Keedy blew the top of his head off. His body slammed back against his service vehicle and began to slide to the ground.

Blocka! Blocka!

Two more straight up top!

"Baby, let's go," Keedy screamed.

"Oh, shit!" Mayhem exclaimed, looking down at the policeman's body. Shit had gone all wrong!

He knew that they had to get away from there, fast. It was broad daylight and dozens of witnesses surrounded them. Several had snapped pictures with their cell phones.

"Fuck! Shawdy, we gotta get out of here." Mayhem grabbed Keedy's arm, and they dashed to their car and peeled off, tires screeching.

When they were a mile or two away from the scene, they ditched the car and flagged down a cab. There was nothing to lose now so Mayhem left the cabbie nodded about a mile from the room and they hiked the rest of the way.

It wasn't until they made it back to hotel that the weight of having murdered a policeman hit Keedy, but she held up well. Mayhem wasn't in custody and that was what had mattered most to her. She had simply reacted on instinct.

"Baby, I was so scared for you," she said. "All I could see was that police arresting you, then I would've been without you."

Mayhem didn't have the heart to tell her that he had was surrendering, not getting arrested. Besides, it didn't matter now. "You did what you had to do, baby," he said, taking her in his arms and holding her.

He felt her body trembling against his. Her tears were wet against his chest. "It's okay, my love. We're together forever now," Mayhem comforted, stroking her hair as he kissed away her tears

When Keedy regained her composure, he told her to pack their belongings while he left to go steal a vehicle.

They had to change rooms before their trail caught up to them.

Chapter 43

With a little luck and a whole lot of prayer, Mayhem and Keedy managed to evade the city-wide dragnet that the police set up immediately after one of their brethren was killed. Their names and pictures were all over the television. The stories on the news made them out to be ruthless and cold-hearted killers.

Mayhem flicked off the TV. He was enraged at how they were portraying Keedy. They had been holed up at this new motel out by Camp Creek Parkway for three days, surviving on candy bars and soda.

As they shared their last Snicker, Keedy remarked, "Hubby, you know what?"

"What's up, shawdy?" asked Mayhem. He fed her the last bite.

"Uh," she paused while chewing, "I never did get to eat my chicken and waffles."

"I messed that up, didn't I? But I promise to make it up to you."

"Doggy-style, I hope." She held the last sip of Mountain Dew left in the can up to his mouth for him to drink.

Mayhem wet his throat with it, then kissed her. "That's how you want it tonight, huh?"

"Yea. And I want to feed you something hot and slippery."

"Talk that shit, shawdy," he said as he pulled his shirt over his head and tossed it on the floor.

Keedy followed suit with her top, and before long her face was down and her ass was in the air. Mayhem put it on her so good, she was snoring and didn't even know that he had dressed and slipped out of the room.

Keedy awoke in a panic when she didn't feel Mayhem lying next to her. She hopped out of bed and checked the bathroom but it was empty. There was nowhere else for him to be in the small room. She dashed to the window and parted the blinds. The parking lot was dark so she couldn't see much.

She told herself that he had probably gone out to steal another car. He had said it was time for them to change motels.

For a split second she considered that he may have abandoned her, but as she glanced down at her rings and weighed everything that Mayhem had proven to her, she quickly discounted the thought. He would never leave her to fend for herself.

Standing at the window with her Nine in hand, Keedy tried to will him to come through the door. As the minutes turned into an hour, then two, panic returned to seize her by the throat. Now the tears began to flow freely.

Keedy turned on the television. It was a little past 11:00PM and the Channel 11 local news was just airing. Her heart almost stopped beating when the newscaster announced a breaking story concerning the continued hunt for two cop killers.

Before Keedy could hear what the reporter was saying, there was a sound outside the door. Grabbing her gun, she tiptoed to investigate. The door opened a crack and the most beautiful sight in the world appeared.

"Hubby!" she screamed with relief. Then she covered her mouth, not meaning to have screeched.

Mayhem had on a jacket and a Braves baseball cap that was pulled low over his eyes. In his hand were bags of Gladys Knight's Chicken and Waffles. "Aww," she blushed, taking them from him.

"I do whatever I gotta do for my wife," he said.

Keedy sat the bags down on the small table and went to turn on the light. "No, shawdy, the lamp is bright enough," Mayhem cautioned.

"Okay." She began taking the food out of the bags. When she looked at Mayhem he had climbed in bed, fully dressed. She thought it strange but didn't comment.

As she pulled the napkins out, she saw that they were soiled with something sticky. It wasn't syrup but it could've been ketchup. She held them up to her eye and her brow lifted. She walked over, flicked the light switch on and the room lit up brightly.

"Turn the light off, baby."

"Yea," she replied, half ignoring him. When she inspected the napkins she saw that what she thought was ketchup was actually blood. "Mayhem, are you hurt?" she asked as she hurried over to the bed.

"I'm good," he groaned.

When Keedy looked down at him she realized that he was sweating heavily and both of his hands covered his stomach. She lifted his hands and let out a cry when she saw that they were covered with blood. "Oh, my god!" she screamed.

"I'll be fine, baby girl. But you gotta get it of here, those folks are going to track me here."

"Mayhem, oh, Lord. What happened?" She sat down on the bed and rested his head on her lap as tears poured down her face in streams.

"I wanted to get you some chicken and waffles, love," he struggled to say. "I stole a car..." His voice went faint. In the background the newscaster was telling the story.

Police were alerted to Gladys Knight Chicken and Waffles on Peachtree when a customer recognized one of the fugitives sought in the slaying of police officer Edgar Tavares. A fierce shootout ensued between the suspect and law enforcement. Two officers were killed and it is believed that the suspect suffered a gunshot, but he avoided apprehension...

"Baby, we have to get you to the hospital," said Keedy. She lifted Mayhem's shirt and saw a big hole in his side and a smaller one in his stomach.

"No—just—get—" He didn't even have the strength to finish what he was trying to say. His eyes closed.

Keedy screamed. "God. Oh, no, no, no, no—please."

Mayhem's eyes fluttered open and he squeezed her arm. "I love you, shawdy. I'm about to go, but I want you to always remember that—" blood bubbled out of his mouth with each word that he forced out.

"I love you, too, baby," she quickly cut in.

"I'm sorry for all of the trouble I got you in," he continued.

"Baby, please don't do this to me," she pleaded as her warm tears rained down on his face.

Mayhem, unable to speak just looked into her eyes, his teeth chattered from the coldness that took control of his body. He had walked to the end of the line and there was only one place left to go.

"I wish I could bear your pain," she whispered, rubbing the side of his face. Her eyes moved down his body at the blood that poured from his wounds. She pressed her hand against his side and watched his warm blood seep through her fingers.

"This shit ain't right," she cried out, lifting her shaking hand back to her face. "I love you, Hubby. Don't go." Keedy broke down.

Though death beckoned with a persistence that could not be set off much longer, Mayhem forced his eyes open once more. He blinked twice, praying that she knew the depth of the love they had shared. A single tear rolled out of the corner of his eye while pain shot through his heart unable to kiss her one last time.

His eyes fluttered open and shut as death came to claim him since he wouldn't surrender to its call.

G'd up to the end, Mayhem fought back. He reached up and rubbed her face. "You're so beautiful. Kiss me—one last time."

Keedy leaned down without hesitation and pressed her lips to his. Her tears drenched his face. His blood stained hers. Their lips remained pressed together until Mayhem took his last breath and his head fell slack.

Keedy held her husband in her arms and let out a wall rattling wail. “Baby, baby, baby,” she cried.

Out of the corner of her eye she caught a glimpse of the Gladys Knight Chicken and Waffles bags. Had he not left to fulfill her stupid request, he would still be alive.

A sob escaped her mouth. She held her true love in her arms and rocked him. “I love you so much,” she gulped. “And you loved me so perfectly even though I had so many imperfections.”

As she looked down in Mayhem’s ashen face, a flood light from outside illuminated the room and the squawk of police radios blasted.

Keedy looked down at what those muthafuckas had done to her man and decided right then and there that they would have to do the same to her. But just like Mayhem had, she was taking a few with her.

Chapter 44

It was over. The love she had waited for all her life was snatched from her heart in seconds.

Keedy continued to cry and cradle Mayhem as she mumbled *I love you* repeatedly. Time stood still as if it understood her need to mourn. However, her grieving was cut short when she heard their names being yelled through a bullhorn.

"This is the police! We have the entire motel surrounded."

"Fuck you," she yelled out, trembling against Mayhem's now dead body.

Keedy looked slowly around the room eyeing what was left of the life she had just spent with Mayhem. Her mother said she would end up amounting to nothing and right there in that shabby motel room, her whole world would come to an end.

But you know what, Ma? I did amount to something. I became the wife of the most wonderful man to ever live and he truly loved me.

"Mayhem, we know you're hurt. Let us get you to a hospital," the designated negotiator yelled through the megaphone.

My baby isn't hurt, he's dead—y'all killed him, Keedy thought to herself.

She reached over and grabbed the gun from Mayhem's waist. After checking the clip like he had taught her, she crawled to the dresser to reload it. She knew that she had to stay low because those bastards probably had snipers out there.

Returning to the bed, Keedy booted up with Mayhem's gun and hers, both fully loaded. She was going to teach them a lesson about taking away the person that gave her life.

She knew that after it was all over people would blame Mayhem for everything that happened to her. They would be so wrong.

Keedy grabbed the hotel note pad and pen from the nightstand and began to pour out her heart. Fuck what anyone might say about her in death, as long as they understood that Mayhem had been her everything.

She wrote fast but poignantly.

When she finished the letter, she grabbed her bold orange lipstick and wrote a defining postscript on the wall above the headboard.

Now she as ready to make them test her G.

"Don't make us come in there. This is our last warning. Give yourselves up!" The command boomed through the hotel window.

Keedy sat the lipstick down and picked up her gun. She kissed Mayhem one last time and said, "Don't worry, baby, I got you."

His eyes were open and she wanted to believe that the expression forever etched on his face wasn't a grimace but a proud smile. "You ain't talkin' 'bout nothin', shawdy," she mimicked him lovingly.

She hugged him tightly. "See you in a minute, Hubby."

Tears rolled down her face as she closed his eyes.

The door boomed with the sound of the battering ram. Keedy leveled her guns and kicked into action.

And so did the S.W.A.T. team.

Long after Keedy lay dead next to her eternal love, the cops' guns and high-powered rifles continued to splatter their bodies with bullets.

Finally, mercifully, the commander gave the order to cease fire. "It's over," he told his squad as he stepped inside the tattered room.

One by one other uniformed men piled in. The approached the bodies with caution, ready to go into overkill if anything moved. Merely, as a formality the commander checked Mayhem and Keedy's pulse. He nodded confirmation that they were dead, but that was obvious to all eyes that stared at their bullet-riddled bodies.

When he stood up, he looked down and saw the notepad lying on the floor next to Keedy's head. He reached down and picked it up and read the words.

Mayhem was my everything.There are not enough words to epitomize how special he treated me and made me feel. You rat bastards may have him pegged as being a criminal thug, but you're wrong! His heart was golden and you took the light he shined into my world and turned it dark.

But, me and my boo went out on our own terms, and that was together.

The commander looked back down at Keedy with a torn heart; he abhorred the crimes that she had committed in the name of love, but he secretly admired her devotion to Mayhem which was summed up by the postscript written in lipstick on the wall.

It read: *Til My Casket Drops!*

BOOKS BY LDP'S CEO, CA$H

TRUST NO MAN

TRUST NO MAN 2

TRUST NO MAN 3

BONDED BY BLOOD

SHORTY GOT A THUG

A DIRTY SOUTH LOVE

THUGS CRY

THUGS CRY 2

TRUST NO BITCH

TRUST NO BITCH 2

TRUST NO BITCH 3

TIL MY CASKET DROPS

Coming Soon

TRUST NO BITCH (KIAM EYEZ' STORY)

THUGS CRY 3

BONDED BY BLOOD 2

RESTRANING ORDER

Coming Soon From Lock Down Publications

RESTRAINING ORDER

By **CA$H & COFFEE**

GANGSTA CITY **II**

By **Teddy Duke**

A DANGEROUS LOVE **VII**

By **J Peach**

BLOOD OF A BOSS **III**

By **Askari**

THE KING CARTEL **III**

By **Frank Gresham**

NEVER TRUST A RATCHET BITCH

SILVER PLATTER HOE **III**

By **Reds Johnson**

THESE NIGGAS AIN'T LOYAL **III**

By **Nikki Tee**

BROOKLYN ON LOCK **III**

By **Sonovia Alexander**

THE STREETS BLEED MURDER **II**

By **Jerry Jackson**

CONFESSIONS OF A DOPEMAN'S DAUGHTER **II**

By **Rasstrina**

WHAT ABOUT US **II**

NEVER LOVE AGAIN

By **Kim Kaye**

A GANGSTER'S REVENGE

By **Aryanna**

Available Now

LOVE KNOWS NO BOUNDARIES **I II & III**

By **Coffee**

SILVER PLATTER HOE **I & II**

HONEY DIPP **I & II**

CLOSED LEGS DON'T GET FED **I & II**

A BITCH NAMED KARMA

By **Reds Johnson**

A DANGEROUS LOVE **I, II, III, IV, V, VI**

By **J Peach**

CUM FOR ME

An **LDP Erotica Collaboration**

THE KING CARTEL **I & II**

By **Frank Gresham**

BLOOD OF A BOSS **I & II**

By **Askari**

THE DEVIL WEARS TIMBS

BURY ME A G **I II & III**

By **Tranay Adams**

THESE NIGGAS AIN'T LOYAL **I & II**

By **Nikki Tee**

THE STREETS BLEED MURDER

By **Jerry Jackson**

DIRTY LICKS

By **Peter Mack**

THE ULTIMATE BETRAYAL

By **Phoenix**

BROOKLYN ON LOCK

By **Sonovia Alexander**

SLEEPING IN HEAVEN, WAKING IN HELL **I, II & III**

By **Forever Redd**

THE DEVIL WEARS TIMBS **I, II & III**

By **Tranay Adams**

DON'T FU#K WITH MY HEART **I & II**

By **Linnea**

BOSS'N UP **I & II**

By **Royal Nicole**

LOYALTY IS BLIND

By **Kenneth Chisholm**

Made in United States
Orlando, FL
26 April 2024

46208625R00153